THE SILVER MARK

CROW INVESTIGATIONS BOOK TWO

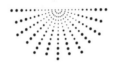

SARAH PAINTER

Siskin
Press

For Cath,
my partner in crime for over 30 years.

CHAPTER ONE

L ydia Crow adjusted the desk fan so that the stream of air was hitting her more accurately and sat back in her broken office chair. The woman opposite was still talking and Lydia forced herself to tune back into the monologue. No. It was still detailing the sex life she and her husband had enjoyed for the previous fifteen years of marriage.

'Always on a Saturday night, unless he had overdone the wine with dinner. Definitely an average of twice a week, though, once you count it all up from when we were first together, and that's what they say is the national limit, don't they?'

That caught Lydia's attention. 'Sorry, what? Limit?'

'Or is it two point five? The average number of times for married couples in England. I'm sure I read that somewhere. So he had no reason to complain. No reason to look elsewhere.'

Lydia slumped back. This was the third infidelity case this week, which wouldn't be so bad if she had other work coming in to dilute it a little. When she had started Crow Investigations she had hoped not to take any at all, especially after the Carter incident up in Aberdeen at her old firm, but it had proved impossible. Despite being rent-free courtesy of her uncle Charlie, living in London wasn't cheap, and she had business costs such as public liability insurance, equipment, transport and registration fees. She still hadn't resorted to honey-trap work, though, and things would have to become a great deal more desperate before that happened.

It was too hot to stay slumped in the padded chair, she could feel sweat sticking to her vest top and the fabric of the seat was itching her legs. She straightened up and took a fortifying glug from her mug. It was a gift from Emma and had a magnifying glass and deer stalker stencilled on the side, which was both faintly embarrassing and very cheering. Lydia had started her own firm after only a year of training at a firm in Aberdeen and every vote of confidence was gratefully received.

'Oh, I couldn't drink tea in this heat,' the woman said, wrinkling her nose.

'It's coffee,' Lydia said, not feeling the need to reveal that it also had a shot of whisky to help counteract the hangover she was still nursing, despite it being four o'clock in the afternoon. Was it her age or were hangovers getting worse?

'So, can you help?' the woman said. 'I just need answers.'

Lydia hated saying 'no' to a paying customer so she

2

did the next best thing and selected her 'top rate card' and slid it across the table. 'Plus expenses.' It was the corporate rate. Not a figure that any private client could afford and it made unwanted jobs disappear out of the door, no fuss, no muss.

'Fine,' the woman said. 'Do I need to sign a contract or something?'

Lydia blinked. 'I need the first ten billable hours paid up front.' That ought to do it. Even for a corporate client, Lydia would have explained her refund policy; that if the job took less time than expected, the client would get some of that extortionate first fee back. But she kept quiet. Nothing like ridiculous sums of money to get rid of an unwelcome client with a dull domestic problem.

'Fine,' the woman said again, a touch impatiently. 'Will you start straight away? I can't live like this.'

And there it was. The anguish in her eyes. The reason Lydia hated doing cheating work. Pain was part of the job. You didn't call on a private investigator when everything was hunky dory and, human nature being what it was, the cause of the pain was usually close by, but still... It wasn't just the dullness of investigating cheating spouses which got to Lydia. It was the unnecessary nature of the misery. All of that pain. And for what? Why couldn't the couples talk to each other, agree that things had gone off the boil in their relationship and either spice it up or agree to an open marriage or go their separate ways. Infidelity cases just made Lydia sad. She opened the top drawer of the desk and gave the woman a contract, realising as she did so that she had managed to

3

forget her name. Or, more accurately, failed to pay attention when the woman introduced herself. She was more hungover than she realised and felt a stab of shame when she imagined what Karen, her old boss, would say about such a lapse of basic observation.

She watched as the woman dutifully printed her name above her signature, reading upside down. April Westcott.

'Thank you, Mrs Westcott. I'll be in touch.'

After Mrs Westcott had departed, Lydia went into her small kitchen and opened the fridge door. It was pleasant to stand in front of the cool air but there was nothing of interest inside. Never mind, she told herself, the cafe downstairs would close soon and then she could investigate its kitchen. If nothing else, Angel had a catering-size fridge which blasted out more cold air than Lydia's little under-counter one.

Back in the office of Crow Investigations, which used to be the living room of the flat and still had a sofa pushed against one wall, Lydia surveyed her domain. Her business had been running for two months and she was still using the rickety flat-pack desk and chair that she had liberated from the tiny office which belonged to the cafe. Now this was a more permanent arrangement, she really ought to give them back but Lydia couldn't bring herself to feel especially bad. Her Uncle Charlie had done his level best to make Lydia stay in this place, above The Fork cafe, and she knew he would consider some ancient furniture a perfectly acceptable cost of doing business.

Her laptop sat in the middle of the beige surface of

the desk, with piles of paperwork and notes on either side. At some point she would need a filing cabinet. And a system. 'Jason?' She looked around for her unofficial assistant. Nothing.

She found him in his bedroom, standing in the corner and facing the wall. 'Are you okay?'

Jason turned slowly and she realised he had a pen in his hand and had been writing on the wall. Again. 'Yeah. Just thinking.' His pale face brightened. 'Do we have a client?'

'Mrs Westcott.' Lydia said. 'Don't get excited, it's another cheating spouse.'

'That's okay,' Jason said, moving so quickly that he made Lydia jump a little. 'Have you added her to the sheet, yet?'

'Just about to,' Lydia said. She followed Jason to the office, sticking close and enjoying the way he cooled the air around him.

He watched intently as Lydia added Mrs Westcott to the basic spreadsheet she was using to track clients and accounts. Now that he was able to touch things well enough to hold a pen and make coffee, Jason was fascinated by the possibilities offered by the laptop and Lydia's phone. The internet seemed magical as far as Jason was concerned. Which wasn't far from true, when Lydia stopped to think about it.

Jason touched the edge of the screen reverentially. 'When am I getting one of these?'

'When we make enough money,' Lydia said. 'I know you just want to download a simulator and play space invaders twenty-four-seven.'

Jason looked up. 'Can you do that?'

'No,' Lydia said quickly. If there was one thing less useful than having a ghost as her assistant it would be having an arcade-game playing ghost as her assistant.

'Are you watching Mrs Lee tonight?'

Lydia felt her headache throb. 'Unfortunately.'

'I wish I could do it, that would be so cool.'

'Trust me, it isn't.'

'But I could be a real help, then,' Jason's face fell.

'You are a help,' Lydia said. 'You are the best assistant I've ever had.'

Jason gave her a long look.

Lydia decided to change tack. 'Maybe if you would let me look into what is holding you here, tying you to the building, we might be able to resolve it. And then you might be able to get out of here.'

'Move on, you mean,' Jason said, his expression thunderous.

'No,' Lydia said quickly. 'Explore the street. Maybe even be able to leave Camberwell. You could see the sights.'

'I've seen them,' Jason said, still looking suspicious and angry, as he did whenever he suspected Lydia might be angling to make him move into the light, or whatever ghosts did when they left this plane of existence and went to wherever spirits went. 'South London,' he said. 'Born and bred.'

'Yes, but there's new stuff,' Lydia ploughed on. 'The London Eye. The Shard.'

'Get me one of those and I could look at them on the

Google.' Jason was gazing at the laptop again. 'You can see anything on there. Anything you want.'

Lydia reminded herself to put parental controls on the laptop before Jason stumbled into porn land. She tried, again, to distract him. 'Seeing things in real life is much better. Wouldn't you like to be able to walk around London again? It would do you good to get out, get some fresh air.'

The words hung for a moment and Lydia wasn't sure if Jason was going to fall into one of his dark moods. Understandably, he found being a ghost a bit depressing. Instead, he grinned, looking fully alive and five years younger. 'I think my condition might be a bit past that,' he said.

MRS LEE WORKED for an insurance broker on Church Street and her husband had engaged Lydia's services to find out whether she was truly going to Pilates after hours on Wednesday and Friday evenings or whether there was something else keeping her out of the marital home.

Earlier in the week, Lydia had followed Mrs Lee from Church Street to the gym in the small industrial estate off Surrey Road and dutifully made sure she had entered the building, changed into her Pilates gear and walked into the class. Two hours later, during which Lydia sat in her old blue Volvo and watched the exit of the gym, Mrs Lee left and went straight back to her and Dr Lee's garden flat near Denmark Hill.

Tonight, Lydia arrived an hour before Mrs Lee's official finishing time at the insurance firm and was rewarded for her conscientiousness when she was just in time to catch Mrs Lee leaving early, five minutes after Lydia had begun surveillance.

Mrs Lee had a bulky handbag over one arm and she looked, to Lydia's eye, light and happy. Instead of getting into her silver-grey Toyota, she walked down Church Street at a fast pace. Lydia got out of the Volvo and followed at a decent distance. It was tricky because there was a bus stop halfway along and if Mrs Lee was getting a bus, Lydia would have to scramble back to the Volvo to follow effectively, or risk getting on the same bus as her target. Mrs Lee passed the bus stop, though, and walked steadily on, turning down Broad Street and then into the leaf-lined Camberwell Grove. The pavement here was a little quieter and Lydia increased her distance. There was a cafe at the end of the road, Lydia knew, and she wondered if that was Mrs Lee's destination. The rest of the road was residential. Then, without warning, Mrs Lee disappeared. More accurately, she had stepped off the pavement and onto the paved front garden of a small block of sixties' flats. Like all of London, different eras were all smushed together and the boxy architecture rubbed shoulders with a couple of gorgeous bricked Edwardian houses. Lydia took the path to one of these houses, as if visiting. Mrs Lee wasn't looking, she had rung a doorbell and gone inside.

Lydia waited for a minute before doubling-back down the garden path she had taken, and following in Mrs Lee's footsteps. The door looked like it belonged to a private residence. There were four flats listed with separate bells. One said 'Nails' and Lydia wondered briefly whether it was a surname or the extremely discreet sign for a manicure business. She looked at the buttons for recent-sweat residue but they all looked the same. Since she couldn't tell which buzzer Mrs Lee had pressed, she dutifully photographed them all.

The problem with a residential street on foot, was the difficulty of waiting and watching unobtrusively. Across the road, there was an alley next to a terrace of four houses and Lydia experimented with standing just inside its entrance. She could see the door Mrs Lee had used although she was pretty sure that Mrs Lee would also be able to see her. If she looked directly, that was. Lydia leaned against the wall in her customary 'I'm going to be here for a while' position and crossed her fingers that Mrs Lee was as unobservant as the average person. The average innocent person who was simply going about their life. Yes, maybe Mrs Lee was carrying out an affair and that was, technically, immoral, but Lydia hated feeling like a voyeur on someone else's mistakes. Especially when life was complex. Maybe Dr Lee was a bastard. Maybe he had affairs of his own. Lydia's old boss and the woman who had trained her as an investigator, had explained it this way; if she uncovered infidelity she would either be ending an unhappy marriage or providing the catalyst for it to improve. It was a win either way. Of course, it wasn't always so simple. One of Lydia's early cases had revealed that the woman was not having an affair, but had been trying to leave her abusive husband. The poor woman had very little freedom and Lydia had, luckily, been suspicious of the husband who had engaged the firm's services. Instead of giving him the full report on his wife's activities, Lydia had fabricated a story which kept the woman safe. It still chilled her, though, to know how close she had been to ruining a terrorised woman's chance of freedom.

An hour and ten minutes later, with Lydia's mind pleasantly wandering through a fantasy which involved a naked DCI Fleet, the flat door opened and Mrs Lee walked swiftly away. Lydia caught a couple of pictures of her leaving the block of flats and then followed, her legs cramped from standing still for so long. Mrs Lee returned to Church Street. She was moving quickly and when she got back to her car, she threw her bulky handbag onto the passenger seat with some force. Lydia caught sight of her expression and it looked serious. And determined.

Lydia got into her Volvo and followed Mrs Lee back to her marital home and then drove to The Fork, parking as close as she could, and climbing the stairs to her flat feeling unaccountably weary. She made a large mug of strong coffee and wrote up the report on the evening's surveillance.

Taking a break, she stretched her arms above her head and then treated herself by cracking her neck, shoulders and wrists. The sounds of the city on a warm night wafted through the open window and Lydia felt her low mood lift. This was the life. She was her own boss. Sitting at her desk with the door open, she could see down the hallway of her flat to the front entrance. The retro wood-and-glass door which Paul Fox had sent to her as some kind of weird manipulation tactic still gave her mixed feelings. She hated the giver of the door and the presumption behind the gift, but she loved the film-noir aesthetic and the bronze-leaf lettering. Crow Investigations. Her own firm. Now all she needed was a case that didn't make her soul curl up and die.

CHAPTER TWO

I t was too hot to sleep and the next day dawned bright and muggy, providing no relief whatsoever. Lydia checked her business account and saw that April Westcott had already paid her the required initial fee. After treating herself to a loud sigh and a quick shower, Lydia went down to The Fork to fill her travel mug with coffee before starting the preparatory work on the case.

It was mid-morning and in between the early breakfast and lunchtime rushes. Only three tables were occupied and Angel was on a stool behind the counter, sipping water and looking at her phone. She looked up as Lydia scooted behind the counter. 'Hey.'

'Hey,' Lydia replied. The coffee machine whooshed and liquid poured into Lydia's mug, the scent filling the air. Lydia could feel her synapses waking up just in anticipation of her first sip. Thank God for caffeine.

'Quiet today,' Lydia said, fixing the lid.

Angel shrugged. 'It's still early. Did you see the news?'

'No. What?'

Angel passed her phone which was displaying the BBC app. The headline said the heatwave was set to continue with high temperatures putting London hotter than Miami and a risk of grass fires in rural England. 'Ugh. It's too hot, already,' Lydia said, passing it back.

'What?' Angel glanced at the phone and scrolled down. 'Not that. This.'

The story had changed. Now it said: 'Banker found dead under Blackfriars Bridge.' Lydia scanned the opening paragraph. A man had been found in the early hours of the morning, hanging, underneath Blackfriars Bridge. The story said that the man had been identified but that his details were not going to be released until his next of kin had been contacted.

'I hope it was police who found him,' Angel said. 'Not some poor kids on a night out.'

Lydia didn't know much about Angel. Uncle Charlie had hired her to run The Fork and she was a magician in the kitchen. She had a wife called Nat who played in a band of some kind and Lydia knew she lived in Camberwell because she walked to work. Angel was generally no-nonsense confident to the point of being intimidating but right at this moment, there was a vulnerability in her expression that Lydia hadn't seen before. Before she could ask if she was okay, Angel stood up to take a customer's money and the moment passed.

Lydia raised a hand to say 'bye' and walked out into the blazing sunshine. The news story had shown a picture of the bridge, complete with police tape and cars. The man had been hanging underneath, although the picture didn't capture the body. The news sites and bloggers probably had more detailed shots, which was both the benefit and the curse of the internet. Lydia wondered whether he had been found upside down, execution style, or whether it was self-inflicted. The bridge was very public, but fairly easy to get underneath. Lydia didn't know if that meant it was more or less likely to be suicide. She found the story on her own phone and looked again at the picture, sipping her hot coffee and thinking. There was a sense of familiarity that went beyond the fact that she knew the location. That was it. A suspected money guy for the Mafia had been found hanging under Blackfriars back in the eighties. She called Fleet. 'Who is the bridge guy?'

'Good morning, Lydia. How are you?'

Lydia ignored his sarcastic tone. 'News said he has been identified.'

'Not for public consumption.'

'Yes,' Lydia was impatient. 'I'm not public.'

Fleet didn't answer right away. She could hear somebody speaking to him and background sounds of the office. She could picture his expression as he gave the other person his attention. The laser-like focus in his gaze, the way his face would stay impassive while he processed and planned. When he came back on the line he said: 'Why are you interested?'

'Wasn't there something similar? Back in the eighties.'

'Roberto Calvi,' Fleet said straight away in a tone

that suggested he had already made the connection. 'Financier for the mob.'

'Did they ever get the killer?'

'Insufficient evidence.' A short pause. 'The usual. You know how it is with organised crime deals.'

'Professional job and everybody keeping their mouths shut.' Lydia did know. 'This is a weird one, though. Right?'

'I don't know,' Fleet said. 'I mean, it's a popular bridge.'

'Hanging,' Lydia said. There was something tickling at the back of her mind. It was like the brush of feathers. A black wing. She closed her eyes and felt weight dragging her down. She wanted to lift up, to reach out her arms and feel her toes leave the earth, but something was pulling. It wasn't just gravity. Something physical around her hips. 'Were there weights tied to him? Maybe around his middle?'

Fleet went silent.

'Fleet?' Lydia could still feel the feathers. An involuntary shiver ran through her body.

'Lunch?'

'Yes,' Lydia said, more pleased than was sensible at the prospect.

'Usual?'

'See you there,' Lydia said and ended the call. There had been something between her and DCI Fleet from the first moment they met, a something which turned into a very enjoyable tumble a few months ago, back when she was still kidding herself that she wasn't going to stay in London. Now she was here for good, determined to build a proper business and to prove to her parents, and the whole Crow Family, that she was a success. Ideally, without their interference and without revealing that she wasn't as completely powerless as she had always assumed. She had told Fleet that they had to just be friends, now. He was her main police contact. A resource to be tapped. No longer a tall, beautiful man to be... enjoyed. Sex made things complicated and Lydia was determined to keep things simple. Professional.

Lydia spent the morning in Brunswick Park. It had been newly refurbished and the benches were still in good condition. Lydia found one underneath the shade of a horse chestnut tree and looked over the notes she had taken from April Westcott. She had her husband's name, Christopher, and a list of his closest friends and relatives. Plus, details of his job as a graphic designer and daily schedule. When she had asked April about her husband's hobbies she had pulled a face and said 'he messes about in the garden'. Surveying the details of Christopher's sparse life, Lydia found herself hoping the man was having an affair. Or, at least, sympathising with his need for excitement. If only people could talk to each other. If only Christopher Westcott had sat down with his wife and said 'I'm bored. I'm unhappy. I need to have more sex.' Or more gardening. Whatever. Lydia wasn't judging.

The Hare on Well Street was essentially unchanged since it had been established in 1847 with its glossy black painted exterior, arched windows and ornate bar.

The over-flowing window boxes and hanging baskets outside might have been new, and perhaps the Victorians hadn't been able to order a vegan lunch with their pint of beer, but the place felt timeless nonetheless and Lydia loved it. Nowhere did pubs like London.

Fleet was already inside, sitting in their favourite spot in the corner, a pint of Doom Bar and a curved glass of pale ale on the table. He stood when Lydia arrived and sat when she sat. He had curiously old-fashioned manners which went beautifully with the red-upholstery and dark wood of The Hare. He also dressed like a fully-grown male of the species, which was something Lydia found incredibly appealing. Obviously, she usually saw him in his work clothes and perhaps in his downtime he wore skinny jeans and a cardigan, but Lydia doubted it.

'Are we still being strictly professional,' Fleet said, 'or can I kiss you?'

Lydia felt the heat in her cheeks. Instant and embarrassing. Fleet was playing hell with her tough-as-boots image. 'You can kiss me but it won't mean anything.'

He tilted his head, as if considering and then leaned in. 'Fair enough.' His lips brushed hers and Lydia closed her eyes. Sparks. A bonfire on a moonlit beach. And, behind those impressions, there was something else. A Gleam. Lydia was adept at sensing the magic which ran through the four old families; Silver, Crow, Pearl and Fox. She could sense that there was something in Fleet. Not strong. Probably from way back in his family tree. But it didn't feel like any of the four usual suspects. It was something different. She kissed him back and stopped thinking for a moment. All work and no play, after all. His large hand on the back of her neck sent sensation running through her body and Lydia reciprocated, feeling the springy hair which was neatly clipped, fading to stubble at his nape.

The moment was over all-too-soon. A man with a faux-hawk put down plates of sandwiches in front of them and Lydia caught her breath. She took a long sip of her pale ale and concentrated on deconstructing the tower of bread and salad into something manageable. 'Why do they put everything into an inedible stack?' Lydia pulled out the wooden skewer which was holding the layers in place. 'I would need to be able to unhinge my jaw to fit this into my mouth.'

Perhaps wisely, Fleet chose not to respond. Instead he forked several mouthfuls of side salad before asking: 'How did you know about the bricks?'

Lydia had just put a piece of cucumber into her mouth so she took her time chewing and swallowing before answering. 'I didn't. What bricks?'

'Our man. He had bricks stuffed into his pockets. And you said-'

'I just had a feeling he was weighed down,' Lydia said, shaking her head lightly. 'Although, now you say bricks...' She thought for a moment. 'Wasn't Calvi found with bricks in his pockets? I was probably just remembering that and transferring it. I remember that story. I remember Mum and Dad talking about it in the kitchen when they thought I wasn't listening.'

'It is starting to look very similar,' Fleet said. 'I don't want to say 'copy-cat', but...'

'If you hear hoofbeats,' Lydia said.

19

'Yeah, but round here, it's just as likely to be a zebra.'

Lydia wasn't sure how to respond to that. It sounded like an opening to talk about the Crow Family and their weird reputation, but that was a tricky area. Lydia was never sure exactly how much Fleet knew about her world, and the whole area was further complicated by the rules of the Family. They came first, naturally, and didn't tend to be open with people outside of blood, but Lydia wasn't sure of the exact lines. How much was public knowledge, how much was secret. And then there was the ever-present fear that Fleet would write her off as a lunatic. Londoners, especially those in Camberwell, knew of The Crows. And the others. But how much they believed was another story.

They had finished their sandwiches and Lydia was draining the last of her ale, supressing a small burp at the end. 'Pardon.' The only downside to delicious beer and totally worth it.

'You said you had a feeling.' Fleet was regarding her over the rim of his pint glass.

'That was the beer. Bubbles.'

Fleet didn't smile. 'About the bricks.'

'I didn't say bricks,' Lydia reminded him. 'I don't know anything about it. I swear.'

'No Family gossip?' Fleet's tone was carefully casual.

Lydia shook her head. 'Are you going to tell me his name?'

'Why do you care?'

'I'm bored.' Lydia pushed her plate away and leaned

back against the red velvet upholstery. 'I've had nothing but cheaters for weeks. It's depressing.'

'And you think a murder would cheer you up?'

'Not suicide, then?' Lydia sat forward.

Fleet closed his eyes briefly. 'No. We don't think so.'

'Execution?'

'You really must stop looking so pleased. It's disturbing.'

'Oh, come on' Lydia said. 'You love it, too. Who was he?'

'Robert Sharp. Business analyst at Sheridan Fisher. Single, as far as we know, and lived in a flat in Canary Wharf.'

'Nice for some,' Lydia said automatically.

'He had ID in his wallet. And house keys.'

'Money?'

Fleet shook his head. 'No cash to speak of, but a couple of credit cards and he was still wearing his Breitling watch.'

'So not a robbery. Any ideas on motive?'

'It's not my case,' Fleet said, turning his palms up. 'Not my manor.'

'All right,' Lydia said. 'Any guesses? Just for fun.'

Fleet regarded her for a moment. 'You are a little bit scary, you know that?'

'So I've heard,' Lydia waved a hand.

'Stay out of this one, though,' Fleet said, his voice serious. 'It's not our area.'

Lydia nodded while privately planning to ignore Fleet. It wasn't her area at the moment, and that was the problem. She wanted to move.

LYDIA WENT BACK to her flat for the afternoon and stripped to her underwear. Sitting at her desk with the oscillating fan pointed directly into her face, she did a little research on Christopher Westcott. It was hard to summon the enthusiasm but if there was one thing Lydia was proud of, it was her work ethic. She had taken on a job and so she would do it to the best of her ability. Besides, Crow Investigations needed to build a reputation in order to get word of mouth clients. That was how the PI business tended to work. You couldn't just take an advert out and hope they came flooding in. People needed to trust the investigator they were inviting into their private lives, which meant personal recommendations. Plus, cashflow was always important. Lydia already had a list of wants regarding surveillance equipment, not to mention a more reliable and comfortable car. And then there was the little matter of keeping body and soul together. She wasn't sure how long Uncle Charlie would let her eat out of the kitchen at The Fork. Probably until he realised she wasn't going to play ball with whatever plans he had laid for her.

Christopher Westcott ran a graphic design agency. The office address was in Soho, but a quick call to April confirmed that Christopher worked out of his home office and that the address on the website was just a forwarding service. April's suspicions were centred on Christopher's work-related trips. They had become more frequent over the last year and regularly involved overnight stays. When she asked him about the trips he said they were important networking opportunities and that he needed to 'press flesh' in order to land big contracts. An unfortunate choice of phrase, given April's concerns.

A buzzer sounded and Lydia clicked to close the tabs she had open on her laptop. She had installed a pressure-sensitive pad under the grotty carpet on the top set of stairs which led from the toilets of the cafe to her flat. That way, she had warning that somebody was on their way. Moments later, she heard footsteps on the landing and a dark shape loomed behind the rippled glass of her front door.

Lydia pulled on her vest-top and a pair of jersey shorts, and went to the door. She used the chain, even though she recognised the outline of her Uncle Charlie. She could feel him, too; the tang of crow magic over-whelming her senses. There was no sense in letting Charlie know her abilities, though, so she called. 'Who is it?'

'It's me,' he said, his voice amused like he knew that she knew.

She opened the door and regarded Charlie through the narrow gap. 'This is a surprise.'

'I've brought coffee.'

Lydia opened the door wide. 'It's almost too hot for coffee.'

'Almost,' Charlie said, smiling.

She accepted the black-and-white espresso cup which Charlie had clearly just brought up from the cafe downstairs and retreated behind her desk. 'What can I do for you?'

'Can't a proud uncle just visit his niece?'

Lydia took a sip of the strong coffee, feeling the caffeine jolt her synapses. The taste of feathers was thick in the back of her throat and she could see a shimmer around Charlie. He was wearing a button-up shirt with the sleeves rolled up above his elbows. The tattoos on his forearms were moving in a distracting manner and Lydia made sure she didn't focus on them. The last thing she needed was to alert Uncle Charlie to the fact that she could see them as they truly were. As far as the boss of the infamous Crow Family knew, Lydia was a damp squib. A powerless nothing and a disappointment.

'How are Daisy and John doing?'

'Better,' Charlie said. He sat in the client's chair. 'They are very grateful.'

'I'm sure,' Lydia couldn't hide the sarcasm.

'They are,' Charlie lent forward. 'You played an important role.'

'Maddie's still missing, though,' Lydia said. 'I didn't solve anything. Didn't bring her home.'

'They know she's alive. They know that she has left of her own accord. And,' Charlie spread his hands. 'They know it's for the best.'

Lydia raised her chin. 'I suppose.'

Charlie looked around the room. 'How's business?'

'Busy,' Lydia lied.

'You need money, you just tell Angel. She'll give you shifts downstairs. Anytime you want. Flexi-hours. No contract. Cash in hand.'

'I'm fine,' Lydia said.

Charlie's face darkened and Lydia caught a glimpse of the other Charlie. The Head of The Family, capital-letter Charlie, and she added: 'But, thank you. I'll keep it in mind.'

'I only want to look after you, Lyds. I promised your father I'd keep you safe.'

'I know,' Lydia said. 'And I appreciate it.'

AFTER CHARLIE HAD GONE, Lydia knocked on Jason's bedroom door. He didn't strictly need a bedroom, as he didn't strictly sleep, but Lydia knew he often lay on top of the striped duvet and pretended. He called it medita-tion and said, having had years of practice, he could maintain the position for six or eight hours and achieve a dream-like state. If he wasn't dead, he would've been able to write a self-help book on the subject.

Jason was in the corner of the room with his back turned. He was writing furiously on the wall which was covered in formulae. He turned, Sharpie in one hand and a fuzzy, far-away expression which Lydia thought of as his 'maths look'. That was another thing Lydia had discovered in the last couple of months; Jason loved mathematics and had been on track to professorship at UCL when he had died. The physical ability that Lydia's presence seemed to give Jason had started with him being able to shove and push, lift and throw large objects, and open the fridge door. With practice, he had regained fine motor control and the first thing he had done when scratching out on a pad of paper with a pencil was to write a series of numbers. 'Primes,' he had said, catching Lydia's look of confusion. 'I love primes.'

He had moved quickly on from pencil and paper to a pack of Sharpies and his bedroom walls. Lydia didn't know how she was going to explain it to Charlie, but it made Jason so visibly happy she hadn't the heart to ask him to stop. Besides, Charlie had no reason to go into the spare room. And she could paint over the marks.

'Sorry,' Lydia said. 'You're busy.'

'I've got time,' Jason said. He capped the Sharpie and shoved it into the pocket of his grey suit jacket. It was such a natural action that Lydia found it hard to believe he hadn't, miraculously, come back from the dead. Then he motioned for her to sit down and the illusion evaporated. Jason often looked fully corporeal these days, giving weight to their theory that Lydia was somehow amplifying whatever energy kept his essence together and functioning in spirit form, but it was a state that could shift in an instant. Either when he moved quickly and there was a strange blurring around the too-smooth or too-jerky motion. Or sometimes when Lydia had been out of the house for an extended period, on surveillance or visiting her parents, and he acquired a very slight translucency in direct light.

'Any idea what a business analyst does? At a firm like Sheridan Fisher?'

Jason frowned. 'Not really. Why?'

Lydia told him about Robert Sharp. 'I'm just wondering about motive.'

'We've got a murder case? That's huge.'

'Not officially. But I'm going to work it. Good practice.'

'Is that all? Just practice?'

'What do you mean?'

'Nothing,' Jason's gaze kept straying to the wall and Lydia could see he was itching to get back to his beloved calculations.

'What are you working on?'

'Just a new proof.' Thankfully, Jason had given up trying to explain his research in detail to Lydia.

'Is it going well?'

'Too soon to say,' Jason's eyes were shining as he spoke. 'I just-' He stopped for a moment and, if he had been alive, he would have probably taken a deep breath. Instead he just paused, motionless for a couple of seconds. The words which followed came out in a rush. 'I've had so much time to think. I've been running proofs and ideas in my mind for years but it was so slow. Not being able to write things down. To pin the thoughts down in a concrete way. I've always needed to see things written down, described visually, and now I can. It's just incredible.'

'I'm happy for you,' Lydia said.

'I mean, think about it... I have this unique perspective on reality and time,' Jason waved his hands. 'Who knows what I will be able to work out. Maybe I could discover something truly ground-breaking?'

Lydia wasn't sure what to say in the face of such unbridled enthusiasm. It made her slightly uncomfortable and, something worse, a little bit jealous. Lydia realised something important. She didn't just need to work the Sharp case for practice or even for business-development purposes. She needed some more enthusiasm, more passion, in her world. When the dead guy in your house is living a better life than you, she thought, it is time to seriously up your game.

CHAPTER THREE

Sunday was the day that Lydia visited her parents, without fail. If she wasn't doing a surveillance job, of course. Or had been up too late the night before drinking shots and listening to Jason talk about the Fibonacci sequence. Or when she couldn't face it.

She was due at midday, sharp, but her phone rang at eleven. 'It's too hot in the house,' Lydia's mother said. 'We can't breathe.' Then, mutinously, 'I'm not doing a roast.'

Lydia tamped down the urge to cancel. 'Park? We could find a shady spot.'

She met her parents on the way to Kelsey Park, just around the corner from a quiet side street where she'd found a perfect parking spot. She would be able to make a fast getaway after lunch, at least.

'Lydia!' Her father recognised her and drew her in for a quick, hard hug.

'This isn't natural,' her mother said, indicating the

road. 'The tarmac is melting. It's like the seventies all over again.'

'It's a beautiful day,' Henry said. He looped his arms around both of their shoulders. 'A picnic with my two favourite girls.'

'Women,' Lydia corrected, and received an evil look from her mother in payment for her feminism.

When they got to the local park, it appeared that everybody else in Beckenham had the same idea. The dead grass was covered with people and picnic blankets, with every demographic represented. Families with small children, entwined couples, loners wearing headphones, and groups of teens laughing loudly and calling to each other. The areas underneath the spreading branches of the trees were packed solid as so many people sought the cool shade.

Lydia's father walked blithely onward, heading straight into the crowd of lounging bodies as if they were no more than the waters of the Red Sea and he expected them to part for him. Which is exactly what they did. Lydia hung back and watched as people rolled out of the way of Henry Crow's feet, some scrambling to their feet and gathering bags and hats and small children to make way. Henry didn't glance at them, seemed no more aware of them than he was of the sky or the grass. He just moved through the rapidly thinning crowd to the base of a tree where he turned and sat, leaning against the trunk. Lydia's mother was right behind him and she had already put down her bags and begun to spread out a blanket on the ground when Lydia caught up.

As always, Henry's mental acuity seemed to have

degraded in the short time they had spent together. He shaded his eyes with one hand and peered up at Lydia, suddenly uncertain. 'I think I know you, don't I?'

'I would hope so, Dad,' Lydia said, smiling to show that everything was fine, even while her heart twisted.

'Lydia, darling,' her mother's voice was a touch louder than usual, and Lydia knew she had used her name deliberately, 'would you like ham or cheese?'

'Cheese,' Lydia took the clingfilmed roll her mother was holding out and sat down.

Her dad accepted a ham roll but began picking bits off and putting them onto the grass.

'What are you doing? I'll take it if you don't want it,' Lydia's mum held out her hand. She avoided Lydia's eye. Embarrassed.

'Sorry, love.' Henry obediently took a bite and chewed while Lydia tried to make conversation to cover the sudden awkwardness, the pall that Henry's worsening health cast over their small party.

A small dog was running around in wildly excited circles with a boy of about eight or nine. Lydia focused on the happy sounds. 'They're both going to get dizzy,' she said and her mum rewarded her with a small, grateful smile.

'You're family, aren't you?' Her dad was frowning at her. He looked angry but Lydia could feel his fear.

She shifted on the grass in order to get her hand into the back pocket of her jeans and produced a gold coin.

Her dad relaxed back against the tree. 'Knew it.'

'I'm your daughter,' Lydia said. No more pretending this wasn't happening. 'Lydia.'

He nodded. 'We've got to be careful, Lyds.'

'It's all right, Henry,' her mother selected something else from her bag. 'Have some grapes.'

Henry ignored her and Lydia couldn't bear it. Her father had always been so loving, so unfailingly polite and caring with her mother. That was the worst thing about the memory lapses. It wasn't just that he couldn't remember them, it was that he couldn't remember himself.

A few minutes later, Henry's eye was caught by some tweens playing with a ball. They were kicking it half-heartedly across a small circle of unoccupied grass, the heat of the sun already sapping their motivation for the game, despite their youth. He still seemed agitated and his forehead creased as he watched, his hands balling into fists. 'If Dad catches them with that, there will be trouble.'

Lydia looked at her mum. Her father was so much worse than she had ever seen. She thought about Jason's theory, that it was Lydia's presence which was making her dad worse, powering up his disease in the way she seemed to power up Jason's life force.

'Wasting time,' he muttered quietly, venomously. 'They should be keeping a lookout, not messing like that.'

'It's okay,' her mum said, 'really, darling, everything is fine. I promise.'

'You don't know what he's like,' he sat forward, lowered his voice to a whisper. 'Listen, Charlie forgot one thing one time, just one thing, and he whipped him. There was blood running down his back.'

Lydia dug her fingernails into her palm and then re-wrapped her uneaten cheese roll. Her appetite had gone.

'He is frightened,' her dad said, suddenly. 'He knows it's all gone to shit. Everybody knows we haven't got it anymore. We're weak. He's frightened about that. He needs to just let it all go, but he won't. He can't.'

Lydia took her dad's hand and squeezed gently. She had only the vaguest memories of Grandpa Crow. He had been old, of course. Impossibly old, it had seemed. And he had a face that didn't smile easily. Hard eyes that were black and shiny, like the back of a beetle, and a tall, thin frame. Uncle Charlie was tall, but thickset with it. Heavy muscular shoulders and a wide chest. Henry, her dad, looked much more like Grandpa's son. He was strong, and still fit for his age, but he tended to slimness. When Lydia looked in the family photo album, and saw images of Grandpa Crow as a middle-aged man, she could see how her father would look if he didn't laugh as often.

'He's always talking about the glory days, but they're gone. They're not coming back and that's a good thing.'

'Quite right,' Lydia's mother said. She patted her husband's leg. 'Would you like some lemon cake?'

He blinked. 'Too hot. Let's get ice lollies.'

'I'll get them,' Lydia stood up, torn between wanting to escape and wanting to listen to her dad. It was heart-breaking, but while his defences were down, he might talk more openly about their family history than he ever had before. She wasn't proud of that thought, but it was there nonetheless. She knew that the Crows had a dodgy reputation, which stretched back to the bad old days when they had operated on the wrong side of the law, offering protection and loans and problem-solving to members of the community, whether they wanted it or not.

Lydia went to the kiosk on the edge of the park and bought a Magnum for her mum and two Soleros. When she got back, Henry was dozing, his head tipped back against the tree, so she ate both ice lollies as quickly as she could, the fruity ice melting. She was licking syrup off her wrist when her mother said something unexpected. 'When I met your Grandpa, he told me that your dad was the strongest they had seen in the family for decades.' She shook her head. 'He hid it from me. He protected me. He protected us both.'

'I know, Mum. Meeting Madeleine, that whole business, made me appreciate your choices. Bringing me up here,' Lydia waved her lolly stick to indicate the park and beyond. 'She is really messed up. And I still don't know exactly what part Uncle Charlie played.'

'You know why we told you stay away from him, then. You see it?'

'I do. I swear.'

She smiled sadly. 'But you're staying at The Fork.'

'I am,' Lydia said. 'I can't turn down free rent, and the location is really good for my business. And I'm being careful.'

'Money isn't everything. And we could help you out, if that was an issue. We've got some savings.'

Lydia waved this away. 'Thank you, but I'm fine. Honestly. And it's not just the rent. I like the place.'

Lydia struggled for something to say that didn't involve her ghostly flatmate. She wasn't going to leave Jason. It would be like killing him. 'Angel is nice and the cafe downstairs makes it feel safe.'

Mum gave her a look which spoke volumes, all of them heavy with scepticism.

Lydia reached across and hugged her quickly. They weren't an especially cuddly family, but the scent of Mum's perfume and shampoo sent her back in time to childhood. Sitting on her knee, having a plaster applied to a graze, hiding her face in Mum's shoulder to avoid having to speak to people at a party, her hand gripped tightly as they crossed a busy road. 'I really am being careful,' she said quietly.

Mum squeezed more tightly for a moment and then let go. 'Eat your roll,' she said. 'You look half-starved.'

THE NEXT MORNING, Lydia woke up with good intentions to focus on her Crow Investigations work (while avoiding being sucked into Crow Family business by Uncle Charlie), exercise more often and cut down on her alcohol intake. The usual Monday-morning bullshit.

She started off well by searching for the address of the flats she had observed Mrs Lee visiting. Then she added 'manicure' into the search and tried again. A Facebook page revealed a home business offering gel nails and 'unique designs'. She copied all the information into her report and forwarded it to Dr Lee, suggesting that he check the state of her nails. There was a good chance that Mrs Lee had been getting knock-off gel manicures and not rolling in the bedsheets. Which, unless Dr Lee had very strong views on nail art, would be a happy ending.

After typing up her notes and sending them over to Dr Lee, Lydia looked at the boxes of books she had brought from her flat in Aberdeen. Unpacking them would be a sign of permanence. Something important and grounding. Something she both wanted and feared. Of course, it was too hot to contemplate the task at that moment. And she still needed to sort out some book-shelves, which meant added expense and hassle. Lydia turned away from the boxes, telling herself it was a job for another day.

Instead, she went back to her laptop and logged into one of the paid-for databases she had learned about during her work at Karen's investigative firm. Before training, Lydia had been in blissful ignorance of just how easy it was to find people; their places of work, home addresses, telephone numbers, criminal and driving records, the names of their pets, and favourite restaurants.

Robert Sharp's finance firm was in the City. More precisely, it was in the Gherkin. Lydia stood outside the bullet-shaped glass-tessellated skyscraper and scoped the reception area. It was filled with large displays of spiky foliage, as well as several dark-suited guards, three shiny-looking receptionists and a doorway scanner like at airport security.

The hexagonal panes of glass of the Gherkin were mirrored black and, up close, the iconic building had more than a little of the Death Star about it. Lydia knew that the chance of anyone at Robert Sharp's place of employment letting her in for a look around and a casual chat with his co-workers was minimal, shiny new business card or not. Instead, she started calling the nearest office plant-hire and maintenance firms to find out who supplied Sharp's company and got lucky in no time. Luckily enough they had a very simple staff uniform of a navy polo shirt with a small embroidered logo on the chest and beige cargo-style trousers. Lydia visited the nearest Gap store for the polo and trousers, and then went to an upscale florist. Lydia bought a plant large enough to be slightly awkward to carry, in the hope that the empathetic reaction to a small woman struggling with a heavy object would make people wave her through a little quicker than they might otherwise.

'Delivery for Sheridan Fisher. PlantLife.'

'You need to sign in.'

Lydia balanced the enormous plant on the desk and scribbled a name she had cribbed from the staff gallery on the PlantLife website.

'Third floor.'

The Sheridan Fisher offices were large and open-plan and filled with quiet work sounds. 'Excuse me,' Lydia stopped a harried-looking woman in a grey trouser-suit. 'Can you direct me to Mr Sharp's desk, please? I have a delivery.' She hoisted the plant a little, making it appear even heavier than it was.

The woman frowned. 'Over there I think.' She pointed to the far corner. 'Joseph Hazeldine will know. He works with him.'

Lydia was surprised that the woman hadn't reacted

to the name but, perhaps she hadn't been questioned by the police. Lydia assumed they would have visited by now, though, and that that would have started a chain of office gossip. Perhaps the place was too big and impersonal for that to have happened. Or they were really living the London life and had cultivated a 'don't ask, don't care' attitude to their colleagues. Perhaps the sight of the police trawling through and asking questions was completely normal. Lydia had absolutely no idea. The world of high finance, corporate analysts and city boys, was completely beyond her realm of experience. She half-expected to see a load of coked-up young men, snorting lines off the toned stomachs of strippers and shouting 'buy!' and 'sell!' at random intervals.

In the corner the woman had indicated there was a cluster of four desks with little partition screens, two of which were occupied. 'Mr Hazeldine?'

A man with floppy blonde hair and a bright purple tie looked up from his computer screen. He smiled at Lydia, seemingly happy for a distraction. 'Is that for me?'

Lydia forced a friendly smile. 'For Mr R. Sharp, I'm afraid. Do you know where I can find him?'

'That's his desk,' Hazeldine said, pointing to the empty desk opposite. Lydia nodded and busied herself with arranging the plant in the corner, behind Sharp's desk. Again, she was surprised that Sharp's colleague didn't seem to know about his death. Of course, Robert's identity hadn't been reported in the news, but surely the Murder Investigation Team in charge of the case had to have been in, asking questions.

Sharp's desk was neat and there were no handy

documents laid out on the plain surface. Nothing, in fact, except for a small action figure of a female superhero Lydia didn't recognise next to the monitor and an empty smoothie bottle in the rubbish bin.

Lydia didn't know what she had expected. Not exactly a black ribbon on the guy's chair or full-mourning outfits on his co-workers but something. Some indication that a man who had spent most of his waking hours in this spot had, just recently, been callously killed.

'Do you know when he'll be back,' Lydia had crossed back to Hazeldine's side of the desk and was leaning against it.

'No, why?' He leaned back in his chair and looked up at her, his gaze lingering on her chest before meeting her eyes with a challenging smile. Hazeldine still seemed friendly enough but there was an edge in there, too. Lydia's normal senses, the ones she used as a woman all of the time, ticked up a little. She resisted the urge to straighten up, and widened her own smile. 'He's supposed to sign for the plant. Is he often out of the office?'

'Shouldn't be,' Hazeldine said. 'He's been off sick a lot recently, though. Lightweight.'

'Oh well,' Lydia said, properly keen to get away, now. Hazeldine had given a snorting little laugh and she knew, suddenly, that his affable demeanour was thin veneer over something darker and more volatile.

'Some people can't handle this job, you know. They're not built for it.'

'What is it you do, here?' Lydia forced herself to seem perky. Interested.

'Analysis.'

Well, that was helpful, Lydia thought.

As she stepped out of the open-plan office and back into the hallway, a woman in a dark suit stopped her. For a heart-stopping moment, Lydia thought she might be undercover security, but a second glance at her red-rimmed eyes and wan expression revealed a different truth. 'Are you here for his things?'

'Sorry?'

'Rob's stuff. Are you here to clear his desk. I saw you over there,' she gestured to the corner of the office.

'No,' Lydia said. 'I'm actually an investigator.'

The woman nodded, as if this was only to be expected. She knew, then.

'Did you work closely with Robert?'

'No, not really. I just...' the woman took a visible breath. 'We were friendly. He was nice.'

'When you say friendly...'

'Oh. No. Nothing like... Nothing like that. I'm married.' She used her fingertips to swipe underneath her eyes. Then looked around as if worried she was being observed.

'Shall we?' Lydia indicated the hall and they moved out of the office and away from the desks and ringing phones.

The woman pulled a face. When she spoke, it was all in a rush. Like the words were escaping from the prison of her mouth. 'You can't show weakness, here. It's not the done thing. Especially if you don't have a dick. Sorry.'

Lydia waved a hand to indicate she wasn't offended. 'So, you liked Robert, then? He was nice?'

She nodded.

'And you are?'

'Anna Croft. My boss told me about Rob yesterday. He knew we chatted. He'd seen us together at the Christmas party. Not together together. My husband was there, too.'

Lydia nodded to show she understood. 'Did Rob have lots of friends, here?'

A short laugh. 'Nobody does. No time.'

'How had Rob seemed recently? Any problems at work?'

Anna shook her head. 'Not that he would have said. It's not that kind of place.'

'He was getting on fine, then. Seemed happy enough?'

'He'd taken a few sick days recently. But he seemed fine when he was here. More than fine, really. He was always really calm. Nice. Good at listening, you know?'

Lydia nodded, again, not wanting to break the woman's flow by speaking.

'Most people aren't, but Rob was...' She took a deep breath, trailing off.

'What did you mean 'more than fine'? When did you last see him?'

'Last week sometime. Maybe the Wednesday? He had just been, I don't know, more energetic than usual. Kind of caffeinated.'

'That's normal round here, I bet,' Lydia said. 'It seems pretty intense.'

'Not for Rob,' Anna said. 'I always thought he was going to get out of here. Retire early and live in a caravan or something. I've really got to get back to work. Sorry.'

'Thank you for your time,' Lydia said. 'Can I just get the name of your boss?'

Her eyes widened. 'Haven't you already spoken to him? I don't want any trouble.'

'Why would you be in trouble?'

The woman just shook her head. 'I've got to get back to work.'

'Here's my card,' Lydia said. 'And I'm very sorry for your loss.' Anna Croft was already walking away, her spine as straight as a prima ballerina. Lydia watched her leave with admiration. Discipline, strength and self-control. Perhaps she ought to take up dancing.

CHAPTER FOUR

That evening, Lydia had ignored the muggy heat that was still lying across the city and dutifully attended her circuits class. She was in her third set of conditioning sprints, her legs and arms burning with effort and her lungs dragging in oxygen with harsh rasps, when she felt her senses fire. Electricity ran through her body in a short, sharp, shock, and she knew there was power in the room. It burned the back of her throat and stung her eyes, screaming that it was a danger, that it meant attack. Instantly, she dropped to the floor and rolled onto her back, legs ready to kick out. Lydia had been working on her upper-body strength, but she knew her legs were still her best bet in a defensive situation. There was nobody there.

Lydia looked around, hunting for the source of danger she had felt so keenly. Everything normal. The instructor, a well-muscled woman with bleached white-blonde hair, crossed the room with a concerned expression on her face. 'You okay, hun?'

'Fine,' Lydia said, climbing to her feet. 'Just thirsty.' She knew she still looked like an oddball, but the excuse gave her a chance to escape to the side of the room where her water bottle and towel were waiting. The sensation had already faded. Gone as quickly as it had appeared, which made absolutely no sense. Lydia scanned the room of sweating exercisers casually, while swigging from her water bottle. Nothing unusual. And she wasn't getting a Family vibe from any of them. If she had she would have been surprised as she ought to have felt it the moment she walked into the room at the start of the class. Lydia closed her eyes for a moment, partly to ease the gritty sensation and partly to try to recreate the flash of magic she had felt. It hadn't been Crow or Fox, that was definite. She was pretty sure it hadn't been Pearl or Silver, either. Partly because she could identify them easily and partly because the flash had been so strong. Pearlies had been growing in strength, but they still had a very mellow, inviting sort of energy, not something spiky and hot. And Silvers were excellent liars, had the gift of the gab and could charm you with wordplay or could argue that the sky was on the ground until you began to doubt your own eyes, but their abilities were the remnants of their old power. When Lydia sensed a Silver, she saw just a thin outline of magic. An after-image.

Maybe her power was misfiring. A thought which gave her an unexpected jolt of terror. She had always thought she was a nothing when it came to Crow power.

The daughter of the heir to the Family, the great Henry Crow, just a big fat zero. Her whole life, all she had been able to do was sense the power in others and identify its origin: Silver, Pearl, Crow or Fox. Since moving back to London, though, she had realised that there was something a little more. She seemed to amplify the power in others, too. At least, that was what Jason thought. Before she had moved into the flat above The Fork, he had been unable to touch anything, had been a true wraith. Now, he could hold a pen and, to Lydia, he looked fully solid and alive most of the time. She had just been getting used to the idea that maybe she wasn't such a useless Crow after all, and the thought that maybe it was all going to disappear was unpleasant. A malfunctioning Crow. That did not sound good.

Lydia took a few more deep breaths. The weird feeling had gone. Everything is fine, she told herself. Get back to the laps, sweat out whatever weirdness had just happened. Then she realised she was being watched. A man Lydia hadn't noticed before was stretching out his hamstrings, but he was looking in her direction with a steady gaze. She had thought 'man' because of the width of his shoulders but his face looked very young and boyish. His dark skin was gleaming with sweat and his brown eyes were fixed on her as if they knew one another.

She wasn't getting a power-sense from him, so maybe he was looking because he was interested. Lydia was torn between feeling flattered and her desire to be utterly anonymous and unnoticed while exercising. Especially if she was going to start having mid-workout freak-outs. Rolling her neck to ease the tension, she closed her eyes for a moment and blocked the room and her admirer out. In that moment, in a single split-second, she was falling. Thrown over the edge of the roof terrace at The Fork and plunging toward the concrete, air rushing past her face. She opened her eyes quickly and felt the sensation drain away, although her heart was hammering and her insides were cold. She crouched down, touching the floor for security and waited until she didn't feel like throwing up anymore. This made no sense. If she was going to have trauma flashbacks, why not the time her cousin had almost choked the life from her? Not flashbacks to something that hadn't happened. It had been threatened, but it hadn't happened. *It hadn't happened.* 'You're fine,' Lydia whispered to herself, more as an experiment than anything else. Feeling a little better, she straightened up. The boy who had been staring had gone. She looked around the gym to be sure, but there was no sign. Unable to shake a feeling of unease, Lydia button-holed the trainer. 'Do you know the guy who just left?'

'What guy?'

Lydia described him. 'He was here a moment ago so he must have just left.'

The trainer shook her head. 'Doesn't ring a bell, sorry.'

Lydia gathered her things and left. She kept a look out for the man/boy, but there was no sign. It was official. *She was losing it.*

BACK AT THE FLAT, Lydia knew she must have still been feeling freaked out, as she found herself confiding in Jason. Predictably enough, his solution involved testing her abilities. 'I told you, I don't know how.'

'What about your coin trick? How do you do that?'

'It's not a trick,' Lydia said. Then, catching herself, she added. 'What coin trick?'

Jason smiled. 'When you're thinking, one appears out of nowhere and you flip it over the back of your knuckles.'

'Oh,' Lydia felt embarrassed to have been observed. It was by a ghost, but still. Charlie would call her sloppy. 'I don't know how I do it. I just think about a coin and it appears.'

'Does it work with other things?'

'Like a million pounds in used bank notes? Sadly not.'

'Does it always work?'

'It's not like working or not working,' Lydia said, her mind stumbling as she tried to articulate something she had always known and never examined. 'It's more that the coin exists all the time. It's mine. It's part of me like my thumb is part of my hand.'

'What would happen if you tried to get more?'

'I have one,' Lydia said. 'I don't know how I would get more.'

Jason put one hand to his mouth and regarded her for a moment. 'But have you ever tried?'

'I don't know how,' Lydia said. 'I told you.' Her chest was suddenly tight and she wanted out of the conversation. Something must have translated to her expression because Jason wavered and, for a moment, he looked less solid than usual.

'I'm not trying to be obtuse,' Lydia went to the sofa and sat down. Her legs felt shaky and it had nothing to do with her workout. 'And I feel really stupid. I don't know why I haven't thought more about this stuff, questioned it all.'

'It's not stupid,' Jason said. 'We always think that whatever we grew up with is normal. I thought everybody did logic puzzles to relax.'

Lydia managed a smile. 'Weirdo.'

Lydia stood outside Sharp's address. The purpose-built block of flats was like nothing in Camberwell. Curved balconies, smoked glass, and gleaming stonework. A lot of very modern looking and no doubt very expensive horticulture outside and, according to the website Lydia had studied, a state-of-the-art gym and swimming pool in the basement. It was only recently completed and there were still a few units available to buy. For those who fancied blowing a million and a half on two bedrooms. This was London so Lydia thought she was used to insane property prices, but even so... She shaded her eyes and looked up, trying to imagine the kind of people Sharp had rubbed shoulders with on a daily basis in a place like this.

The woman behind the desk in the large open-plan lobby was very attractive. More than that she was a Pearlie. Maybe not central bloodline, but definitely related. There was a sheen to her skin, a lustre that made

Lydia want to reach out and stroke her cheek. Her mouth flooded with saliva and she was suddenly ravenously hungry. *Feathers. Beak. Claw.* She repeated the words until her mouth stopped watering and her mind cleared enough to approach the desk.

She had a lie at the ready, but changed her mind at the last moment and produced her business card, instead. 'I'm here about Robert Sharp, one of your residents.'

A pink tongue darted out and moistened her lips as she studied Lydia's card. Then she turned perfect almond-shaped eyes, edged with black kohl onto Lydia. 'You're here to see Mr Sharp? He's-'

'Dead, yes. I know. I'm an investigator and I want to ask his neighbours a couple of questions.'

'That's out of the question, I'm afraid. If you're not with the police I can't let you through to harass our residents.'

'I'm not a journalist.'

She pursed her lips and it was everything Lydia could do not to vault over the desk and kiss her. And Lydia had always considered herself, for the most part, heterosexual. The Pearlie powers of attraction were clearly running strong.

'You're not police,' the woman said. 'You've got no right. And our residents value their privacy.'

'I bet they value their security, too,' Lydia said. 'Doesn't look great when one of their number ends up swinging under Blackfriars Bridge.'

The woman tilted her head. 'That's Blackfriars. This is Canary Wharf.'

Lydia smiled. 'Yeah, I got that. I'm a long way from home, here. Camberwell isn't half as swanky.'

Her eyes widened a little and, for a moment, her glowing beauty dimmed.

'Yes, Lydia Crow. One of those Crows.' She tapped her business card. 'The Crows.'

The woman opened her mouth, but no sound came out and then she closed it again.

Lydia leaned on the desk. 'I can see you know what that means. You're a Pearl, aren't you? We don't have any problem with Pearls. Not for a very long time, anyway. And isn't that nice.'

'Please,' the woman's face creased into a pained expression. 'I can't help you. I'll lose my job.'

'Nah,' Lydia said. 'I guarantee no one will complain. Especially if you let me into his flat. Let me have a little look around. I probably won't need to go banging on doors at all, then. Probably get everything I need on the quiet.'

The woman picked up a walkie talkie and pressed a button. A few moments later, a security guard in a grey uniform strolled through the door. 'Can you take Ms Crow to see unit forty-five.' She held up a hand, as if anticipating an objection. 'I know it's not on the market, yet, but this is a special favour.'

THE FLAT WAS DROP-DEAD GORGEOUS. Provided your vision of beauty was monotone, open-plan, and filled with statement lighting and glass. A folding glass wall led from the living space to the balcony and the skyline view of assorted skyscrapers and water was truly spectacular. It was like being in a different London entirely. One of shining metal and modernism.

Lydia did a quick walk around while the security guard waited, fiddling with his phone. Sharp's personal belongings were few and far between and it was as if he had moved into a showhome with hand luggage only. Which was entirely possible. Even with his job, this address had to be a stretch on the mortgage. 'How long had Mr Sharp been here?'

The guard looked up. 'Not long. Same as everyone. New build, innit?'

In the bedroom there were a couple of paperbacks on the nightstand, both sci fi, and a ratty checked dressing gown which looked like Robert could've kept it from childhood. The ensuite revealed Colgate toothpaste, Imperial Leather soap, and a supermarket own brand antiperspirant. Not exactly the high-end toiletries you would expect in a home of this calibre and cost.

Back in the living space, Lydia checked the kitchen cupboards. A box of sugary cereal, a bag of pasta and jar of tomato sauce. The fridge had cheese and grapes, an entire shelf of champagne, and a pack of Budweiser. 'No one has been to clear out his stuff, then?'

The guard looked up. 'Is that full?'

'Yeah.'

'No, then.'

Lydia pulled a face. 'Thanks.'

'You done in here? I need to get back.'

'Almost.' Lydia felt a little bit nauseous and figured it

was the heat of the day, combined with the stale, shut-in air of the flat.

The guard heaved a dramatic sigh, as if Lydia were keeping him from vital duties. Or perhaps he felt unwell, too.

There wasn't much storage and she had checked every drawer and cupboard. She turned slowly, looking for ledges or tops of furniture. Then, she took a dining chair and, moving methodically around the room, used it to stand on while she ran her hands across every concealed space. Just dust.

She sat on the dark grey sectional sofa and eyed the coffee table. It was shaped like a large pebble and looked like it was moulded from one piece of plastic but when she leaned forward and touched it, it was textured and more solid. Some sort of ceramic or resin. She ran her hands over the smooth sides, checking for a hidden catch. Nothing.

On the opposite wall there was a huge television hung on the wall and, underneath, a long low cabinet with a glossy white finish. There was a large table lamp with a complicated blown-glass base and a couple of spiky plants which were either plastic or doing an excellent job of appearing so. There was something tucked behind the larger of the plants and Lydia crossed the room to have a closer look. It was a silver figure of a knight in full armour, carrying a sword and shield. The figure was about six-inches tall and was mounted on a circular base with lion's feet. It looked antique and as out of place with the rest of the décor as the Imperial Leather soap had been in the bathroom. She took several photos of the figure from as many angles as she could think of and some close-up shots of the underneath of the base where there were markings and a maker's stamp.

'Time to go,' the guard said, finally out of patience.

CHAPTER FIVE

B ack at the flat, Lydia took a bottle of beer from the fridge and spent a satisfying minute rolling the cold glass around her face and neck. It was past six and the heat was still thick across the city. Lydia had windows open but there was zero air movement. She considered stripping off all her clothes, but the thought that Jason might appear at any moment was inhibiting.

Her phone rang, and she saw Paul Fox's number. Paul Fox had phoned Lydia a couple of times over the last few weeks and she hadn't picked up. He had sent over a thick A4 envelope via courier, too. Lydia hadn't opened it, hadn't even touched it, in fact, and had just told the courier to take it straight back. She hadn't told Charlie about Paul's involvement with her cousin, Maddie. She figured that Maddie turning out to be psychotic, and Charlie's own culpability in the whole affair, made the Fox family's role pale into comparison.

Besides, the last thing anybody needed was tensions to rise between the Families. The Foxes had always been the trickiest. Not to mention the most unpredictable. She hesitated, looking at her phone screen and wondering whether it would be better to just speak to him. 'What?'

'Hello, Little Bird.'

The instant he spoke, Lydia felt the Fox tang. It vibrated through her body and set her fight or flight instincts on high alert. 'Don't call me that,' Lydia said, immediately regretting it. Now he would never stop. 'What do you want?'

'Just checking how you are settling in. Wondering if you're ready to take on a new client, yet?'

'I'm fully-booked.'

'I'm not surprised,' Paul said. 'Flying around all over the place for Uncle Charlie, I bet.'

Lydia produced a coin from the air and then held onto it, tightly. 'Is that all?'

'You should be friendlier to me.' Paul's voice was no longer gentle, there was a thin meanness coming through.

'Is that a fact?'

'You remember what a good friend I can be, Little Bird.'

'I remember lots of things,' Lydia said. 'How is dear Tristin? Is he speaking to you again?' Tristin Fox, head of the Fox Family and probably the only person to strike fear into Paul Fox's heart.

'What?'

'After you hooked up with Maddie Crow and she

56

went rogue and then dear old Tristin had to smooth things over with the cops. I bet that went down well.'

'You are way off,' Paul said, after a pause, but Lydia could feel a reduction in his energy.

'Why do you want me to work for you so badly?' Lydia said. 'You know I don't want to help you, you know I don't trust you, so what is this about? If you're just trying to irritate me then, congratulations, job done, but surely you've better things to do. Unless,' Lydia paused theatrically, 'you don't have anything better going on? Unless bothering me is your new hobby because you truly don't have anything more interesting in your life. I do hope not, that sounds terribly sad.'

'You shouldn't speak to me like that,' Paul said, his voice tight. 'Things have changed.'

'So you keep saying,' Lydia said. 'But it all feels like business as usual around here.'

'Like you would know. You are the precious little princess, kept away from all the dirty work.'

He was echoing Maddie's words and she wondered just how much she had spoken to Paul in the time they were together. Hell Hawk, they could still be together. Maddie had done a disappearing act again, but that didn't mean she wasn't hiding out with Paul. Just that the Crow Family weren't looking for her this time. For all Lydia knew, Madeleine could be standing right next to Paul, now, listening to her every word. The hairs stood up on the back of her neck.

'Next time I send you a parcel, you'd do well to open it.'

'I'm busy,' Lydia said. 'Fully-booked. No room at the inn. No space in my diary.'

'You'll change your mind.'

'I won't, Lydia said. 'So stop trying.'

Paul cut the call suddenly and without saying good-bye. Lydia looked at her screen for a moment and wondered whether she had won that round or not.

Jason shimmered in the doorway looking anxious. 'Who was that?'

'Paul Fox,' Lydia said. 'Fishing for information or just trying to annoy me. Not sure which.'

'That doesn't sound good,' Jason was shaking a little and, now that Lydia was looking properly she could see he looked properly upset.

She stood up. 'Hey, it's all right.'

'He's bad news,' Jason said.

'I know,' Lydia held her hands up, uncertain whether to try to pat Jason or not. She was surprised to find that she wanted to put her arms around him. 'It's okay, though. He's just trying to annoy me. He must be bored.'

'What if it's more than that?'

'I whisked Maddie out from under his nose, he's just trying to assert dominance or show me that he's not beaten or something equally macho and inane. I'm not playing his little power games so it doesn't matter.'

'I don't like it,' Jason said, still vibrating gently.

'Look,' Lydia rummaged in her desk drawer. 'I bought a new pack of Sharpies. Different colours. Why don't you do your maths thing. You'll feel better.'

'I'm not a child,' Jason said. 'Technically, I'm older

than you.' But he took the pack of markers and disappeared into his bedroom.

THE WARNING BUZZER sounded and Lydia took a slug from her beer before going to open the door. She was just in time to see Fleet round the corner of the landing.

He stopped when he saw her lounging in the entrance. 'You expecting someone?'

Lydia raised her bottle in salute. 'Just you.'

Fleet walked along the landing, his bulk filling the space. He had come straight from work and was carrying a leather bag and his suit jacket, but had loosened his tie and rolled up his shirt sleeves. 'Spooky.'

'That's me,' Lydia said, she stepped back to let him into the flat. 'Beer?'

'Please,' Fleet threw his jacket and bag onto the client's chair, and sat on the sofa Lydia had pushed against one wall.

Lydia passed him a bottle and their fingers brushed. Suddenly, the tiredness of the day evaporated and she felt her senses kick up. She watched as he tipped his head back and took a long drink, his throat moving as he swallowed, then headed back into the kitchen to get some nuts. Okay, it was time to move away from Fleet before she jumped him.

'Good day?' Fleet called as she dumped salted cashews into a washed-out takeaway tray.

'Frustrating,' Lydia said, presenting him with the snacks.

Fleet put the tray on the floor. 'Tell me about it.'

Lydia bent down to scoop some cashews and then joined Fleet on the sofa, making sure not to touch him as she sat. 'You first. Catch any bad guys today?'

Fleet leaned back. 'Picked up a couple of kids for street art.'

'Street art?'

'Well, they said it was art. Couple of spray-painted cocks and a carefully-worded stanza on the human condition. And who the hell knows anymore?'

'Stanza?' Lydia regarded him over the rim of her beer bottle. 'You talk fancy for a copper.'

Fleet looked mock affronted. 'I'm educated.'

'I'm not,' Lydia said, cheerfully enough.

'Your turn,' Fleet pointed with the neck of his bottle. 'Tell me all about your frustrating day. And give me your foot.'

'Why?' Lydia instinctively drew her legs up, curling her feet underneath her body.

Fleet looked amused. 'So I can rub it. Ease your aching muscles.'

'My feet are fine,' Lydia said.

'I have skills in other areas,' Fleet said, his voice low and teasing.

'Stop that,' Lydia said. 'We're just friends.'

'I'm just being friendly.'

Lydia gave him a severe look. 'I am downgrading you from friend to source.'

'Source?'

'Of information,' Lydia said. 'So if you want to sit on my sofa and drink my beer, you'd better give me some.' She hesitated, feeling the blush ignite her face. 'Information. You'd better give me some information.'

Fleet looked like he was trying not to laugh.

'Have you made friends with the investigative team, yet? The MIT on the Sharp case?'

'Why are you so interested in Sharp?'

'A man has been murdered.' Lydia was going for the moral high ground, but Fleet didn't look impressed.

'Plenty of those,' Fleet gestured with his beer bottle. 'Why are you so fixated on this one?'

'I don't know,' Lydia said. 'I think the method just feels like a big 'fuck you' to the whole city. It was designed to be seen, to cause fear or send a message, and I don't like it. It's disrespectful.' Lydia was surprised at her own words. She sounded like Uncle Charlie.

Fleet was no longer lounging. He sat forward. 'I do agree, I'm just not sure I want to tank my career over it.'

'Fair enough,' Lydia said, trying not to feel too disappointed.

'There are very strict rules about taking actions within the Met. We have a database where every single move is documented and there are all kinds of procedures and rules in place to ensure things like chain of evidence are maintained.'

'I know,' Lydia said. 'I understand.'

'Having said that,' Fleet continued. 'Coppers are still coppers. We talk to each other. And it turned out that I do know someone on the MIT for Sharp. Ian Weatherby. Good guy. We trained together.'

Lydia sat forward, mirroring Fleet's position. 'Please tell me you've recently reconnected.'

'Funnily enough, we have.' Fleet became serious. 'He's actually been having a rough time of it recently. Trouble at home.'

Lydia dug her finger nails into her palm to curb her impatience.

'But we got around to the case and the main line of enquiry is looking for companies who may have lost out on the stock exchange or during sales deals when he valued them.'

'That's his job? Valuing entire companies?'

'Right,' Fleet said. 'As far as I can understand, anyway, which isn't very far. He provides the analysis on which the final valuation is based, I think. The guy's job description would make an excellent alternative to sleeping tablets.'

'It's deliberately obtuse,' Lydia said with the instinctive dislike of cloak and dagger. Yes, her Family were known for it, but obfuscation was entirely appropriate when you belonged to an ancient, magical family with age-old feuds and had survived a couple of witch hunts... Less so when you were a corporate behemoth with enough financial and political power to change the wider society. Or she was just being a hypocrite.

'Isn't it a bit unlikely that a company would take out a professional hit on some worker bee in another large corporation?'

'Maybe,' Fleet said. 'But like you said, it seemed like a message. Maybe it wasn't so much Sharp himself as what he represents. Maybe he was just the most convenient option, the notepaper that came to hand when they went to scrawl a letter... Know what I mean?'

Lydia nodded. It was a horrible thought. A person considered as disposable. A means to an end.

'He lived alone and background checks haven't exactly turned up a thriving social life. It seems the guy worked and slept and that was pretty much it.'

Lydia wanted to talk to Fleet about the knight figurine. She valued his opinion and, though she felt pathetic for admitting it, she wanted the connection that would come from talking. Fleet must have seen the conflict written across her face.

'What did you do?'

'What makes you think I did something?'

Fleet reached out a hand, cupped Lydia's cheek. 'We've been through this before. I'm on your side.'

'You're also a cop.'

'You contravened any laws recently?' He smiled fondly. 'Big ones, I mean.'

Lydia let herself lean into Fleet's hand, just for a moment. 'There was something weird at Sharp's flat. Something out of place.'

Fleet moved his hand and Lydia's face felt cold. 'You broke into his flat?'

'Definitely not,' Lydia said, robustly.

'Then how?'

She spoke over him. 'But I saw this. I've been chasing it up.' She pulled her phone out of her back pocket and thumbed the screen, bringing up the images. 'Look. It's expensive.'

'He wasn't short of a bob or two,' Fleet said, studying the pictures. He looked up. 'You saw his flat, so you know that. Which we still need to discuss. If you didn't break and enter-'

'But it didn't fit,' Lydia persisted. 'With his other stuff. With his life.'

'If someone killed him over this,' Fleet handed the phone back. 'Why didn't they nick it?'

Lydia slumped back. 'I don't know. It's weird, though. Right?'

'I suppose,' Fleet said. 'People are weird, though. You can never tell what people will be into in their spare time.'

'True,' Lydia thought about Mrs Lee and her clandestine manicure visits and the many other odd little habits she had observed over the last couple of years of investigating.

'Speaking of which...' He let the sentence trail away, while maintaining eye contact. His pupils were dilated and Lydia could read his meaning clearly. They were both consenting adults. They were both off the clock. She swallowed hard. 'Don't look at me like that.'

The corners of his mouth lifted. 'Why not?'

'You know why. We're just friends, now. Colleagues.'

'Friendly colleagues.'

'Emphasis on the colleagues,' Lydia said.

'If you insist,' Fleet said. He saluted her with his beer bottle. 'Shame, though.'

Lydia pushed down the flare of attraction which was threatening to ignite into a forest fire, burning down all of her good intentions, her self-restraint. She drank her

64

beer, instead, and turned her thoughts to the dead analyst, swinging from Blackfriars Bridge with bricks in his pockets.

CHAPTER SIX

Lydia was out on the roof terrace. The low railing was digging into her stomach and she could feel her centre of gravity shift as she tipped forward. Something was pushing from behind and she was going to fall and there was nothing she could do to stop herself. She tried to move her arms, to grasp the railing, but they were glued to her sides. She was as thoroughly paralysed as if she was bound head to foot in rope. Still, she strained against the invisible bonds. She tried to turn her head to see who was pushing her, to reason with them. Was it the man? The hit man sent by Ivan. Professional gaze, dead inside. But that had been a mistake. That had been a hit meant for her cousin Madeleine. She was dreaming. Lydia suddenly knew she was dreaming. It was probably just a delayed reaction from that awful day. Her first day back in London when a man with a gun had tried to make her take a swan dive off the roof. She willed herself to wake up.

'No chance,' Maddie's voice was in her ear. Clear as if she was really standing there and not a figment of Lydia's subconscious. 'You are stuck here, now.'

'I don't want to fall,' Lydia said.

'Nobody wants to fall,' Maddie said. 'But it's the landing you really ought to worry about.'

Lydia felt the brush of feathers against her cheek and then the horizon tipped and she was levered over the railing. She was falling, air rushing, stomach swooping.

The grey concrete was getting closer and bigger, fast. Too fast. Impossibly, Maddie's voice was still in her ear, as if she was falling with her. 'Come on, Lydia. You know how to fly.'

Lydia woke up. She was sweaty and her heart was galloping and, for a moment, she lay with a hand on her forehead and thought about crying. The feeling passed and logic swam back into the foreground. Paul Fox had phoned her and made her think about Maddie. That was why she had dreamed about her. Carefully ignoring the flare of danger she had sensed at the gym and the possible mis-firing of her Crow intuition, Lydia filed the dream under 'weird one-off' and got out of bed. She took a long shower, rinsing away the dregs of the dream, and dressed for work. Black vest top, black skinny jeans, hair tied back. The clothes which meant action, business, and strength.

In the small kitchen, Lydia found a fresh mug of coffee ready-made on the side. She couldn't see Jason but she said 'thank you' out loud, anyway. A waft of cool air and the scent of citrus smoke heralded his appearance and, when she turned around, he was in the doorway. 'I left you alone last night,' he said.

'Right,' Lydia said, saluting him with her mug. 'Thanks?'

'In case you wanted some privacy with your visitor.'

'Ah. Very thoughtful,' Lydia said. She was about to ask him, politely, whether he had had a good evening, when she noticed his expression. It was intense. 'You okay?'

'Are you with him, now? DCI Fleet.'

'No,' Lydia said. 'We're just friendly colleagues. It's too complicated otherwise.'

Jason nodded. 'Good excuse.'

'It's not an excuse,' Lydia said, 'it's good sense. You know there are things about me, about my family, he can't know. And he's my police source. That's a professional relationship and I shouldn't cloud it with the messy stuff.'

Jason's mouth turned up at the corners. He pushed the sleeves of his grey suit jacket a little further up his arms and affected to lean against the wall. He didn't quite manage it – there was a narrow gap of air between his shoulder and the solid surface, but Lydia was impressed, again, by how fully alive he appeared these days.

'Oh come on,' Jason said. 'You know you're emotionally withholding.'

'I am not.' Lydia was stung.

'Uh-huh,' Jason said. 'You have a lone-wolf complex.

You think you have to do everything on your own and everything in your own way. It's not a criticism.'

'It sounds like a criticism.'

'Well, it's something to be aware of, that's all. You can't do everything yourself. Not forever.'

'I know that,' Lydia said out loud, while thinking, *I bloody well can.*

STEPPING AWAY from the main Holborn thoroughfare with its Starbucks and Sainsburys Local, Lydia turned down Chancery Lane and back in time. She knew lots of the buildings nearby had been built by the Knights Templar, one of Henry Crow's bedtime stories had involved a family myth about a newly-arrived Crow helping one of the Knights in his hour of need, and gaining a boon in return, but she hadn't known that the headquarters of the Law Society was here, too.

Her focus, today, was on the silver vaults. Lydia couldn't shake the feeling that the unusual silver figurine was important in some way. It had been so completely out of place, with both Robert's relative youth and the modern aesthetic of the flat. It was another hot day and Lydia was grateful to walk into the shade of the tall Georgian buildings. The entrance to the vaults was through a tasteful doorway set in a white-fronted edifice, complete with black railings. Lydia would have assumed posh flats or an accountancy firm, if it hadn't been for the understated blue sign which announced The London Silver Vaults. Inside, Lydia descended five levels underground to the arcade of shops, now housed in the old safe rooms. Originally, the vaults were a stronghold for London's wealthy and the first safety deposit in the capital. All kinds of companies, households, individuals and even criminals kept their valuables in the place, and it had never been successfully burgled. Even a direct hit from a bomb during the Blitz hadn't damaged it. Silver shops had been trading here since the thirties and each shop was housed behind a thick iron door, in one of the old safe rooms. There was still a massive vault beyond the arcade of shops, and on any other occasion, that would have been what interested Lydia, but today she needed information.

Most of the shops were third generation or more, and their proximity to each other would either result in a close-knit community or a nest of vipers. Crossing her fingers for the second, Lydia walked past open doorways which shone with glittering silver and the lustre of gilt, to roughly halfway down the arcade. She was working on random, just waiting for her gut to lead the way. Her dad always said that Crows had an innate sense of direction and she hoped it was true.

Vault seventeen was fitted with dark wood and glass cabinets, with royal-blue velvet in open cutlery drawers and small snatches of the blue-painted walls, the only colour other than glistening, shining silver, as far as the eye could see. A giant cabinet to Lydia's right was filled to capacity with cups, vases, platters, bowls, tureens, and fifty other shapes she could not name, all intricately laced with filigree or embossed or etched or moulded with curlicues and flowers. Silver chandeliers hung from the ceiling in a forest of branching arms and twinkling lights, and larger items like an enormous circular serving tray, propped upright to fit into the space, and a wheeled wooden structure topped with a huge silver capsule, so smooth and shiny that its surface mirrored every item around it in perfect detail.

'Carving trolley.' A voice emanated from a tall narrow display case, topped with two intricately modelled silver grouse and an art deco candlestick the width of Lydia's thigh. 'Late nineteenth century.' The owner of the voice appeared. It was a small, strangely ageless man. If Lydia had been writing a report, she would have had to put his age at somewhere between forty-five and seventy. He was bald and pale and had large dark brown eyes which were startling against his pallid complexion. He blinked and, a small hiss escaped his thin lips. 'What do you want, Magpie?'

Lydia tasted metal on her tongue. 'Just some information. Your help. If you are willing?'

He didn't move and his expression remained hostile.

'It's not much,' Lydia said, trying to radiate calm.

'We don't like magpies down here, they tend to have a problem controlling themselves. All this shine.'

Lydia spread her hands, showing that she wasn't holding one of her coins. 'It is stunning, that's true. But I just want your help with a small identification. Nothing bad. Nothing dangerous. Absolutely your area of expertise.'

The taste of metal was still there, it was spreading around Lydia's mouth and she felt, just for a moment, like she might gag. 'I just want to know what this is.' Lydia took her phone from her pocket and found the first image. 'Here. It's a medieval knight figure. I'd love to know more.'

The man glanced at the phone despite, clearly, not wanting to. And then he took a step forward, holding out a hand for the device with one hand and putting half-moon spectacles which were hanging around his neck on a silver chain onto his nose.

'Is this yours?'

'A friend's. They received it as a gift and would like to know more about it.'

The man shook his head at the obvious lie, but seemed unable to draw his gaze from the pictures for long. He scrolled through the gallery. 'German, I think. See the porcelain face. That's typical of the type. Late nineteenth century, possibly early nineteen hundreds...' He stopped. Peered more closely. 'Ah, yes. Neresheimer. You can see the mark, here,' he tilted the phone and Lydia looked dutifully at the photo she had taken of the base. 'And I think that's an import mark, too, I would need to see the piece with my magnifier to be certain. But I think that's Muller import for Chester, 1903.'

'Is it genuine?'

He glanced at her. 'It certainly appears so. I assume you want a valuation?'

'Ballpark would be handy.'

'Well, very cautiously, and with the proviso that I would need to see the item to confirm, I would guess around fifteen thousand at auction. Maybe more dependent on condition.'

'Fifteen grand?'

'Sterling.' He nodded.

'Thank you,' Lydia said. 'May I trespass on your good favour for a moment longer.' She had no idea where the old-timey speak had sprung from, only that it felt appropriate for the environment and she had a hunch it would go down well with the squirrelly little dealer.

He inclined his head, the light catching the glass of his spectacles in little flashes. 'You may.'

'Have you ever bought or sold a knight figure of this kind?'

'More than one,' he said. 'A couple back in the seventies, early eighties. They had a bit of a renaissance after falling somewhat out of favour.'

'Nothing recently?'

He hesitated and Lydia wondered if it was for effect. One thing she had learned as a PI was that some people bloody loved their moment in the spotlight. They would draw out whatever meagre bit of information they had, develop their role from casual bystander to key witness, with a mix of exaggeration and dramatic pauses. It was usually easy enough to spot, the self-aggrandising was always a big giveaway.

'I don't like to give out details about my clients.'

'I understand that,' Lydia said, 'but this concerns a young man's death, I thought you might make an exception in the circumstances. For the common good.'

The man's lip curled. 'And what is your stake in the matter? What role did you play, Magpie?'

'I'm looking into it, trying to find the person or persons responsible. I'm an investigator.' Lydia showed him her card. 'Take it. Call me if you decide you might be willing to divulge the details of the customer in question. If not, no worries. I understand that you have to operate within the confines of your professional code of conduct.'

'Very well,' the man said, looking confused at Lydia's retreat.

'May I just note down your name, Sir?' Lydia had her notebook out and ready. 'Just for my records.'

'Chartes,' he said, stiffly.

'First name?'

'Guillaume. Shall I spell it for you?'

'Got it,' Lydia said. 'I'm sure DCI Fleet will be able to decipher my approximation, anyway. He's smart like that.'

'DCI Fleet?'

'Well,' Lydia pulled an apologetic face which had exactly no truth in it, and explained that, as Chartes wouldn't give her the name of the client she wouldn't be able follow it up and would, instead, be duty bound to hand the lead over to the police. And they would follow it up with a warrant. 'I hate to give a good lead away like that,' Lydia said. 'It doesn't look great for my business as the police won't give me any credit for it, and my own professional pride will be dented, naturally, but I can't, in good conscience, leave any stone unturned in the pursuit of justice.'

Guillaume looked absolutely furious. 'You'll run to the police.'

'They are on the side of the community,' Lydia said. 'You've nothing to worry about if you've done nothing wrong.'

'I suppose they'll come down here with their uniforms and cars? Scaring away my customers, making me look bad.'

Lydia shrugged. 'I have no idea.'

Guillaume retreated to the back of the shop, returning moments later with an iPad. He scrolled and tapped for a few moments before giving her the name and address of the customer.

'You delivered it?'

'Yes,' he scowled. 'Not personally, of course. I used a courier. I suppose you want that, too?'

'Please,' Lydia said sweetly.

Guillaume gave her the phone number for the courier company. 'Not my usual,' he said. 'They were busy.'

'Thank you,' Lydia said. 'You've been most helpful.'

Guillaume glared at her, his pale thin lips disappearing, and Lydia decided it was time for a hasty exit. No sense in pushing her luck and, besides, she had everything she needed. For now.

CHAPTER SEVEN

April Westcott called to tell Lydia that her husband, Christopher, was going to a design conference in Greenwich at the end of the week. Although he could feasibly get home, he had told April that he needed to stay at the venue for the whole shebang to take full advantage of the networking opportunities. It was perfectly reasonable. Lydia wouldn't have chosen to haul arse from Greenwich to Twickenham and back if she had the money to choose otherwise, either. It was going to be a long surveillance job, though. Forty-eight hours to cover, as April was insisting that she keep eyes on him the whole time. She told April as much, giving the woman an out in case she had decided there were better ways to spend her cash. But no. 'Don't let him out of your sight,' April said, her voice brittle. 'I need to know. I can't live like this. I can't stand the uncertainty. It's going to destroy us.'

'All right, then.' Lydia went over a few more details before pocketing her phone.

'Jason?' Her ghostly assistant was in the small kitchen, making coffee. And it was odd how ordinary that felt.

He poked his head out of the doorway. 'Yeah?'

She filled him in on the details. 'So, I'll be out Wednesday, Thursday, Friday.'

'Away two nights?'

'Have to be,' Lydia said, not relishing the prospect. She was already tapping on her laptop, looking for a reservation at the conference venue. Typically, given the short notice, it was fully-booked. Marvellous.

Jason carried a mug carefully across the room and placed it on Lydia's desk. 'What will happen to me?'

'What do you mean?' Lydia was scrolling through listings on a hotel booking site, before her brain caught up and she realised she wouldn't be able to stay elsewhere. Eyes on him the whole time meant camping out in the hotel lobby and her car. Two nights of that without anybody else to take a shift was going to be brutal. And all to watch April's husband attend a conference. Lydia found herself hoping he got up to sexy nonsense super-quickly so that she would be able to take a few snaps and call it a job done. That was the problem with adultery work; it made you cynical.

Jason was hovering by the desk. 'You haven't been away for that long before.'

Lydia thought about it. That couldn't be right, could it? She must have stayed with Emma. Or her parents. 'What about other jobs? I've done long shifts before.'

'Not that long. Not without coming back here at all.'

'Well, it isn't that long. Only two days. I know you'll miss me...'

'It's not that,' Jason said, clearly impatient.

'Charming.'

'I don't know what will happen to this,' he picked up Lydia's coffee mug with exaggerated care. 'How long before the Lydia effect wears off?'

'Right. Yes. Sorry.' Lydia was half-listening, back on the conference website and hoping for alternative accommodation options. She knew she wouldn't be sleeping much, but a room to set up as base would be better than snatching a nap in the reception area or her car. Less conspicuous, too.

'And we haven't been testing it. Your ability. You said we would, that you wanted to know more, but every time I bring it up you're too busy.'

'I am busy,' Lydia said. Looking up from the screen. 'I'm running this business on my own and I need all the work I can get, but it's not easy covering everything. I'm knackered and I'm doing my best.'

Jason looked properly hurt, now, and Lydia mentally kicked herself. 'I mean, I have you. And you're a big help. Really.'

'That's my point,' Jason said. 'If we worked on this,' he gestured between them. 'You might be able to power me up some more. If I get strong enough I might be able to leave the building and then I could do surveillance. It's like you said before, I should get out of here. It would do me good.'

Lydia perked up. 'You know I think it might be your

past that is tying you here.' She tried to be tactful. 'Your passing.'

'No,' Jason shook his head. 'I'm not interested. I told you.'

'If you would let me look into how you died, then maybe that would help... Let you move around more freely.'

'No!' Jason was shimmering, his outline vibrating. Lydia watched him control himself with effort. 'I don't want that. It's too risky. There's a reason I don't know what happened when I died. We don't know what would happen if you told me. But if you could power me up. Use your mojo,' Jason traced shapes in the air. 'Then, I could be a proper investigative assistant. I could be your partner.'

'I've told you, I don't know how.'

'Where else are you going to find someone who will work for free? Someone who doesn't need sleep? Or food?'

The man made sense. Lydia had been managing fine, but it was jobs like the Westcott one which brought home how hard it was to fly solo. In Karen's firm there had been a core staff of four and a host of regular free-lancers. Long surveillance jobs were done in shifts. 'But how? I haven't the first idea-'

'Isn't this stuff, I don't know, passed down through the generations. Isn't there a magic book or something in the Crow Family archive.'

'We don't have a Family archive,' Lydia said. 'At least, not as far as I know. And I've never heard of the 'The Big Book of Crow Magic' or anything.'

'Didn't your parents keep you away from all that, though? I mean, how would you know? There could be a whole training school and they might have burned your letter.'

Lydia gave him a look. 'You've been reading again, haven't you? That sounds like Harry Potter.'

Jason's face lit up, as it always did when he talked about books. 'Oh God. Yes. Years and years with no entertainment and now... You have no idea what it's like to be able to pick up a book and turn the pages. Speaking of which, can you bring me some more?'

'Of course. Anything in particular?' Lydia had started to pick up piles of paperbacks in the local charity shops and bring them home for Jason.

'Thrillers. Crime. The last Harry Potter.'

'No problem.'

'And your instruction manual so we can work out how you work.'

'You're still on that, then.'

'Seriously, Lydia. How can you not be more curious? Don't you want to know how your Family powers work?'

Lydia shivered.

'Sorry,' Jason said, looking suddenly concerned.

'It's fine,' Lydia said, still shivering. She wrapped her arms around her body and hugged and then, realising it made her look weak, dropped them and got up to go to the kitchenette. She ran the cold tap until it was freezing and filled a pint glass. She couldn't put it into words, couldn't explain to Jason why she felt such dread at the thought of delving into the Crow Family power. The Family history was murky and in the bad old days, being a Crow meant being part of something people feared. Protection rackets, heists, and Feathers-knew what else. These days, Charlie said he was all about protecting the local community and Lydia was pretty sure the Crow Family businesses were, at least mostly, legit, but there was a solid reason Henry Crow had abdicated his throne. The mysterious powers which had run through the Crow bloodline for centuries were now a vestige of their old majesty. Gold coins and a little bit of persuasion. Heightened intuition. The mere idea that there might be more, as in the case of Maddie, had brought out the very worst in Charlie. The hunger for the old magic. But what was the phrase, better the devil you know? Perhaps it wasn't an entirely daft idea to find out more. Knowledge was power and all that. She didn't have to do anything with that knowledge, after all. It would still be her choice.

Henry Crow stayed at home a lot, happy with the company of Lydia's mum and the snooker on the TV, but Lydia knew that he still had a Thursday evening ritual of visiting his local. On the corner of her parents' road, The Elm Tree had been a fixture of Lydia's upbringing. Drinking cola on the small patio which was called, rather grandly, the garden, and learning how to play pool with her mum. The Elm Tree had been refurbished in the last few years and now the exterior was bright white, the porticos and bay window adorned with fresh window baskets, overflowing with blooming flowers and greenery. Inside the pub remained largely untouched. It had been scrubbed clean and the walls were no longer nicotine-yellow, but the interconnecting rooms, snug sitting spaces, and old wooden bar with its collage of photographs and cardboard bar mats were all intact.

The new owners had strung up fairy lights as a nod to modern tastes and there were a few more comfortable bench seats, upholstered in navy velvet, but it was still recognisably the venue from Lydia's childhood. Henry Crow was sitting in his usual place, an open newspaper and almost-finished pint in front of him on the round table.

'Hi Dad,' Lydia said, 'hope you don't mind me crashing your quiet time.'

'All I have these days,' he said, standing to hug Lydia. 'Always good to see you, Lyds. You know that.'

Lydia went to the bar and got a pint of his favourite and a soda and lime for herself. She wished she hadn't brought the car and could have a proper drink. Now that she was here, she felt suddenly weirdly shy about talking to her dad on his own. She realised how much of a buffer her mum's presence had become.

Back at the table, things went downhill rapidly. Her dad looked up from his paper and said, 'hello', as if they hadn't just greeted each other.

'How are you?' Lydia said, sitting opposite her dad.

Henry was frowning at her, as if trying to place her. Lydia couldn't believe the difference a couple of minutes had made. Was Jason right? Was she powering up whatever was making him ill? It was painful but it seemed true; Lydia made him sick.

'I'm all right, love,' Henry said. 'You?'

Lydia passed her dad his pint of beer and he took a long appreciative slurp, like a man who had just crossed the Sahara. 'Feathers, that's the stuff.'

Lydia took a sip of her soda, the ice cubes clinking against the edge of the glass.

The pause lengthened, and then he spoke. 'Did Charlie send you?'

'Sorry?'

'Sweet talk from a pretty face. Not really his style, but I guess he's getting desperate.'

Lydia opened her mouth to correct him, but he was staring down at his drink and his expression was odd. Halfway between fear and longing.

'I've told him I can't. I won't do it to Lydia.' He shot her a look full of anger. 'And I love Susan. Pretty faces are not the way to go. I'm a faithful husband. You tell him that.'

Hating herself, Lydia forced a quick nod. 'What does Lydia think about it all? If you don't mind me asking.'

His forehead creased. 'She's a baby. She doesn't know a thing about it and she never will.'

'Right,' Lydia said.

'And I promised Susan when we decided to have children... We promised each other.'

'I'll tell Charlie, then. It's a no go.'

'That's the deal. I'm out and so is my daughter. He's not training her and neither will I.'

Lydia paused, weighing up whether she was really going to do this. Then she ploughed ahead. 'What about her heritage? Shouldn't she know?'

Her Dad's focus sharpened and, in a split second he went from being her father to a stranger. 'I don't think you should be pushing me on this... Do you, darling?'

Lydia managed to shake her head but she didn't trust herself to speak. The malevolent energy coming from a man she had loved and trusted her whole life was hard to bear.

He smiled, still channelling the Henry Crow who was heir to the Family. He seemed taller, meaner, and infinitely sharper. 'Now I know you're just doing as you're told, following orders from my dear brother, but I've got a little word of advice for you.' He leaned in very slightly, still smiling and said: 'Just because I'm out of the business, doesn't mean I won't snap every bone in your body if you don't stop asking stupid questions.'

SHAKEN, Lydia sat in her car and stared out of the windscreen for a few minutes before calling Emma. 'I'm in the area,' she said, looking around at the leafy streets. The sense of space and reduced pollution levels ought to make her breathe more easily. Instead, she felt her lungs constricting and a band wrapped tightly around her shoulders. 'Come round,' Emma said immediately and Lydia felt the band loosen slightly.

Lydia took her boots off in the hall. Emma had already poured two glasses of wine. 'I've got the car,' Lydia said.

Emma shrugged. 'Stay over if you want.'

'Maybe,' Lydia eyed the red wine with longing. 'I'll start with tea. Want one?'

While she dealt with the kettle administration, she asked about Maisie and Archie. 'Maisie's asleep and Tom is reading to Archie.'

'How are they?' Lydia chucked the teabag into the bin and followed Emma to the living room. It was covered with books and toys and the coffee table was overflowing with plastic dishes, dinosaur figures, and a pile of opened post. Several cushions were on the floor, along with a blanket and a circle of soft toys. It was still the most beautiful room Lydia had ever seen in real life. Emma had impeccable taste.

'Will Tom mind me crashing your evening?' Lydia knew she ought to make more of an effort with her best friend's significant other.

'He'll probably go back to work after Archie is down.'

'Busy?'

'The downside to connectivity,' Emma said, drily. 'Never actually leaving work.'

Lydia had no concept of a work-life balance, herself, but she said. 'That doesn't sound good,' to show she was normal.

After they had caught up with the news on Archie and Maisie, Emma told Lydia a story about someone they had both known at school who had started a charity providing sanitary products for disadvantaged girls and had been given an award. They drank to her excellent work and Lydia decided she would definitely move onto wine just as soon as she had finished her tea.

Emma was looking at her with a strange expression, though. 'We haven't done this in a while.'

The guilt hit Lydia in the solar plexus. 'I know,' she said. 'It's been a bit mad-'

Emma waved her wine glass. 'When you stayed, I thought you would be around a bit more. I know you're busy and that our lives are very different. I chose this, I know that. I just miss you.'

'I miss you, too,' Lydia said. She felt like crap but it wasn't guilt. Well, not just guilt, anyway. It was sadness. 'I will be better.'

'I will try, too,' Emma said. 'It's a two-way street. I'm so wrapped up in my mum-life. I know that I'm not the friend you need in your life right now.'

'That's crazy-talk.'

'No, it's true. I can't go out drinking or dancing,'

'I don't dance,' Lydia said, trying to lighten the tone.

'I can't help you with your business stuff. I know your schedule is nuts and it would be helpful if I was more flexible,' Emma stared at her wine, not looking Lydia in the eye. 'I know I'm a nightmare. I need, like, a month's notice to do anything not involving the kids.'

'You are a brilliant friend,' Lydia said. 'The best. Now stop talking balls.'

Emma sniffed. She took a big swig of wine and managed a watery smile. 'Okay.'

'Anyway, I need to update you on my love life...' Lydia paused. 'Assuming you're still interested in that kind of thing now that you're a sedate older-lady motherly type with Play Doh on the brain.'

Emma threw a cushion at Lydia's head. 'Shut up. And tell all.'

Lydia settled more comfortably on the sofa and,

hugging the cushion as she spoke, she told Emma about her dismal failure to stay away from Fleet.

'It sounds like he can't stay away from you, either, to be fair.'

'Well,' Lydia gestured to herself. 'Who can blame him?'

'True,' Emma said. 'So, it's going well? You're at that lovely stage when you can't keep your hands off each other?'

'I need to keep my hands off him, though. That's the problem.'

'Why?'

'He's a copper,' Lydia said promptly.

'And?'

'You know my family,' Lydia said.

'Not really,' Emma said. She was serious again and her wine glass was empty. It had gone quickly.

'Well, you know enough. And it's not just that. I have to keep things professional. He's my source. My contact in the force. I can't risk losing that for a... A night of fun.'

'Sounds like bollocks,' Emma said. 'You're pulling your usual.'

'My usual?'

'You're Martin Blank.'

This was an old argument and not one Lydia felt like having. 'I am not Martin Blank.' Grosse Point Blank was one of their all-time favourite films and she and Emma watched it so many times when they were teens that they could both recite along to the whole thing. It did not, however, mean that she wanted to be likened to

Martin Blank. Well, she did. But not by Emma who she knew did not mean it as a compliment.

She put her mug down on the table, next to a plastic T-Rex. 'I've got an early start tomorrow.'

'You're leaving?' Emma's voice was strangely flat.

'Better had,' Lydia got up. 'Sorry. Let's have a proper night soon, though, yeah?'

'When you don't have an early start,' Emma said, in the same monotone. Her mouth was a line of unhappiness and Lydia knew she should stay, make things better, but she didn't know how. On her way home, Lydia felt the guilt gnawing in her insides until she admitted the real truth; it had been easier to leave.

CHAPTER EIGHT

Instead of her office, Maria Silver suggested The Seven Stars. It was an old pub, backing onto the Royal Justice Courts and established on the doorstep of Lincoln's Inn, one of the most prestigious Inns of Court, where barristers have been learning their trade and paying their respects since the early fifteenth century. Not surprisingly, it was a known drinking hole of the legal establishment. Maria was playing an at-home advantage without actually inviting a Crow into her workplace. Smart.

The heatwave had cooled in intensity a little, but hadn't yet broken. A period of intense sunshine like this would surely have to end in thunder and torrential rain but, for now, the sky was still clear blue. Outside The Seven Stars was mobbed. Drinkers often stood around outside pubs in London, spilling out across the pavement and, on quiet roads, into the street, and the warm weather had only amplified this tendency. Stretching down the street, past the legal-wig shop next door to the pub, and beyond, people were sitting on the pavement. Settled in as comfortably as if they were in their own living rooms.

Lydia pushed her way into the darkness of the pub. The cosy fug of a London boozer welcomed her inside. It still smelled of smoke from the generations that had enjoyed tobacco within its walls before the ban, and the light glinting on the gilt lettering on the mirrors, the polished brass and warm cherry wood of the bar, all invited Lydia to sit down, have a drink, forget her cares. It was a kind of magic, really, and it was no wonder that the place had been thriving since 1602 when it had served homesick Dutch sailors coming in off the Thames.

Having obtained a large coke with ice, Lydia avoided the attention of a young barrister, high off his first case who wanted to celebrate by buying her champagne, and scouted the interior for Maria. Right at the back and leaning against the dark green wall, was Maria Silver. She was petting a black cat which was sat on a tall wooden bar table and purring loudly enough for Lydia to hear as she approached.

Lydia introduced herself and Maria nodded before turning her attention back to the cat. It was wearing a white ruff around its neck and, unusually for a cat, seemed to be okay with the fancy dress. Lydia had heard rumours that this pub had a resident cat and she wasn't entirely thrilled to see they were true. Her eyes were already starting to itch from its fur.

Lydia waited for Maria to speak, trying to appear

unfazed by the situation. In theory they held the same status; Maria was the daughter of Alejandro, head of the Silver family. But then Lydia's father had abdicated his position, which made things a little blurry. Plus, the official line was that the Family stuff was in the past. That nobody cared anymore about relative status or power. Which, of course, was laughable.

'Something is amusing you?' Maria raised an eyebrow. 'It had better not be Cicero. He is easily offended.'

On cue, the cat gave Lydia the haughtiest look she had ever seen on a feline. Which really was saying something.

'You wanted to see me?'

'I heard from a friend of a friend that you've been asking about Robert Sharp.'

'Do lawyers have friends? I thought it was just clients.'

Maria smiled. 'That's detectives you are thinking of. And solicitors.'

Lydia took a welcome mouthful of her coke. There were a couple of ceiling fans, but they were just moving the warm air around.

'You are going to stumble across it eventually and I thought I would save you the trouble. Sharp had engaged our services.'

'That's very public spirited of you. Have you extended the same courtesy to the police?'

'Naturally,' Maria said. 'And this courtesy is by way of a peace offering. Continued good relations.'

It clicked. 'Your dad made you call me.'

Maria's eyes flickered and her mouth hardened. That had pissed her off. And no wonder. Hot-shot legal mind, aged somewhere in her forties, and still at the beck and call of her daddy. 'No,' she bit off the word.

'So, what did Sharp want?'

'My department specialises in protecting large companies' intellectual property assets, as well as defending them from bogus claims, libellous lawsuits, all the usual hazards involved in doing business. An individual is not our remit, but Sharp's case was taken as a favour to one of our existing clients, JRB.'

'What does that stand for?'

'I believe it's just the founder's initials. It doesn't mean anything in particular.'

Lydia noticed that Maria had side-stepped the question but she wasn't sure why. 'Why did they want you to look after Robert?'

Maria shrugged. 'We didn't ask.'

'And what kind of trouble was Mr Sharp in?'

'I have no idea. We didn't get that far.' Maria turned her attention back to the cat, who was nuzzling its head on her forearm with its tail high in the air, its back a steep curve. 'His first appointment was scheduled for next week. Cancelled now, of course.'

'Obviously,' Lydia said. 'And he definitely gave no indication of the nature of his issue when he made the appointment? Nothing in email?'

'I didn't speak to him, my secretary did.'

'Can I speak to your secretary?'

Maria stopped petting the cat and it straightened up in fury. She looked at Lydia for a few seconds as if weighing something up in her mind and then said. 'If you must.'

LYDIA HAD BEEN PLANNING to go shopping for food on the way back to the flat, but the muggy heat sapped her motivation. Keeping to the shade as much as possible, she headed back from the station, hoping to beg a late lunch from Angel.

The Fork was busy, with most of the tables filled and a buzz of chatter and the gentle clink of cutlery on china. Lydia didn't recognise the kid behind the counter but she had a more immediate problem. Uncle Charlie was holding court in a corner table, and his dining companions were not Crows.

Lydia hesitated in the doorway, wondering whether she should simply head straight upstairs and deal with the hunger. She was sure there was half a packet of crackers kicking about her kitchen. Maybe even a heel of bread. Uncle Charlie looked straight at her, though, his face breaking in to a welcoming smile. It was the smile of a card sharp welcoming a mark and Lydia felt her spine stiffen in response. He raised a hand and beckoned her over.

He stood to greet her, holding her shoulders and kissing each cheek. The full treatment which, Lydia assumed, was for the benefit of the onlookers. The men at Charlie's table also got to their feet. A beat too slowly for proper politeness, but still.

'My niece,' Charlie said. 'This is Lydia. Lydia, this is Julius and Marko.'

'Charmed,' Lydia said. 'Listen, I won't keep you. I'm just getting some takeaway.'

'Join us,' Marko said. He flashed a bright white smile with a tiny jewel embedded in one of his incisors.

The cafe wasn't table service. You ordered at the counter and took a number for your table, but Charlie stayed on his feet and signalled the boy who was ringing up a coffee cake and a cola for a woman who, now that Lydia was looking in her direction, had an odd vibe.

'Another piece of lasagne for my niece,' Charlie's voice carried easily over the hubbub of the room and several people looked up. Lydia slid into the seat by the window to try to end the scene as quickly as possible. Declining the invitation was clearly not an option. Her phone buzzed and she glanced at it quickly, hoping for a work emergency that could spirit her away from this awkwardness. It was a text from Emma:

Archie wanted me to send you this.

A second message was a photo of a felt-tip drawing of a stick figure with long black hair, drawn in violent slashing scribbles, and round yellow circles orbiting her flung-apart arms. The mouth was drawn in crimson and it wasn't smiling or frowning, just a grim straight line.

She thumbed a quick reply:

I love it! Please thank him.

After a moment's hesitation, she added:

Be round soon.

Another moment and she added 'Love L' and a kiss. Jason said she was emotionally withholding which clearly wasn't the case.

Charlie had sat down and he moved his own plate

and glass over to his new position. The guy from the counter arrived and hurriedly put down a bundle of cutlery wrapped in a paper napkin and a basket of fresh bread.

He was in the process of turning away when Charlie clicked his fingers. The boy turned back, looking terrified. 'You want something to drink?'

'A Coke, please,' Lydia said. To Charlie she said. 'Don't click your fingers at people, it's rude.'

There was a silence and Lydia wondered which way it would go. After another beat, in which Julius and Marko appeared not to breathe, Charlie smiled a genuine smile. 'You're right, of course.' The kid escaped back to the counter and Lydia concentrated on tearing a piece of bread into chunks and then slathering each piece with butter. The sun was shining through the upper part of the window, bouncing off the metal salt and pepper shakers in burning spears of light.

'Julius was telling me about his start-up. It's, now let me get this right...' Charlie paused for a moment. 'Brand awareness using guerrilla marketing-tactics combined with a holistic social-media strategy.'

Lydia almost choked on the bread she was chewing. She looked at Julius and wondered what possessed the man to come to Charlie. It sounded nothing like the usual Crow Family fare.

'Not our usual,' Charlie said, echoing Lydia's thoughts. 'But interesting, no?'

Lydia swallowed her mouthful and pulled a non-committal expression. She had zero desire to get involved and even less to be seen endorsing a deal that might go south at a later date.

'So,' Julius's eyes flicked nervously from Lydia to Charlie. 'I need two hundred to get up and running. That will keep things afloat until the profits kick in. I have a projection, here,' he reached for a large phone on the table and tapped the screen.

'You're good for it,' Charlie said, leaning back. 'I know that.'

He turned to Lydia, just as Angel arrived with a plate of lasagne, which she put in front of Lydia. 'Enjoy,' she said, not smiling. But then Angel hardly ever did. She cast a professional look over the meals that were in progress. Charlie's plate was empty but Julius and Marko had hardly touched their pasta. Now that Lydia knew they were visiting Charlie Crow to ask for a loan, she could imagine their stomachs were closed for business. 'Everything okay with your food?'

'Perfect, as always,' Charlie said.

Angel pointed at Lydia. 'Eat up, skinny-girl.'

Lydia had demolished most of the bread and still felt like she could eat three times the portion of lasagne on her plate, so she dug in. Forking food and ignoring, as much as possible, the wrap-up chat between Julius and Marko. Julius did most of the talking and Marko's voice, when he did join in, was very deep, very smooth. Looking at her food, and not her dining companions, Lydia found herself growing warm every time Marko spoke. She looked at him, curious now, and caught the faintest gleam on his skin. He turned his face and the light on his cheek made the skin there appear pearlescent. For a moment turquoise, lilac, pink and lemon yellow danced across his skin in a wave, like the iridescent interior of a shell. And then he moved and the mother-of-pearl was gone.

'Keep in touch,' Charlie said, as Julius slid out of his seat, followed by Marko.

'Very nice to meet you, Lydia,' Julius said. And then they walked out of the cafe into the boiling sunlight. Lydia watched them through the window, hanging in the doorway for a moment, pulling out sunglasses and putting them on, before sauntering across the street.

'What a waste,' Charlie indicated the almost-full plates of pasta.

'They were too intimidated to eat,' Lydia said. Mainly because she knew it would make Charlie happy, and she had vowed to be a little more careful about pissing him off. The dream with Madeleine had felt like a clear warning and, while it was probably just random images from her subconscious, it seemed like a good idea to take heed, anyway. Maybe her subconscious had noticed something that she hadn't. That lizard brain that had kept her ancestors alive by spotting danger. Well, she wasn't going to look a gift horse in the mouth. Or a gift lizard. Whatever.

Charlie smiled. He pushed his plate away and leaned back, producing a gold coin and flipping it over the back of his knuckles in an easy movement. 'So, what did you think of them?'

'Your new investment?' Lydia chased a piece of lasagne crust with her fork.

'It's nothing new,' Charlie said. 'Just business as

usual. I lend them capital, they pay it back with interest. It's good to encourage development in the community.'

Lydia concentrated on chewing and avoided looking Charlie in the eye. It was no longer the bad-old-days and Lydia was pretty sure that extortion, protection rackets and actual loan-sharking were not on the table, but that didn't make her uncle and his various minions saintly. The only reason Charlie cared about community development was in order to line the Crow Family coffers. And maybe to secure his reputation as the benevolent Godfather of Camberwell.

'A reasonable rate of interest, I assume,' Lydia said, keeping her voice light.

'Well,' Charlie spread his hands. 'If they were able to convince a regular bank, they would be able to benefit from those rates. I'm taking a risk, it's only fair that I'm compensated for that risk.'

They both knew that there was no risk. One way or another Julius and Marko would pay Charlie back. Lydia just hoped that these days it would involve working for Charlie, rather than losing body parts.

'Did you trust them, though?' Charlie's tone had turned casual. Hyper-casual. Suspiciously casual. 'What impression did you get?'

Lydia immediately felt herself stiffen. He doesn't know, she told herself. He doesn't know anything. 'I have no idea,' she said.

'It would be so useful to know if there were any little surprises. In my line of work, surprises are rarely good.'

'I can imagine,' Lydia said.

'So, there's nothing you can tell me about them?'

'Like what?'

'Lyds,' Charlie said. 'Come on. Be straight with me.'

Lydia opened her mouth to argue that she had no idea what he was driving at and then she caught a warning in his expression. 'Nothing from Julius,' she said. 'But Marko is a Pearlie. A little, at least.'

Charlie nodded. 'That's useful. Thank you.'

Lydia lined her knife and fork on her plate. 'How long have you known?'

Charlie slung an arm around her shoulders. 'I'm family. I've always known.'

She gave him a long look. 'I am pretty good at detecting bullshit, too.'

He laughed. 'All right. Your dad isn't as tight-lipped as he used to be. That's all.'

Lydia looked away to hide her anger. He had taken advantage of Henry's compromised mental faculties. The fact that she had done the same did nothing to improve her mood. Guilt and anger swirled together in a bitter brew.

'He's my brother,' Charlie said, as if reading her mind. 'I didn't do it deliberately, but sometimes he forgets who he is talking to these days. Last time you were visiting, before you moved back, he let it slip.'

'Christmas?' Lydia remembered that visit. Charlie and Dad in the living room, watching snooker and drinking whisky, while she helped Mum wrestle a beef joint into its pastry jacket.

He nodded. 'The specifics were interesting, but it wasn't news, you know? You're Henry Crow's daughter.

There was no way on this sweet earth you weren't going to have some talent.'

'That's why you want me here?' Lydia indicated the cafe. 'So that I can sit in on your business meetings. Suss out who is who and whether they are packing.'

'Only if you don't mind,' Charlie said. 'Just an occasional favour, but I wouldn't want to make you uncomfortable.'

It sounded perfectly reasonable and that, Lydia knew, was the problem. There would be more, there always was. And a big pile of stuff that Charlie wasn't telling her. Still. She shrugged. 'It's the least I can do while I'm living here rent free.'

He smiled and gave her shoulder a squeeze with his gigantic hand. 'We've got to stick together. Times are changing.'

'So I heard.'

'So, tell me about your life. Are you settled into the flat? Got everything you need?'

'Yeah, it's great.' Lydia pictured the blank functionality of the space and was surprised at the warmth she felt. It had only been a few months, but it felt like home. The security system she had installed helped, as did the lack of rent. A free flat in London was enough to give anyone a hot flush.

'And business is good? You're getting clients. I can put the word out, if you need-'

'It's good,' Lydia broke in. 'Busy.'

'I knew you'd land well,' Charlie said. 'You making friends?'

'Friends?' Lydia said.

'It's important to enjoy life. Not just work all the time.'

'I'm fine,' Lydia said, 'Honestly, I'm living my best life.'

'Hmm,' Charlie twisted his lips. 'I don't know. I think it's all work, all business. Angel says you don't have friends visit, only clients.'

'Is she your source?' Lydia regretted the words as soon as they were out. Karen would not be impressed.

Charlie didn't glower, although his bland expression was scary enough. 'I'm your uncle. I'm your family. I'm allowed to worry.'

'I know,' Lydia said. 'And I appreciate your concern, but I'm happy. Honestly.'

'Okay,' Charlie raised his hands in mock surrender. 'Although, you need to tell your police contact to be more respectful of your time. Or you won't have any opportunity to make better friends.'

And there it was. The information he had been leading up to. Lydia put her hands in her lap and linked her fingers together to stop herself from fidgeting. 'He is a friend,' she said. 'And a very useful contact. A bit of both.'

'That's what I was afraid of,' Charlie said. 'He's police. A copper. I'm sure he seems very reasonable, very helpful, but you can't ever forget what he is.'

'I know,' Lydia said.

'Do you?' Charlie shook his head. 'Henry always coddled you. Wanted you away from all of this,' he waved a hand. 'But you're here, now. Living here.

Working here. And you can't ever forget that you're a Crow and that has to come first. Every time.'

'I know,' Lydia said, again. 'Really. I get it. I'm careful. I don't talk about the Family.'

'Does he ask, though?'

'No,' Lydia lied. 'I ask him questions, not the other way around. The information flows one way only.'

'You make sure of it,' Charlie said. 'And don't get too friendly.'

Lydia stood up. 'I have to get back to work. Thanks for lunch.'

'Any time, Lyds. You know that. I look after my own.'

CHAPTER NINE

Robert Sharp was no longer front-page news. One dead analyst didn't merit the spotlight for very long, despite the public way he had been killed. His name had been released, which had resulted in a flurry of attention at the beginning of the week but, Lydia assumed because the journalists had drawn a similar blank as the police on friends and family, it had blown out quickly. There didn't seem to be anything interesting about Robert Sharp's life to dig into in the aftermath of his death. Lydia had asked Fleet if the police were treating it as gang-related, instead. Some group deciding to emulate an old Mob-killing for kudos. Fleet had said that it was the main line of inquiry. His expression was sceptical, though.

'You don't think it's right?'

He had shaken his head. 'Too tidy for that. Gang retaliation is messier. Nastier.'

'Nastier than hanging?'

'Much nastier.'

Lydia hadn't asked him to elaborate.

Maria had given Lydia a direct telephone number and a name. She had made it clear that Lydia was not welcome to visit her office in person, but that she could question her secretary, Milo Easen. When he answered, it was clear he had been briefed to give the barest of bare details. He confirmed that Robert Sharp had telephoned to make an appointment with Maria Silver.

'The appointment was for next week, correct?'

'Yes. That was our next available time. He was flagged as a priority.'

'Not that high a priority. It was over a week between his call and the appointment and it obviously wasn't quick enough.'

Easen was silent. Then he said: 'Ms Silver is extremely busy, like all the staff here. If Mr Sharp had been flexible as to who he saw for the initial meeting, we would have been able to accommodate him sooner, but he was not.

'Fair enough,' Lydia said. 'Do you know why he was so fixated on Maria?'

A slight pause. 'She has a formidable reputation.'

'What was the nature of Mr Sharp's problem?'

'He didn't say.'

'No indication at all? Is that normal? For you to arrange an initial appointment without any kind of briefing notes for your boss? That seems like an inefficient use of her time. Especially when she is in such high demand.'

Another short silence. 'I had been told to expect Mr Sharp's call and instructed to give him an appointment within the next two weeks. No questions asked.'

'Does that sort of thing happen often?'

'No,' Easen said, 'but then we have a very full roster and rarely extend our client base.'

'Speaking of clients, what can you tell me about JRB?'

This time there was no hesitation whatsoever. 'Absolutely nothing.'

After finishing the call, Lydia stared into space for a few minutes, thinking. She had already Googled JRB and found the kind of bland corporate website which told the world exactly nothing about their business, except that they could afford a top-notch designer. Going through company records for the directors yielded a couple of names which she dutifully looked up. Again, they had minimal web presences. It was hard to know if that was, in itself, suspicious, or whether both men were just very old school.

Lydia leaned back in her office chair and considered whether fanning herself with a piece of paper would be worth the effort. A sudden drop in temperature preceded Jason's appearance. 'Oh, that feels good,' Lydia said. 'Stand closer.'

'Still hot?' Jason said. 'I can't feel it.'

'You're lucky,' Lydia said.

'Yeah, that's me,' Jason said, his voice dry.

'Sorry,' Lydia said. 'It's the heat. It's making me stupid.'

Jason walked around the desk, which Lydia appreciated, and lightly wrapped his arms around her upper body. Instantly, her skin rose in goosebumps. A few seconds more and she began to shiver. He moved away. 'No, don't. It's so nice to feel cool.'

LYDIA WAS STRETCHED out on the thin hard carpet of her ex-living room. From this angle, her desk reared up in her peripheral vision and she had a panoramic view of the stains on the anaglypta ceiling.

'What are you doing?' Fleet had been in the tiny kitchen, fixing them both dinner from the supplies he had brought; salad, cheese, fresh baguette, and olives. Lydia heard him cross the room and put plates down onto her desk. 'We could eat outside. It's so warm-'

'No!' Lydia said quickly, sitting up. 'In here's fine.'

He gave her a funny look so she followed up with 'we'll get dive-bombed by pigeons.'

'They wouldn't dare,' Fleet said but, thankfully, dropped the matter. He took his plate and a glass of orange juice and sat on the sofa.

Lydia got to her feet and plucked an olive from her plate. The intense salty flavour flooded her mouth and she realised that she was starving. The heat masked hunger. Or perhaps it was her level of distraction. Her mind had been so taken up with her open cases and the case that she wasn't even supposed to be working, all the while trying not to think about her weird dreams. She had a sense of growing unease which had no logical reason. It was exhausting.

'You're miles away,' Fleet said. 'Anything I can help with?'

Lydia blinked and focused on Fleet. 'Tell me you convinced Ian to let you see the crime-scene photos.'

'I've seen the crime-scene images.' He popped an olive in his mouth and chewed.

Fleet was so casual that it took a second for Lydia's brain to catch up to what he had said and to understand that it was actually what she wanted to hear. 'And you wasted time with food?'

'I was hungry,' Fleet said, wiping his hands together and leaning to one side to pick up the black rucksack he used for work. 'Now, I shouldn't have these. It goes without saying that I am definitely not doing what I'm doing right now.' He crossed the room and opened his laptop. The screen sprang to life and he navigated to a folder and clicked to open a handful of files.

'Of course,' Lydia said. The files were JPEGs. She looked up at Fleet. 'Won't there be a record of you copying these?'

'Ian knows a guy in IT,' Fleet said. 'Hopefully he knows what he's doing.'

Lydia peered at the photographs, concentrating on the close-ups of the bindings used on Sharp's wrists and ankles. Plastic zip ties. There were red marks where he had struggled against his bonds, cutting into his flesh, and Lydia deliberately noted them down in her notebook to avoid thinking about the picture of human suffering they painted.

The bricks that had been stuffed into Sharp's suit jacket pockets were also photographed carefully. 'They're not new,' Lydia said, touching the screen with her fingertip.

'Nope,' Fleet said. 'Victorian, apparently. Ian's put a request to trace their origin, where they might have been bought or found, but no luck yet.'

'Reclamation yards?'

'Yeah, that kind of thing. Old buildings that haven't been completely salvaged, yet. Problem is, there are a lot of old bricks in London.'

Lydia nodded. She was looking at another of the pictures. Sharp's body was attached to the ironwork girders underneath Blackfriars bridge. Even though he had been strung up near the bottom of the curve of the bridge, relatively close to where the Thames met the embankment, his feet were well off the ground. 'How hard would it be to do that?'

'Physically you mean?'

'Physically, logistically. How was it not caught on CCTV for starters? And there must have been a group. And some pretty tall, strong people.'

'A professional crew,' Fleet said. 'They sprayed the cameras in the area. Official line of enquiry is that it's definitely organised crime. Sharp got tangled up in something and got himself made an example.'

'An example for what, though?'

Fleet shrugged. 'Something to do with his valuation work at Sheridan Fisher? Maybe he didn't follow instructions for some reason, stopped playing ball. Or maybe he did something accidentally. Valued a company poorly that he didn't know belonged to his benefactors.'

'What's the investigation looking like?'

'Slow,' Fleet said. 'Just between us, they're winding it down. Reason Ian let me take a peek at these. He's desperate.'

'But it's murder.' Lydia felt like a child for pointing out the obvious. There were a lot of murders in the capital, she knew, but even so.

'Yeah, but there aren't any other leads. And he doesn't have family clamouring for results. Or a high-profile name. MIT are doing their best, but they are squeezed, just like everyone else. Ian's had half his team pulled onto other tasks already.'

'Good thing I'm helping out, then,' Lydia said, joking.

'You stay out of it,' Fleet said, not joking at all. 'If this is organised crime, you do not want to poke around.'

'I think you're forgetting who I am,' Lydia said, surprised at how insulted she felt.

Fleet had gone very still. 'I haven't forgotten. And if you got into trouble with some gang, how long before your uncle starts a war?'

Lydia was so used to worrying about the four Families, that she never spared a thought for the normals. Their gangs seemed inconsequential, insubstantial. Looking, again, at the image of Robert Sharp swinging beneath Blackfriars, was a sobering reminder that it wasn't just the old magical families that had teeth.

Lydia opened her eyes and confronted the inside of her duvet cover. Her head felt sweaty where she had been buried underneath the covers and she fought her way out, almost panicking. More dreams. Stepping out onto her roof terrace and then being tipped over the railing. The swooping sense in her stomach of falling and Maddie's voice in her ear, telling her to fly. 'I can't fly,' she had said. Screamed, really. Lydia's throat clicked as she swallowed and she reached for the glass of water next to her bed. After swigging from it, her head cleared and she frowned. It was unlike her to be organised enough to leave a glass of water next to the bed. Sometimes a diet cola bottle or last night's whisky dregs. And what was that noise? As the nightmare cleared and Lydia woke up, she realised that there was a dragging sound next door. And then a thump.

'Jason?'

At once, she remembered. Fleet had been here. They had sunk a few drinks, which accounted for the woolly-feeling in her head and the pounding behind her eyes. Lydia climbed out of bed, relieved to find she was still wearing her jersey shorts and vest top. They hadn't had drunken sex, then. She was staying strong. Keeping Fleet at arm's length. Keeping things professional.

She remembered, now. She had been feeling rebellious. Charlie telling her who she could and couldn't be friends with had made her open a bottle of bourbon after they had finished looking at the crime scene photographs. So, this outrageous hangover was Uncle Charlie's fault.

Gripping the now-empty glass in one hand, Lydia

trailed out of her bedroom and stopped. Fleet was crouching in the corner of her living room-slash-office. He had stacked bricks and planks of wood to make a bookcase and had just opened one of her cardboard boxes of books.

'What are you doing?'

Fleet looked up. 'Morning, my exceedingly drunk friend.'

'I wasn't drunk,' Lydia said. She frowned, trying to remember, but it intensified her headache.

'Right,' Fleet said. His smile could only be described as a smirk and Lydia didn't like it.

There was an empty bottle of whisky on the desk and two tumblers. 'What about you?'

'I was very restrained,' Fleet said. 'I slept on the sofa, though, hope you don't mind. It was pretty late when you passed out.'

'You were drinking, too,' Lydia said. She had a vague memory of playing poker. An image of Fleet singing along to the Beatles, although that didn't seem likely.

'It was a great night,' Fleet said. 'Until you started raving about flying.'

Oh no.

'I don't rave,' Lydia said in her most-withering tone.

'Eat,' Fleet pointed to the kitchen. 'And there's coffee.'

'Coffee?' Lydia headed into the tiny kitchenette. A pile of neatly rinsed and squashed beer cans were next to the sink and Lydia had a flashback to chugging an entire can just to prove that she could. She cringed. On the side there was a bakery box filled with croissants, pain au chocolat and a custard-filled pastry, and a large cafetiere. Lydia poured a mugful and ate a pain au chocolat in three large bites. She found paracetamol in the end cupboard and swallowed two with half a glass of water. Carrying another pain au chocolat and her coffee, Lydia felt strong enough to face Fleet.

'Thank you for breakfast,' she said. 'What is this,' she gestured to the shelves.

Fleet was lining books up and he didn't look around. 'I saw you hadn't unpacked these and figured you needed a bookcase. This is just a temporary measure. I know it's a bit low-end. It's easy to move, though, and you can replace it with proper furniture whenever you want.'

'I like it,' Lydia said. 'Where did you get the wood?'

'I had some left over from when I did mine.' Fleet glanced at her, then. 'I know you'll probably need more. I can fill the whole wall, if you want.'

'And you just had this with you?'

'I brought it round last night in the car. Then we got distracted.'

The man had brought her bookshelves. And pastries. And coffee. Lydia felt slightly stunned. 'Thank you,' she said, sitting on the sofa. At least they had been distracted by extreme drinking and not anything more complicated. As a solution to their mutual attraction, it had merit. Although her hangover said otherwise.

'I'm not filing these,' he said, still placing books. 'You'll have to alphabetise them yourself.'

'Or not,' Lydia said, around a mouthful of buttery, chocolately flakes.

'Or not,' he agreed. 'If you prefer the element of surprise, I suppose. The unexpected serendipity of reaching for a Terry Pratchett and ending up with a Nigella cookbook.'

Lydia took another sip of coffee. 'You organise yours, then.'

'Oh, yes. I'm a great believer in the Dewey Decimal system. And I lied about the Nigella. The only cookbook I have is a Madhur Jaffrey.'

Lydia couldn't imagine owning a cookbook. 'We are very different, you and me.'

'Opposites attract,' Fleet said, standing up. Once he had finished filling the last shelves, he turned his attention to the empty boxes. 'You want these flattened for the recycling?'

'I might keep them,' Lydia said. 'Just in case.'

'Thinking about moving?'

Lydia drained her coffee. 'You never know what's around the corner.'

'That's true.'

Lydia stood up and began un-taping the boxes, flattening them. She caught Fleet smiling at her and said, defensively. 'They're just easier to store like this. I'm still keeping them.'

'Shall I put them in your spare bedroom?'

'No, that's all right,' Lydia said, thinking about Jason. Then a thought hit her. 'You slept on the sofa?'

'Passed out is more accurate, but yeah.'

Happy that it hadn't just been her in a state, Lydia was still confused. 'Why didn't you use the spare bed?'

Fleet frowned. 'I don't know...' Then he shook his head. 'That's right. I tried. Couldn't get the door open.'

'You *were* drunk,' Lydia said lightly. 'It's not got a lock.' She would have to speak to Jason about stopping people from going into his room. It was his room, but still. Fleet might get suspicious about randomly-impossible-to-open doors. Mind you, the sight of a load of mathematical equations all over the walls would have taken some explaining, too. And this kind of trickiness was just one of the many reasons she couldn't start anything more intimate with Fleet.

CHAPTER TEN

After Fleet had left, Lydia tried to distract herself from her impossible love life with a bit of work. She had a call scheduled with Dr Lee. She read over the report she had sent through, reminding herself of the details of a case which felt as if it had happened a lifetime ago. She needed to be on the ball, couldn't afford a bad review at this stage. Sadly, she needed plenty more cheating spouses to keep her in whisky and crisps. What she really wanted was to build up enough capital so that she could pay a deposit on a flat and have six months' rent as a buffer, just in case she ever had to leave The Fork. Free rent from Uncle Charlie was very useful, but it made keeping her business separate from Charlie's world immensely difficult. She hated to admit it, but her parents had been right.

Things didn't get any less depressing with her client phone call. Dr Lee was very upset and it took Lydia's most soothing voice and lots of leading questions to get him to explain the issue. Not her strong suit.

'She doesn't have fancy nails,' he said, finally. 'They are plain. Cut straight across with scissors. She doesn't like long nails, says they get in the way when she is typing. At work.'

'Right,' Lydia said.

'You said it was nails, that she was having them done,' his voice was halfway between anger and tears.

'It was a possibility,' Lydia said. 'Would you like me to resume the investigation?'

'Of course,' Dr Lee said. 'It's not finished.'

'I just thought you might have changed your mind...' Lydia always liked to give clients an out. It probably wasn't great for her bottom line, financially, but there was so much stirred up in these cases. The past sediment of long-term relationships which, once whipped into the present, clouded the whole river.

'I need to know,' Dr Lee said.

'Okay, I'll be in touch.' Lydia finished the call and made her second coffee of the day. She ignored her unusable roof terrace and leaned back in her office chair, staring at the ceiling and trying to keep her mind on the Lee case. Dr Lee was a paying client and she ought to be thinking about her next steps in tailing his wife. Instead, she couldn't stop seeing the figure of Robert Sharp suspended beneath the ironwork of Blackfriars bridge.

She closed her eyes and gave in. Robert Sharp had a fifteen-grand silver statue and priority treatment at a premier law firm and, if Lydia's hunch was correct, a sweet deal on the rent of a fancy flat in Canary Wharf.

All in all, it added up to a tidy package. He was clearly very valuable to somebody. Lydia filled a glass of water and drank it while she stared out of the window, thinking. The sounds from the street, ever-present, were particularly loud as the heatwave continued. A group of teenage boys were shouting and laughing and Lydia leaned forward to see what was happening. They were in mismatched football kit and clearly heading home after a friendly kickabout. One boy poured a bottle of water over his head without breaking stride and another shoved his friend playfully in the shoulder, causing him to step out into the road.

Of course, Mr Sharp might be valuable to a whole group of somebodies. A family, for example. Lydia didn't want to jump to conclusions, but the fact that a Silver-run law firm was involved was suspicious. Lydia called Charlie, acting before she could talk herself out of it.

He picked up instantly. 'All right, Lyds?'

'Yeah, fine,' Lydia ignored the tug in her stomach. Charlie had sounded so like her dad for a moment. 'What do you know about the Silvers?'

A slight hesitation. 'Lots. What are you after?'

'Would they represent an organisation of flexible morality?'

'In a heartbeat. Why?'

'Do you know JRB? It's a registered company and the website uses words like 'consulting' so you haven't a bloody clue what they're about.'

'Doesn't ring a bell,' Charlie said. 'Not exactly memorable, though. Sounds like a hundred other things.'

A car horn blared, followed by a flurry of clearly enunciated swear words. Lydia closed her eyes and tried to organise her thoughts. 'There's this guy. He's a nobody. Mid-level analyst in the City. But someone is looking out for him like he's important, like he knows something.'

'You think he's into blackmail?'

Lydia opened her eyes. 'You know what? He could be.' Lydia had been focusing on Sharp as a victim. The way he had been killed had been so horrible and so public and his possessions in the flat had seemed so meagre, it had painted a certain image in Lydia's mind. 'He could have exhorted favours and money.'

'And it doesn't have to be related to his job. It could be personal. He might have stumbled across some information or have a personal vendetta against someone, some kind of relationship connection. Or he might have set things up. Could have gone looking for dirt on someone with a lot of cash and a reputation they don't want tarnished.'

Lydia was frustrated. If Fleet could get her a list of Sharp's known associates, she could see if anybody fitted the description. Of course, the police had no doubt already thought of the angle. She was being slow. Had been too distracted by the anachronism of the silver knight. That could just have been a payment for blackmail in lieu of a traceable bank transfer.

'Is this guy dead by any chance?'

'Very,' Lydia said.

'Could easily have been into blackmail, then,' Charlie said. 'That often goes wrong.'

Lydia decided not to ask exactly how much experience Charlie had in that particular arena. The less she knew, the better. As always.

'Don't be a stranger,' Charlie said as Lydia ended the call.

'Impossible,' Lydia said out loud to the empty room.

She looked at her phone screen for a moment and then called Fleet. 'Have they looked into who was paying rent for Sharp's flat?'

'Are you still on this?'

Lydia didn't bother to answer, just waited for Fleet to carry on.

'Not on the phone,' he said. 'I'll come round in a bit.'

LYDIA WORKED while she waited for Fleet. She organised her case notes for the various jobs she was running and updated her accounts. Jason was in his room, sitting on the bed cross-legged and staring into space. Lydia couldn't tell if he was deep in thought, meditating or powered-down in his version of sleep, but he didn't react when she knocked and walked in, so she left him to it.

Fleet was in shirt sleeves and he handed a carrier bag to Lydia when he arrived. She opened it and saw a bag of ice cubes. 'Lovely. Thanks.'

Fleet filled a couple of pint glasses from the tap, ripped open the bag and added cubes to each.

Lydia took the proffered glass and drank gratefully before rolling the cool surface against her cheeks and the base of her neck. 'When will this bloody heat end?' It was reflexive, the same words that everybody in the city was saying on repeat. If the old Gods had still existed, it would have been like a prayer.

'Shall we go outside?'

Lydia thought about her roof terrace and felt an instant stab of visceral fear. 'Let's just sit by the window.' It was wide open and Lydia dragged both office chairs in front of it.

'So, I spoke to Ian and got a progress report.' He held up a hand. 'Don't get too excited. Suspects are still thin on the ground.'

'Did they find out who was paying his rent?'

Fleet nodded. He took a notebook out of his pocket and flipped it open, reading from his notes. 'Rent paid by Robert Sharp.' He held a hand up as if anticipating an interruption and carried on reading. 'Five weeks before his death, Mr Sharp lived in a house-share up near Hampstead Heath. Modest rent by London standards, Oyster card was one of his biggest outgoings, along with his computer and gaming costs.'

'Gambling?'

'Online RPG, elves and wizards sort of thing.'

'So what happened five weeks ago?'

'No idea. Ian hasn't made headway, either. Sharp just upped and left. His housemates weren't especially close, describe him as 'quiet, kept to himself, tidy,' not exactly illuminating, and they have no clue why he gave notice. Apparently he didn't share his plans with them. In fact, one member of the house,' Fleet glanced at his notebook, 'Serena Hapzburg, said that he told her to mind her own business when she asked and she was surprised because he had never been rude like that before. Quiet, but nice.'

'Were those the words he used? Did she say that he said 'mind your own business'.'

'Not exactly,' Fleet said. 'Apparently he told her to "fuck off out of his face".'

'That's a bit aggressive.'

'Under stress, perhaps?'

'Personality change due to drug use?'

'Could be,' Fleet looked thoughtful. 'MIT hasn't found any evidence of drugs, but maybe it was one time. If he was slipped something really nasty it could have messed him up. Unusual but not unheard of. The brain is a funny thing and it can react that way for some people, if they've got an underlying pathology waiting to be unlocked.'

Lydia remembered a guy at her school who had smoked weed a few times, along with everyone else but, unlike everyone else, had ended up in a psych ward. Of course, it was possible he had been doing a lot more than weed or a lot more weed than most. She was basing her information on the rumour mill of a bunch of teenagers but still, it had always stuck with her that drugs were unpredictable. That what might be a night or two of fun for most, could end the life of the unlucky. Drugs were like magic in that way, at least according to the stories her Dad had sometimes told. Back in the glory days, when power was running through the Crow family like electricity, there had been some unfortunates who pushed too hard and burned out. And some whose minds just couldn't take the old magic in the new world and their minds had gone soft. Left with pudding brains, dribbling in the corner of a care-home lounge, unable to recall their own names.

'Ian's not pursuing the drug line,' Fleet said. 'He's a smart cop and I trust his judgement. He's interviewed Sharp's associates, been in the house and his place of work, and spoken to the family. If he's not feeling it, then I reckon it will be something else.'

'But what?'

'I have no clue.'

Lydia drained the glass of water. It felt good in the heat but mainly made her want to have a cold beer. It was still early, though, and she had hours of work ahead. 'I thought someone else would have been paying for his flat. It just didn't look like something he would choose.'

'Well you were right. It wasn't something the old Robert would have chosen, as far as we can tell. So something changed.'

'I just don't see how he got in with people who would do what they did,' Lydia said. 'I thought either he was being paid off for something he knew or black-mailing the wrong people.'

'Ian is working on the assumption that he got into the wrong place at the wrong time. He was having some kind of life change, maybe sparked by drugs, maybe a breakup, some family news we haven't discovered yet. Maybe he was just stressed out at work and he didn't get to the doctors or talk about it with anyone and it built up until he had some kind of breakdown. That could change his behaviour.'

'The new flat was him trying to run away from his feelings?'

'Could be.'

'And then, what? He's just walking down the wrong street one day and gets snatched up by a random psycho with a flair for the dramatic? Some guy who loves the old mafia stories and has decided to pay homage with a Blackfriars Bridge hanging.' Lydia couldn't see it. 'Have they worked up a timeline on his last hours?'

Fleet flipped a couple of pages in his notebook. It looked tiny in his large hands, but his writing was small and neat, lines of tidy script in fine black ink. Lydia forced herself to look away from those deft long fingers. They were too distracting.

'Thursday 24th. He left work early at five-forty. Most on his floor stay until half six, seven, as a matter of course.'

'Stressful work environment. Pressure?'

Fleet nodded. 'Tick in that column for the breakdown theory. Then he used his Oyster card to go to Whitechapel. We've got him on camera coming out of the station. We've got him going into the Sainsburys on Cambridge Heath Road where he bought a Twix and a four-pack of Peroni, and then we don't see him again until he uses his Oyster card at Aldgate. Presumably on his way home.'

'We don't have the end of that journey?'

'No,' Fleet said. 'It's a bit odd, but not beyond the bounds. Could be the gate was glitching and he beeped out and it didn't register the information for some reason. Gremlins in the software.'

'Or he beeped his Oyster card at Aldgate Station but changed his mind and didn't go through the gate. Have you seen the CCTV?'

'I'll ask Ian,' Fleet said.

'What's in Whitechapel?' Lydia mused out loud. 'He hasn't got friends there.' And it's not the area for the Silvers, she added silently. The silver knight statue was still worrying away at the back of her mind.

'Not as far as we know,' Fleet said. 'Could have been meeting new people. Could be some East End business types. That could lead in a bad direction.'

Of course, the Fox family lived in Whitechapel. Lydia didn't remember them ever executing people in such a public manner, but, as Charlie kept saying, things had changed. If the Fox family were trying to reassert their crime family cred in the East End of London, it was a possibility that they would carry out a stunt like this as a show of strength. Or a demonstration of their skills. Lydia shuddered.

'What is it?' Fleet was watching her.

'Just trying to connect Sharp's life with his ending. It doesn't fit.'

Fleet shook his head. 'It's not right.'

CHAPTER ELEVEN

Lydia wasn't sure how Charlie would react to a possible Family connection to her case. Especially since it wasn't really her case, at all. She had a suspicion he wouldn't approve of her getting involved. But she couldn't stop thinking about the antique knight statue and how utterly out of place it had been at Sharp's sterile flat. And now there was Sharp wandering, apparently aimlessly, around Whitechapel the day before he died.

She turned up at his house, anyway, hoping to hear something useful. Charlie was in the middle of work, his laptop open on the dining room table and piles of paperwork spread around the surface. It wasn't a side she associated with Charlie. The mundane realities of running several businesses in a (possibly) criminal empire.

'You're busy,' Lydia said.

'Always got time for you, Lyds,' Charlie said.

Once they had exchanged a few words about the continuing heatwave, Lydia judged that enough politeness had been delivered and she could launch in. She decided to stick to questions about the Silvers. Charlie was more likely to lose his mind if she brought up the Foxes. 'You said things had changed,' Lydia began. 'What is the current situation with the Silvers?'

'I thought you didn't want to know about that stuff?' Charlie said, crossing his arms. He looked surprised as if this was the last thing he expected her to bring up. And a little bit relieved, too, which set Lydia wondering what he had been worried she was going to say.

'We're cordial, yes? Alejandro made Maria speak to me as a matter of courtesy.'

Charlie looked pleased with that.

'But would we use the firm if we needed legal help?'

A shutter came down. 'We don't need lawyers.'

'What about when Maddie was in trouble? There was the driving offence and-'

Charlie waved his hand. 'Wasn't needed. We have enough friends.'

'But if we did need help with something, something really big. Silver and Silver specialise in business crime, cartels, fraud, corporate protection.'

The tattoos on Charlie's arms began to move and Lydia fought the urge to take a step backward.

'Hypothetically, it's possible. Not really our level, though. We're a small business. Community stuff. They deal with international conglomerates.'

'So I've read.' Lydia had spent all morning reading

up on Maria's previous cases. 'Maria just prevented Aden Naser from being extradited back to Yemen for historical crimes. He was up on a cartel charge in the UK, and the sentencing guidelines had a minimum of four years prison time. Maria got him eighty hours of community service.'

'They're good, gotta give them that,' Charlie said.

'That's one word for it.'

'You want something to drink?'

Lydia could see through the glass doors to Charlie's decked seating area where there was a folded newspaper and a discarded mug on a metal table. 'Just water, thanks.'

Charlie filled a glass and they went outside where the noise instantly increased. Not just the usual street sounds of the city, but with bird chatter and song. A row of jackdaws and magpies sat along the top of the tall fence and the copper beech at the end of the garden was filled with small birds. A crow flew across and landed on the back of a wrought iron bench and called her name with an uncanny impression of Charlie's voice.

'Good morning,' Lydia said respectfully. The crow let out a harsh caw and flew off. Turning back to Charlie, Lydia was struck by how tired her uncle looked. There were hollows in his cheeks and salt-streaked stubble was visible on his jaw in the bright sunlight. 'Is everything all right?'

'Yeah, course.' Charlie pulled a pair of sunglasses out of his shirt pocket and put them on. 'Everything's peachy.' He moved the conversation on with a barrage of questions about The Fork, her investigative business and whether she was getting work, updates on family members Lydia hadn't seen in years or, possibly, had never even met.

Lydia let him lead. The sun was hot on her bare arms and the sound of the birds was relaxing. She thought about setting up feeders and putting some pots out on the roof terrace. It was stupid not to use it. Just because some guy had once nearly tipped her over the railing to her death was no reason not to use it.

Charlie's mobile buzzed. He turned it face up and glanced at the screen before turning it over on the table again. His expression hardly changed but Lydia saw a micro-change, the barest flicker of displeasure. 'Something's wrong.'

'Something is always wrong,' Charlie said with a forced smile. 'Price of leadership.'

'Do you want to talk about it?'

Charlie shook his head. But then he said: 'Just a new gang. Kids who don't know any better, haven't been taught their history. Making trouble with the established drug trade and breaching the peace.'

Lydia knew that Charlie wasn't a fan of the drug trade, but that he was a realist. If you kept it regulated, the way the government ought to be doing, you kept the violence to a minimum and ran off chancers who sold really bad product. It wasn't pretty, but it prevented some poor school kid from snorting a lungful of pure soda bic and dying on their first experiment, and the corner shops from being knocked over by low-level gangs. The addicts still lost out, of course, but then they always did. They needed legal product to stop them getting into trouble and decent healthcare and properly-funded addiction programs.

'What are you going to do?'

Charlie smiled his shark smile. 'Give 'em a history lesson.'

THE CUSTOMER NAME from Guillaume Chartes was Yas Bishop. The address was in Bayswater and a bit of judicious web research threw up that Star Street was lined with Grade II listed Georgian terraced houses. A small three-bed version could be Lydia's for a mere one point five million. More interestingly, Lydia used her background search software tools to cross reference other known details and discovered that Ms Y Bishop had listed JRB Solutions as her employer on her mortgage application documents.

Lydia rang the landline listed and a woman answered after only three rings. Lydia was momentarily surprised, she didn't think anybody answered an unknown number to their landline anymore, and had been prepared to leave a message. 'Is that Yas Bishop?'

'Yes?'

'Ms Bishop, my name is Lydia Crow and I'm an investigator. It's nothing to worry about but I was hoping to ask you about a silver statue you purchased last month.'

'I'm sorry, what? Who are you?'

Lydia repeated her introduction. 'I just wondered whether the knight statue you purchased from Guillaume Chartes last month was for yourself or a gift for somebody else?'

'I haven't bought anything. I don't know anybody of that name. A knight did you say?' A high-pitched laugh. 'Why would I want something like that?'

Lydia hadn't been expecting full cooperation but a flat refusal was odd. 'Yes, a silver knight. German, dated early nineteen hundred.'

'I don't understand... Who are you? Why are you calling me about this?'

Lydia opened her mouth to explain, again, but Yas was still talking. 'Why have you called me? I don't... I was expecting a call but I wasn't expecting...' Yas trailed off. Then, in a voice that was pure terror. 'Is this a test? Is this the call? Oh God. Oh God. I'm sorry. Can we start again? I didn't realise.'

'Ms Bishop, it's okay. This isn't a test. You aren't in any trouble.' There was a click halfway through Lydia's last sentence and then the dialling tone.

Hell Hawk.

LYDIA DID a bit more research on Yas Bishop and discovered that she hadn't updated her social media accounts for six weeks. Prior to that, she had shared many pictures of a small beady-eyed dog, peppered with the obligatory food shots and the occasional sunset. There could be a number of reasons, of course, but it seemed significant that she had also had a change in behaviour. Lydia searched Yas's friends on Facebook and sent a few friend requests. It only took one of them to let Lydia in and she would have access to Yas's full timeline.

THERE WAS something about that statue. She was sure of it. Lydia decided to head back to the vaults and see if she could get more from Guillaume. Since she was in the area, Lydia decided to visit the JRB head office, too.

The office was listed as Chichester Rents which turned out to be a narrow passageway between eighteenth century buildings off Chancery Lane. The passage was lined with delis and high-end takeaways serving sushi and vegan burgers and above, a stack of concrete cubes with large square windows, housed the modern offices.

Lydia located what she assumed was the entrance to the offices, but it took discreet to another level and didn't list company names or even numbers. Lydia pounded on the wooden door and pressed all of the unlabelled buttons on the door bell. After five minutes of this, as well as trying the door to check it was locked, she had to admit defeat. JRB truly weren't open to visitors.

The silver vaults were located further down Chancery Lane. Lydia couldn't help but feel it was all very cosy. The weather was close to breaking, Lydia could feel it in the air, as she walked down the street checking building numbers. There was an electricity that wasn't unlike the feeling Lydia had when she sensed Family power. A roll of thunder, far off in the distance, rumbled as Lydia opened the outside door to the vaults. She descended to the passage and, unlike her previous visit, there were a couple of other shoppers in the passageway. A couple in front turned into a shop which seemed to specialise in cutlery. Lydia made her way to Guillaume's shop and stood for a moment outside, dumbfounded. The steel door to the old safe room was shut. There was no sign above or on the door, nothing to suggest that a business resided inside. Lydia went to the shop next door. A woman with black hair in a chic bob and a bejewelled black jumper smiled in welcome as she walked into the shop. It was an Aladdin's cave, just like Guillaume's, with a selection of shining silver antiques of every size and shape. 'Just looking?' She smiled in a friendly way. 'Help yourself, dear. Ask if you need help with anything.'

'Actually,' Lydia said. 'I was hoping to pop next door. Guillaume had a teapot I was interested in and I was wondering if you knew when he would be open?'

The woman frowned. 'I'm sorry, do you mean the jewellers? They're by appointment only, dear. You can find their details online, I believe.'

'No, Guillaume Chartes. He sells a mixture of stuff. There was a big carvery trolley in the middle of the place. You couldn't miss it.'

'If you're after one of those, I can source it for you. If you give me an idea of your budget...'

Lydia could feel the conversation getting off track. 'No, I need to see Guillaume. If you have contact details for him, by any chance? Or know when he is likely to be open again. Does he usually take Wednesday off?'

'I don't know a Guillaume,' the woman looked distinctly less friendly now. She looked wary, in fact, as if suddenly realising that Lydia was unhinged in some way. 'But the shop on that side,' she pointed in the direction of Guillaume's, 'has been empty for months.'

CHAPTER TWELVE

Lydia made her way to the hotel in Greenwich for the design conference. It was actually closer to Deptford, in one of the big chain hotels, but Lydia could understand the organiser's decision to bill it as Greenwich. Swank-appeal. She waited until the crowd had moved through the reception area and the majority of attendees had picked up their name badges from the table where they were laid out. A young woman in a black skirt suit was sitting behind the table smiling as if she was paid by the centimetre. Through open doors, Lydia could see a multitude of trade stands set up in an exhibition area and there were several bi-fold screens displaying the conference schedule. Talks and work-shops with titles like 'The New Modernism Aesthetic' and 'What About Monochrome?' were listed with times and locations and there was another table laden with glasses of orange juice, sparkling water, and a thick green sludge that Lydia assumed was blitzed kale or some other horror. Another three young, black-suited and widely grinning people hovered behind the refreshments table and Lydia noted that she could always pose as a staff member if the name-tag situation didn't pan out.

She took a glass of water and had a closer look at the suits. Not matching, which was good.

Christopher Westcott ought to be here by now. Lydia confirmed his attendance at the name tag table. His was gone. There were twenty or so tags left and she scanned them quickly before picking one up with a female name. 'Welcome to the symposium,' the woman said. 'Please help yourself to a complimentary drink.'

Lydia hoisted her glass of water. 'Way ahead of you.'

With no way of knowing into which of the panels Westcott had gone, she took a management decision and headed to the bar. A glass of red wine killed an hour and then a wander around the exhibition space. The trade stands were a motley mix of software, printer companies, advertising agencies and architects. An earnest man from a tech company tried to sell her a tablet computer with a digital pen and she picked up several free key rings, pens, sweets and a branded travel mug.

Lydia was just wondering whether Jason's idea of powering up enough to leave the flat was, in fact, an excellent one and just how quickly she could manage it, when she caught sight of Christopher. He was chatting to a woman a couple of stands ahead and took a glossy brochure from her before moving on.

Lydia tailed him to the restaurant and ate an overpriced plate of spaghetti while he sat at a lone table and played with his phone for an hour or so. The networking opportunities had either been greatly exaggerated or he had been stood up for a lunch meeting. Lydia would have laid money on the former, as Christopher didn't look around or give any sign that he was expecting a dining companion. He had a complimentary tote bag which was stuffed, having seriously ransacked the exhibition area, and Lydia steeled herself to follow him into one of the mind-numbing talks after he had finished massacring his berry cheesecake.

Her mobile vibrated and she answered it, keeping Christopher in her peripheral vision.

'Hello? Hello?'

Lydia pulled the phone away from her ear as Jason's voice yelled through the microphone. She hastily thumbed the volume down button the side of her phone before replacing it in position. 'Stop shouting, I can hear you.'

'Sorry,' Jason's voice was now a hoarse whisper. 'I'm out of practice.'

'I know,' Lydia said. She had bought a retro-style touch-tone phone with a cord and receiver to make Jason feel at home with the landline that she'd had installed. His motor control was easily good enough to pick it up and press the buttons, but he hadn't had cause to use it, yet.

'There's someone here.'

'What?' The line was filled with loud static and Lydia thought she might have to ask him to shout again.

'Someone is here. They rang the bell and waited outside the door for ages and then they tried to come inside.' Jason's words were rushing, tumbling over the crackly line.

'A client?'

'A woman. Brown hair, approximately five foot six.' He hesitated. 'Can I say she looks Indian? British Indian. Or is that racist? She has brown skin, but I don't know if I can say that. I mean, this is a description. A report. But it feels racist.'

'It's not racist to describe the colour of a person's skin for the purpose of clarity or identification.'

'I thought I wasn't supposed to see race. I thought that if you noticed it, it meant you were racist.'

'That's very eighties,' Lydia said.

A slight pause. 'Well, duh.'

'Ahh,' Lydia was at a loss as to what to say. Foot in mouth was one thing. Continually reminding a person that they were out of their proper time. Stuck because they had died three decades ago. 'Sorry, sorry.'

'It's okay,' Jason said, although his voice indicated otherwise. 'I'm trying, you know. I'm trying to-'

'I know,' Lydia said. 'You're just so normal and so real these days. I keep forgetting... I keep forgetting you're new to all of this.'

'Okay,' Jason sounded mollified. 'I followed her downstairs to the cafe and I heard her speak to Angel. She sounded northern. Northern English, I mean.'

'Right. Good.' Lydia still couldn't work out why he was freaked out. 'I know we're not exactly in demand, but it's not that weird that a potential client might...'

'She's trying to break in.'

'What?'

'Right now.' Jason still sounded relatively calm, but his voice wavered a little. Either he was moving the receiver away from his mouth, or he was doing that strange vibrating in-and-out of existence thing he did when he was upset. 'There are little scraping noises like someone is picking the lock.'

Lydia opened her mouth, but nothing came out.

'Trying to pick it, anyway. It's been going on a while.'

Lydia put her finger in her ear and hunched away from the noise of the bar. Jason was difficult to hear, now, and she needed to concentrate. Her first instinct was to run outside to her car and race back to Camberwell. To confront the stranger. To protect her home. But she couldn't leave her post, and she had no real idea of what she would do if she could even get there in time.

'Lydia?'

'I'm thinking.'

'Shall I call the police?'

'No!' Lydia's reaction was instant and instinctual. Then she reconsidered. 'I'll call Fleet. Hang tight. Don't worry. She's probably just an opportunist. She won't make it in and, if she does, there isn't much to nick. Just hide in your room until she's gone.'

'I don't like it,' Jason said.

'I know. But she can't hurt you. She doesn't know you're there and she won't know. I'm going to call Fleet, now. I have to hang up to do that. It's okay, Jason. I promise.'

Jason made a sound of shock, a sort of yelp. 'Sorry,'

he said a moment later. 'There was a banging. I thought she had got the door.'

'She'd better not smash my nice glass,' Lydia said. 'I don't suppose you want to slip outside and scare her away? Put a sheet over your head-'

'I can't,' Jason said.

'It's okay, I'm only joking. Go hide. I'll call Fleet.'

Lydia ended the call. Her ghost was terrified. And she understood completely. She had brought two murderers to the flat in the short time she had lived there. No wonder he was antsy at the thought of an uninvited visitor. His ability to pick things up, to write his maths proofs on the wall, to turn the pages of the paperback books, all relied on him convincing himself that he wasn't dead. That he was a live, solid human being. A body which would affect the physical world. Naturally, that same conviction would make him feel fear for that same physicality. A thought struck Lydia. Could he be hurt? Had she powered Jason up in order that he could then be harmed? That was a sobering thought. Lydia reached absent mindedly for her drink, readying herself to call Fleet. She glanced over the rim at the place Westcott had been sitting. He wasn't there.

Feather and Claw. Hell Hawk. Lydia stood up quickly and waked out of the bar, looking left and right in the hope she would catch sight of Christopher Westcott. She called Fleet as she walked. He sounded sleepy. Or stoned. Which was an odd thought. Fleet didn't strike her as the type. 'Did I wake you?'

'Nah. You're all right.'

'There's somebody trying to break into my flat.'

'What? Now?' Fleet was instantly awake. His voice sharp and clear.

'Don't worry, I'm not there.'

'Good. Wait... How do you know there's somebody trying to break in?'

'Anonymous tip,' Lydia said, thinking on her feet. 'A concerned citizen just called me.'

'That makes no sense. How do they have your number? Are they a neighbour?'

Lydia ignored that question and repeated Jason's description of the intruder. 'Can you go there? If you're quick, you'll catch her at it.'

'If I'm very quick,' Fleet said drily. 'Where are you?'

'Deptford.'

'My condolences. I'm on my way.'

Lydia fast-walked into the hotel lobby, expecting to see Christopher at any moment. She had only looked away for a few seconds, he couldn't have gone far. Turning in the lobby, it hit her how stupid she was being. He had probably just gone to the loo. Back in the bar, Lydia wandered past his table. Still empty and no sign that he was intending to return. No coat, or half-finished drink. Of course, he might just be cautious. Or not have had a coat in the first place. If he was staying in in the hotel and wasn't intending to go outside... Lydia headed in the direction of the toilets. She hesitated outside the door for a moment, before walking into the gents. If Christopher was using the facilities, he would almost-certainly remember the woman who had accidentally wandered in and caught sight of his penis. However, it would be worth it to have eyes on him,

143

again. It wasn't as if he was presumed dangerous and he had no reason to be suspicious, either.

'Oops, sorry,' Lydia said. There was a short-ish young man at the middle urinal and another just coming out of one of the stalls. Neither of them was Christopher and she had clocked that the other stalls weren't occupied.

Another circuit of the bar and Lydia had to admit the sad truth; she had lost her mark. She was about to call Mrs Westcott and swallow the indignity of asking her client whether she happened to have the room number that her husband was staying in. The client who was paying her handsomely to stick like glue to her wandering spouse. Her finger hesitated over the call button before she had a better idea.

In the hotel reception, there was only one member of staff behind the desk. Lydia was pleased that it was a young-looking woman, guessing she would be easier to intimidate. She hated herself a little bit for the observation, but there it was. Not letting the woman finish her polite greeting, Lydia cut across her while drumming her finger nails on the counter top. 'I've locked the key in my room.' She snapped her fingers for good measure. 'Westcott.'

'One moment,' the woman said, fingers tapping quickly on her keyboard. A tiny frown between perfectly-plucked brows. 'I'm very sorry, Ms Westcott, I can't find your details here.'

'My husband booked it, Christopher Westcott. Do you need me to spell it? It's double 't' at the end.'

'No, that's all right...' Another pause and more

tapping. 'I'm very sorry, but I can't find your room in the system. Are you sure of your dates?'

'Of course,' Lydia forced herself to snap, staying in character. 'He's here for the conference.'

'Oh, that could be it,' the woman visibly sagged with relief. 'There might be a block-booking under the conference name. Hang on a tick.' More tapping. Then, 'nothing, I'm afraid. There was a block booking but that has since been superseded by individual check-in details. No one called Christopher Westcott. She frowned. What was your room number did you say?'

'Oh never mind,' Lydia said, channelling inner dick. 'I'll go and find my husband, it will be the quickest. He'll have the other key.'

'But, I don't-'

Her phone was ringing and Lydia moved outside to answer it. The air was warm compared to the air-conditioned interior and Lydia moved away from the smell of cigarette smoke which was hanging in the air, courtesy of the nicotine addicts gathered just outside the glass-and-metal entrance.

'There's no one here,' Fleet said and Lydia felt a shock of relief at hearing his voice.

'Nobody?'

'Angel is in the cafe, she let me in. Not happy about it, mind, I think I interrupted her quiet time.'

'No one else?'

'I've been through the whole building. Even checked the cafe's kitchen. Which is another complaint you're going to be hearing when you get home.'

'Thank you,' Lydia crouched down and sat on the

kerb. She hadn't realised how worried she had been until the relief washed over her. She took a deep breath, car fumes and a strange odour that was entirely Deptford. It was strange how the different parts of London had their own unique bouquets. If she went blind, she'd know she was in Camberwell, of course, sensing the Crows without any hesitation, but it was interesting to speculate how many other areas she would be able to identify by nose alone.

'Nothing there,' Fleet was saying.

'Sorry, what? I lost you for a second.'

'Back alley. Nothing. I did have a good look at your door, though, and someone has definitely had a go.'

The relief shrank back. Jason hadn't been mistaken. 'Bugger.'

'You want me to hang around? I can wait until you get home, if you like?'

'I'm out for the night,' Lydia said. 'But thank you. And thank you for heeding my distress call. That's above and beyond.'

'Always.' A pause. 'While I'm here, do you want me to let myself in and look around the flat. Just check on things?'

Lydia imagined Jason having heart-failure. 'No, that's okay. No sign of entry, so I'm sure it's fine.' Then something hit her. 'How would you let yourself in?'

'Kick the door in,' Fleet said, as if it was the most obvious thing in the world. Which of course, it was.

'Oh, right.' Lydia felt a little turned on. She was a Crow through and through. Irritatingly.

After finishing the call, Lydia sat for another

146

moment. She wanted to head straight back to the flat and throw herself onto Fleet. Lucky she had a job to do. Even if it turned out she was crap at it.

So, Christopher Westcott didn't have a booking at the hotel he had told his wife he was staying at. Lydia put her head on her knees and tried to think. Her brain refused to cooperate. It was filled, not with helpful sleuthing suggestions, but with images of a mystery woman attempting to get inside her home. At least it wasn't Maddie. At least that world of terror was still safely out of her life. Haunting her dreams, but still. Dreams couldn't kill her.

Lydia forced herself to her feet and walked up and down the street. She didn't really expect to see Christopher, but felt as if she ought to at least try... The sky was pale purple and the air was cooler than it had been for weeks. Lydia didn't know if it was the unfamiliar area or her sense of abject failure, but she felt uneasy. Unlocking the car, she settled in for a long wait and checked for nearby hotels on her phone. Perhaps if she cold-called them all she would get lucky and find out exactly where Christopher was staying. Or if she trawled every bar and restaurant in the area. He could have got into a taxi, though. Or a car with a friend. Or headed to the tube.

It was hopeless and Lydia banged her head on the back of the seat. Her phone buzzed and she saw Emma's number. She pressed answer and felt her muscles relax at the sound of Emma'a voice. 'Do you know how many times I've played the shopping game this evening?'

'How many?'

'Five,' Emma said. 'In a row.'

'Intense.'

'Five. In a row. Guess how many I won?'

'None?'

'Bingo,' Emma said. 'I was going to play properly, so that I could start teaching Archie that he won't always win, but his little face.... I just couldn't do it. Do you think that's okay?'

'I think you're amazing,' Lydia said. 'I think Archie and Maise-Maise are the luckiest kids in London.'

'Thanks,' Emma said. 'What are you up to? I haven't seen you.'

'I know, sorry.' The guilt punched Lydia in the solar plexus. She had planned to be a better friend. Camberwell to Beckenham was so much closer than Aberdeen, but somehow it still felt like a world away. Life priorities, schedules, work. All the usual excuses.

'It's okay,' Emma was saying. 'I know you're working.'

'Next week? Drinks? I can come to yours if you can't get out.'

'Sounds good,' Emma's voice was downbeat.

'Are you okay?'

'Yeah, it's nothing.'

'What is nothing?'

'Do you think men still go to strip clubs? I mean, married men. Ordinary men.'

'On stag nights, maybe.'

'That's what I thought. It's just a cliche, now, right?'

'Of course,' Lydia lied. She had caught one of her client's husbands stuffing ten pound notes into the g-string of a nineteen year old just last month. Couple of pictures taken with her spy camera and that was another marriage over. Lydia felt the weight stretch across her shoulders.

'Couples go together, now,' Lydia said, trying to distract them both.

'What? No!'

'For kicks, yeah. Spice things up with a little shared thrill.'

'Wow. Does that work?'

'You're asking the wrong person,' Lydia said. 'Long-term relationships are not my forte.'

'It will happen, Lyds.'

'I don't know if I want it to,' Lydia said, the words popping out without consultation with her brain.

'You don't want to be alone forever,' Emma said. 'Trust me.'

Lydia frowned. Emma wasn't alone. Hadn't been since she was eighteen, in fact, and she and Tom had locked eyes in a pub in Camden. She was about to ask if everything was okay at home, when she was distracted by movement on the opposite pavement. A group of young women, appeared from an Italian chain restaurant. They were laughing, talking at full volume and one of them had a helium balloon with the number thirty in pink writing.

And behind them, coming out of the restaurant with his arm slung around the narrow shoulders of a brunette with a pixie cut, was Mr Christopher Westcott. 'Oh, thank feathers,' Lydia said.

'What?'

'Sorry,' she told Emma. 'I've gotta go.'

Lydia picked up her camera and slung her cross-body bag over her shoulder. She waited until Westcott and his companion had got a few metres further down the street before getting out of the car. Lydia knew that it was risky to follow him when the street was quiet, but having lost him once she had no desire to do so again.

She trailed the happy couple to the riverside, past swish-looking blocks of flats and to a decidedly-regenerated part of the waterfront. They sat on a bench on a wide paved area and Lydia snapped a couple of pictures from behind. Christopher had his arm around his companion and was leaning in. The angle wasn't good enough to get a clear picture of lip-action, but it was pretty incriminating nonetheless. Lydia continued walking, crossing in front of them to the river, looking out over the water as if that was her reason for dawdling in the vicinity. She gazed at the view for a few minutes before turning around. Christopher Westcott and his young friend were kissing passionately, oblivious to Lydia and everything around them. Lydia used her phone to take a few shots while pretending to take selfies with the river as her background, before strolling away.

Driving back to Camberwell she was flushed with success. She had finished the job efficiently and would get home in good time to power-up Jason so that he wouldn't fade. She had a report for April Westcott which, although deviating from her forty-eight hour brief, delivered results. She didn't need a partner, could handle everything on her own. She could do this. She had everything under control. The thing that Emma forgot about Martin Blank was that he was really good at his job. He didn't need to join Dan Akroyd's contract-killer collective.

CHAPTER THIRTEEN

Lydia was still feeling invincible when she got back to the flat. She didn't let herself be fazed by the marks around the lock on her front door. After all, whoever had tried to break-in hadn't succeeded. She was perfectly safe.

'We're perfectly safe,' she said to Jason when she coaxed him from his bedroom for a debrief. 'She couldn't get in.'

Jason was fiddling with the cuffs on his jacket and Lydia wondered what that felt like to him. Were they substantial to his own touch just from the force of habit? She opened her mouth to ask but he spoke first. 'I know it sounds stupid given my... Status. But I can't always just disappear. Sometimes I do it when I don't want to and sometimes I want to go, because I'm scared or something, and I can't. And I can touch things, now. You can touch me.'

'I know,' Lydia said. 'I understand and it's not stupid

at all.' She reached out her hand and touched Jason's arm. There was a spark of sensation, the usual strange charge she got from contact with the ghost, but then she felt something else. Soft material. She tensed her fingers, gripping the material in a small bunch and rubbing her fingertips over the weave.

'Bloody hell,' Jason said, looking at her hand. 'What does that mean?'

'I have no idea,' Lydia said, letting go of his sleeve. 'But it will have to wait. Sorry.'

A few minutes later, she had fired up the laptop and opened Facebook. Her dummy account had been accepted by two of Yas's friends and she could now see past the few profile pictures visible to the public. A quick scroll confirmed that Yas hadn't been active on Facebook for over six weeks and that her timeline updates had been pretty sparse before that. A few comedy memes reposted, multiple pictures of the small, beady-eyed dog, and the occasional sunset. Yas was obviously mindful of her privacy, or just disinterested in posting selfies, but Lydia had a look for pictures Yas had been tagged in and found one immediately. A group of dressed-up women, sitting in a restaurant and smiling for the camera. 'Do you recognise anybody here?'

Jason pointed at Yas Bishop. 'That's the woman who tried to break in.'

Lydia was dreaming. She knew she was dreaming but that didn't stop the terror from thumping through her with every wild beat of her hammering heart. The sky was navy blue with a bright turquoise edging the rooftops and chimney stacks. The sensation of being poked in the back, the bruising pressure and the knowledge that the man was behind her and that he was going to force her over the railing and to her death. 'I don't want to fall,' she said, hating the pleading sound in her voice.

It wasn't the hitman who spoke, though. Not the Russian gun for hire who had been sent to kill Maddie and got the wrong Crow. It was Maddie and she sounded exasperated. 'Oh, for goodness sake.'

LYDIA STUMBLED to the kitchen to make coffee. She was half-asleep after her broken night and wondering how much longer the nightmares were going to last. Her subconscious was clearly working through something, but she wished it would hurry up and let her get a full eight hours of shut-eye. The door to the hallway was wide open and the light coming through the glass panel of her front door didn't look right. She rubbed the sleep from her eyes and blinked a couple of times. There was a shape obscuring the glass on the outside. It was rectangular and pale and Lydia had a horrible feeling she knew what it was before she unlocked the door. A padded envelope had been taped to the glass with bright yellow 'police crime scene' sticky tape. More worrying was the fact that her sensor hadn't alerted her to the fact that somebody had visited her door.

Lydia took the package indoors and examined the blocky black handwriting on the front. It was addressed to 'Ms Lydia Crow, Crow Investigations, The Fork'. She flipped it over but there wasn't a return address.

Her landline rang. Lydia walked back to her desk holding the package and snatched up the receiver. 'Crow Investigations.'

'Have you opened it, yet?' The scent of Fox went straight to the back of Lydia's throat. She swigged from the water bottle on her desk before replying, not wanting to sound hoarse. Any sign of weakness, however small, was unacceptable in front of Paul Fox. 'No and I won't be.'

A theatrical sigh. 'Still being hostile, Little Bird?'

Lydia looked at the envelope with loathing. 'I'm putting it straight into the wheelie bin. I am not interested in working for you. Not now and not ever.'

'You shouldn't throw it away. Who knows what sensitive information is inside.'

'What information?' Lydia raised her eyes to the ceiling. She knew she was being drawn but it was hard to avoid.

'I heard you met with Maria the other day. How is the Silver princess?'

'You're following me?'

'Word gets around. You know how it is.'

'This bloody town,' Lydia said. 'What happened to the big anonymous city?'

'Social visit, was it?'

'Yes,' Lydia said. 'I wanted to meet her cat.'

'Typical of a Crow to side with a Silver. Old habits.'

'I'm not siding with anybody. Just myself.'

'Back in the day, the Crows always allied with the Silvers.'

'I know,' Lydia lied. 'And nobody allied with the Foxes. I wonder why?'

'You should cultivate some friends.'

'I have plenty of friends,' Lydia said.

'Like that lovely Emma? Please.'

'Don't say her name,' Lydia said. 'If I hear you have been within one hundred yards of Emma or her family, I will kill you.'

'That was chilling,' Paul said, amusement clear in his voice. 'Say it again. I'm getting goosebumps.'

'Slink off and hide in your den,' Lydia said and hung up. The retro phone made that a very satisfying action and Lydia banged the receiver down once more, for the sheer joy of it.

ONCE SHE WAS SHOWERED and caffeinated, Lydia considered her options. She could take a hint. A silver statue. Rumbles from Paul Fox. She wasn't going to be fobbed off with a meeting on neutral ground this time.

Silver and Silver LLP was housed in a shining glass and metal office building on Fetter Lane, running off Fleet Street. The narrow road was split in time down the centre. On one side, the impressive neo-gothic stonework and clocktower of the Maughan Library and on the other, the shining glass and metal edifice of the modern law office. Lydia had no idea how much it would cost to have an entire building in a prime central and historical area like this, but she would guess it was more money than most people would ever see in a lifetime. Around the corner was Temple Church, built in the twelfth century by the Knights Templar as their English head-quarters and the four inns of court were nearby. This was an area of ancient power and money, where the power lay with those who could tell the best story. Those who understood all the rules and how to bend them to their will, the people who had the knowledge of the esoteric guidelines, both legal and religious, and could help you navigate those murky waters between salvation and damnation. For a fee.

Back in the sixteenth century, there had been a gibbet at the junction with Fleet Street and when an MP had been found guilty of tax-dodging he had been hanged right outside his own front door. Public justice. That it was seen to be done was as important as the justice itself. Things hadn't changed, Lydia thought. The look of things was still as important as the truth of them. More so, usually.

Lydia didn't have an appointment but she persuaded Maria's assistant to let her into Maria's office by dint of ignoring him and walking straight in.

He flapped behind her but Maria just raised an eyebrow. 'Don't worry about it. Close the door.'

Lydia threw herself into one of the leather chairs in front of Maria's vast desk. 'Congratulations on the Gallo case.'

Maria looked momentarily surprised. Then she smiled thinly. 'I'm assuming you are being sarcastic.'

'Why would you think that?' Lydia said. 'Just because you made sure a mob boss will be back on the streets within three months instead of going away for twenty years.'

'I'm excellent at my job,' Maria said.

'And that doesn't bother you?' Suddenly Lydia really wanted to know. 'The man was guilty, that was proven, but you got him less time than some desperate teen junkie who swiped a watch in a department store.'

Maria shrugged. 'Not if I had defended them.'

'That's what I mean. It shouldn't depend on who defends you. It should be fair.'

'Life isn't fair,' Maria said. 'And the social system which means that one person can afford my services while another cannot isn't fair. We don't live in a utopian society with full equality.'

'Yeah-'

'But the law is fair. The legal system in England is one of the best in the world. Nothing is perfect, but it's one of the fairest systems. That's why so many of my clients want me to fight extradition and have their trial in the UK.'

'I thought that was to avoid justice.'

'It's to ensure a fair trial. There are places in the world where you can buy a judgment.'

'But that's what you are, bought freedom. A bought ruling.'

'No,' Maria said with sudden vehemence. 'You buy my services, my expertise, my knowledge of the law, my ability to convince a jury and to tell a good story in court. You don't buy a verdict. You don't buy a bribe.'

'Okay,' Lydia held up her hands. 'But I don't see how you can represent for people you know are guilty. I don't see how you can argue or tell a good story or whatever when you know you're trying to get a criminal off.'

'I don't know that they are a criminal, that's very important.'

'Oh, come on. You must know.'

'I may strongly suspect, but I will not know. Not in the legal sense because it hasn't been proven, yet. That's the point of the legal process.'

'Fine. But you can know they've done bad stuff before, that they have form. Don't you add that to your suspicions? There must be times when you know they are guilty. I know arrogant scumbags. They probably even tell you they're guilty.'

'If they're stupid enough to say something like that to their legal representation then they can't afford me, trust me. Besides, do you believe that people should have a fair trial? That they should be innocent until proven guilty, regardless of their past mistakes?'

'Yes, but-'

'Then you agree with me that it is my duty to do my best for my client. Without a defence that is carried out to the full extent of the legal capabilities to match the prosecution which is doing the same, there can be no fair trial. And that is the basis of the whole system.'

'Have you represented anybody from JRB?'

'No,' Maria said after a quick pause, clearly thrown by the turn in conversation.

'Has anyone in your firm represented them?'

'Our firm is on retainer so it's certainly possible, but I would have to check our records. You can access court records yourself, you know.'

'I know, I was curious as to whether you would tell me the truth.'

Maria tilted her chin. 'I see.'

The phone on Maria's desk chirped and Maria pressed a button. 'Your two o'clock is here,' a male voice said. Presumably Milo.

Maria smiled without warmth. 'You know the way out?'

'Why would JRB give Robert Sharp an antique statue?'

'How on earth would I know?'

Lydia was watching carefully and Maria's answer was perfectly casual. Maybe a little too quick, but then she was busy and trying to get rid of Lydia. Lydia cursed her abilities. If only she had been born a lie detector rather than a power-sensor, that would have been handy.

'It was solid silver.'

Maria's expression didn't flicker. 'I really do have to get on. Some of us have careers, you know.'

LYDIA WAS on her way out of the shiny, shiny building when a kind of wild stubbornness took hold of her mind. She knew it was a bad idea. If harassing Maria Silver was ill-advised, bothering the head of the Silver family and senior partner in Silver and Silver LLP, Alejandro, was pure madness.

She had never met the man, although she knew his name well, of course. Uncle Charlie spoke of him with admiration and this, as well as his role as both a lawyer and a Silver, had formed her opinion of him as slippery and morally ambivalent. A keen legal mind for hire. A business man first and foremost. And, naturally, a Family man above all else.

She asked the way to his office and was directed upstairs. One of many assistants told her that Mr Silver was too busy to see her and that drop-ins were completely unacceptable. Lydia sat down in the small, but comfortable, waiting area, and told the assistant she would wait.

Lydia spent an hour checking her emails and playing a mindless game on her phone. At one point, she was brought a glass of iced cucumber and lemon water, as if her arse-touching-sofa had triggered a politeness protocol that the bevy of assistants in their sharp suits were unable to bypass. Lydia was just wondering how expensive the air conditioning in the building had to be to achieve the perfectly comfortable atmosphere she was enjoying, when a different assistant, or possibly a solicitor or clerk, crossed the room with one hand held out for Lydia to shake. 'Amanda Browning. This way, please.'

Lydia obediently followed and found herself in a large rectangular office. Three walls were panelled in honey-coloured wood while the remaining wall was glass. Outside, a narrow terrace ran the length of the building and, facing the view, a cluster of low uphol-stered chairs with an aggressively modern-retro style and an oval glass coffee table which had probably cost more than Lydia's car.

Alejandro was at a standing desk in the corner, a cup of espresso dwarfed in one of his hands. He drained it hastily and crossed the room to greet Lydia with a kiss on each cheek. 'What an honour,' he said, showing white teeth. The right incisor was a little crooked and it lent him a rakish air. He must have been in his early sixties but his light brown skin was barely lined and he had a full head of black hair, shot through with silver at the temples and in his neatly-trimmed beard. It wasn't his wiry and disturbingly attractive physicality which was bothering Lydia, though. It was the power radiating from him. Not the power she had felt from Maria, which was the power of influence, money, education and a sharp tongue, but a blast of silvered magic which was making standing up difficult.

'What can I do for you?' A hand shot out and, at once, Alejandro was holding onto Lydia's arm, a solicitous expression on his handsome face. 'Are you all right?'

'Just the heat,' Lydia said. 'Outside. In here isn't hot. Out there, though...' She trailed off, glad that the verbal diarrhoea seemed to have trickled to a stop.

'Please,' Alejandro said. 'Sit down. I'll get you a cold drink. Maybe something to eat?'

'I'm fine,' Lydia said as she sank onto one of the low comfy chairs. She was trying to think, trying to work out whether Alejandro had any idea of the strength of Silver magic which was pouring out of his body or any idea of the effect he was having. She felt sick and sweat was breaking out over her torso. Any second now, she would begin shivering and probably look like she had rocked up at his fancy office with a full-on case of bird flu. The taste of silver was in her mouth and she could smell metal. The power she only usually sensed as a memory, seeing it like a photographic after-image, was swirling all

163

around Alejandro like dark grey smoke and seemed to be pouring out of every inch of his skin. She closed her eyes and massaged her temples for a moment.

'You have a headache?'

Lydia opened her eyes. The swirling grey smoke was still there. She clenched her jaw and produced a coin into one hand, closing her fingers around it and squeezing tightly until the smoke was no longer writhing quite as energetically. She focused on the middle of Alejandro's forehead and, that way, could look at him without feeling as if she was going to vomit. Just.

'Is it this, I wonder?' Alejandro pressed a piece of the wood panelling and there was an audible click. A door sprung open and he swung it wide, revealing a recessed cupboard which was lit from within to showcase the contents. On a plinth was a large silver trophy. It was the shape of a tall cup, covered in ornate silver-work flowers and vines, and with two curved handles on either side. Lydia could see that it was the dark silver of a well-handled antique, but at the same time her vision was overlaid by a second layer of colour. The surface of the cup was the brightest, purest silver she had ever seen. It was blinding.

Alejandro's smile was dazzling, too. He looked utterly delighted with his big reveal and the effect that Lydia knew she was failing to conceal. She heard herself retch, and her body was propelled downward, folded over with stomach spasms as her insides tried to urgently relocate.

The cupboard door must have been closed as the next thing Lydia knew she was blinking back tears and looking at the pile of spat-up bile on the carpet in front of her eyes. She straightened up and could only see smooth wooden panelling once more.

'I would apologise,' Alejandro said. And then he didn't.

Well, that was honest, at least. Lydia wiped her mouth with the back of one hand.

'Please,' Alejandro darted forward, a crisp white handkerchief held out.

Lydia took it and mopped her face. 'I think I must be coming down with flu. Stomach flu.' Lydia looked at the mess on the floor, mortification fighting for second-place behind fear and desperate, calculating thought. What on earth was that cup? How the hell was Alejandro so strong? And did Charlie know?

'That's a shame.' Alejandro wasn't trying to hide his look of delight and satisfaction. He sat on the nearest chair, uncomfortably close. He sat on the edge, as if poised for action. 'Do you need to reschedule?'

'Reschedule?'

'This urgent meeting. Whatever important questions you had for me. I assume they are important, my secretary said you were very insistent. And, of course, I know you are a detective, now.'

The sarcastic emphasis on the word 'detective' was barely perceptible, Alejandro's tone superficially neutral. His eyebrow gave the merest flicker of a lift. Somehow, his politeness felt like more of an insult than Paul Fox's open taunting.

'JRB,' Lydia said, lowering the handkerchief. 'Maria

wouldn't tell me what they do, who they are, or why you were so keen to do them a favour.'

'I see.'

'And why were they looking after Robert Sharp?'

'You realise that we operate with confidentiality for our clients. It's a cornerstone of our work.' He raised a hand. 'Much like yours, I imagine.'

'Fair play,' Lydia said. 'But I don't represent murderers.'

'Are you accusing my client?'

'JRB?' Lydia widened her eyes. 'I wouldn't know where to start.'

'The thing about JRB is that they are like many of our corporate clients, they can't be accused of murder because they don't really exist.'

Lydia was still trying to take small breaths through her nose and was gripping the coin in her hand. 'I know you can't convict a whole company of murder,' she managed. 'I'm not an idiot. But the company is made up of people and those people can be convicted-'

'JRB is a web of different concerns, not a unified entity. At least, not in any meaningful sense. And, like a spider's web, if I wave my hands,' he mimed the action. 'It will simply disappear.'

'There are records,' Lydia said. 'Things don't just disappear. Not in this day and age.' Unhelpfully, Maddie's image floated across her mind's eye. She had disappeared with great success.

'Our family have always been lawyers, you know. Barristers, of course, and judges. Legal experts of one kind or another stretching all the way back to when we first arrived in London fresh from our tour of South America. Before reading and writing was widely available, those who could write things down, read the marks on paper, were seen as one step from magicians. The art of deciphering written language, the ability to be loquacious and ebullient and to run verbal laps around our conversational opponent was as likely to land us at the gibbet as the bank. But we learned. We learned that the ability to persuade or bamboozle, to argue or lambast, was like a weapon. And in the right hands that weapon was more powerful than anything else in the capital.'

'Except the pointy end of a stick, perhaps,' Lydia said. 'Or a sharp beak. They're quite dangerous.'

'Quite so,' Alejandro acknowledged the reference. 'The Crows have always been useful allies. The talons to grip, the feathers to hide. Very valuable in their own way.'

Lydia knew he was deliberately trying to needle her, to put her further off-balance and she was annoyed to find it was working.

'I'm a little bored,' Alejandro said, leaning back in his chair and gazing out of the glass wall. 'I've been hearing whispers. I feel as if there is something I'm missing, something I should be doing.' He turned his bright blue eyes upon her. 'Something we've all forgotten.'

'I don't follow-'

'Do you remember the fire that destroyed the House of Lords? In the eighteen hundreds?' Alejandro smiled at her. 'That was us. It wasn't a Silver who piled the tally sticks onto the fire, wasn't our hands which sealed the fate of the building. But it was my great, great, great -

whatever - grandfather who spoke to the men who stoked the furnace. He explained that it would be much easier to pop them all in at once, that the advice to go slow was an invention of their bosses, fat men who lived in comfort and could afford to give orders that they, themselves, would not have to work late to accomplish. Hundreds of tally sticks, dry as tinder, and the whole place went up in an instant.'

'Why?'

'Contracts,' Alejandro said, as if speaking to a stupid child. 'The Houses of Parliament needed a grand rebuild. And all those oriole windows and gothic spires, statues and carved wooden ceilings, all of that stonework and craftsmanship and material, all of those created money for the people in the industry.'

'And you're taking inspiration from your ancestors? Whispering in corporate ears to create contract money for your clients?'

'I didn't say that,' Alejandro said, shaking his head gently. 'It's just interesting, no? The power of the right word in the right ear?'

'And whose ear was Robert Sharp whispering in? Or was it a case of the wrong word in the wrong ear will get you strung up by your neck?'

'Quite so,' Alejandro said. He spread his hands. 'Thus it ever was.'

LYDIA FELT sick all the way home, and very nearly threw up again in the heat of the tube train. Back at The Fork, the new boy was behind the counter and Angel was sitting in one of the central tables, reading a paperback. A couple of other tables had patrons, but it was the quiet time of day. Lydia hated to admit it, but it was nice to walk through the cafe and exchange a few words with Angel before going upstairs. It felt homely. And it was no bad thing that there was a living soul who would notice if she disappeared for any significant length of time. Her line of work wasn't without risk, after all. Throwing up in Alejandro's office had been a salutary reminder of that.

'I haven't seen you much,' Angel said. 'You been busy?'

Lydia had seen Angel that morning, before she had gone to Silver and Silver. So much for her theory. She would have to work on having more memorable interactions with Angel. 'Can I have one of those custard tarts?'

'You got cash, you can have anything on the menu.'

'No cash,' Lydia said. 'I was thinking you might like to sub me one. Out of the goodness of your heart.'

Angel's eyebrows climbed toward her hair line where her hair sprang up. Was it Lydia's imagination or were her plaits standing to attention. Affronted.

'Never mind,' Lydia said, backing away.

That ought to do it, she thought. Better to annoy Angel into remembering her than lie dead somewhere for days before anybody noticed she had disappeared. She was simultaneously proud of herself for the dark practicality and concerned that she was letting the nightmares get the better of her mental health.

Lydia had barely had time to make a coffee when the alarm told her that she had a visitor. She recognised the shape behind the glass but still didn't quite believe it.

Emma wasn't a frequent visitor to Camberwell, let alone to Lydia's new home. Lydia couldn't help feeling nervous as she unlocked the door. Was this a confrontation? A continuation of their near-argument the other night?

'I need your help,' Emma said, as soon as Lydia opened the door.

'Of course,' Lydia moved back, making room for Emma.

Emma walked straight down the hall and into the office, sitting in the client's chair next to Lydia's desk.

'I mean, your professional help. Your services.'

Lydia decided to play along. She sat in her chair and clasped her hands on the desk. 'Okay. What's wrong?'

Emma had clearly been crying but she was dry-eyed and utterly calm, now. 'I think Tom is having an affair.'

'No.' Lydia said, rearing back. 'Absolutely no chance.'

Emma gave a little laugh. 'What makes us so special? You said yourself that everybody was at it. Everyone was lying to their wives or their husbands or unhappy and just looking for a reason to leave.'

'Yes, but it's my line of work, it skews the statistics. People don't exactly come to see a PI when things are going well. It doesn't mean every relationship is doomed.'

'Mine is,' Emma said. She still wasn't crying and her voice was the same, flat monotone. It was terrifying.

'No,' Lydia said. 'It isn't. He isn't cheating. He loves you. And Archie and Maisie.'

Emma visibly flinched at the sound of her children's names and Lydia felt like hell. 'I'm sorry,' she said.

'I don't need you to be my friend,' Emma said. 'I don't want you to tell me everything is okay and that he loves me and that we just need to talk. I want you to be an investigator and do your job. I can pay.'

'I'm not taking your money,' Lydia said.

'You are,' Emma said, her voice grim. 'Give it to charity if you want, but I'm booking your professional services and paying your going rate.' A hesitation and a flash of normality, a half-smile Lydia barely caught. 'How much *is* your going rate?'

'You sure you want to do this?'

'Certain.'

'Right,' Lydia pulled out a fresh notepad. 'Let's start with why you think he is playing away.'

'He's not himself. He's not happy. I can tell he's hiding something.'

Lydia felt herself sag with relief. 'He's not having an affair,' she said, holding up a hand to stop Emma from interrupting. 'I hear people talking about their partners all the time. The ones that are cheating are never described as unhappy. Never. They are more attentive than usual. Funnier. Lighter. Happier.'

'Maybe he's the exception that proves the rule,' Emma said. Her expression was heart-breaking, caught between hope and misery.

Lydia produced a coin and spun it on the table, watching Emma's expression glaze a little as she couldn't help but look at it. 'Take a deep breath,' she said. 'And another.'

Emma did as she was told. 'Are you hypnotising me?'

'Of course not,' Lydia said, although she had been tempted to try. Like most Crows, she had always been able to nudge people's emotions. Emma was so upset, so scattered, Lydia wanted her to feel better. To make her feel better. What were the ethics on nudging a friend's emotions for her own good? If you meant well did that cancel out the tricky violation of freewill aspect?

'He's tried to hide it. Tried to pretend like everything is okay, but I can tell.'

'Let's imagine for moment that it isn't what you think. What else might it be? How is his work?' Lydia realised as she spoke that she didn't know what her best friend's husband did.

'It's fine,' Emma said. 'As far as I know. We don't get a lot of quality time to have actual conversations these days.'

'You're both busy, you've got the kids, you're tired. It's understandable that you're feeling distant and you're worried that something is wrong, but it's just the phase you guys are in. It will get better when Maisie is bigger. You'll get more sleep and-'

'Don't do that,' Emma said.

'What?'

'Treat me like I'm an idiot just because I'm a mum. I'm tired and I'm emotional but that doesn't mean I'm delusional. I'm not imagining this. I know my marriage and there is something seriously wrong.'

'Right. Sorry. Give me his schedule. His work

details, list of his friends, places he goes, gym nights, everything.'

Emma blinked. Then she did and Lydia took notes. Just like any other client.

When they'd finished she said 'leave it with me.'

CHAPTER FOURTEEN

At the door, Lydia hugged Emma goodbye. Jason was hovering in the hallway, obviously waiting to speak to Lydia. It was slightly distracting, and made Lydia feel more isolated than ever. Emma couldn't see Jason, of course, and it just underlined the ways in which they were different. And now Emma wanted Lydia to investigate her husband which could only end up two ways for Lydia, both of them bad. Either she found dirt on Tom and was the gun which fired the fatal shot on her best friend's marriage. Or she proved that Tom wasn't messing around on Emma which would result in a guilt-ridden meltdown. Probably with her confessing hiring Lydia to Tom, ensuring he hated her for ever. And that Emma could never look at Lydia without bringing back all of the bad memories.

Now she was depressed. Jason, however, looked cheerful. 'What's with you?'

'What do you mean?'

'Maths going well?' Lydia guessed.

'I'm just feeling good,' Jason said. 'Strong. And you've not got any client work today.'

'Right... I don't follow. Why is that good news?'

'We could try testing your mojo. Do some experiments.'

'I don't think so,' Lydia said, hating the way his face fell. 'I think I need to investigate our uninvited visitor.'

Jason sagged.

'Do you want to try leaving the flat, though? I could use your help with something. Just behind the building, not far.'

Jason brightened. 'An experiment?'

'Sure,' Lydia said, picking up the envelope from Paul Fox.

Downstairs the cafe was busy and Lydia cut into the kitchen as quickly as possible. It was a hive of activity and nobody questioned Lydia when she took the fire extinguisher off the wall and headed out of the back door.

Jason was in the doorway, looking unsure. 'I don't think I can cross the threshold.'

'Have you tried?'

'I feel funny,' Jason said.

'Sometimes you have to push a little,' Lydia said, glad that nobody in the kitchen was close enough to see her talking to thin air.

'Take my hand,' she reached for him. 'Maybe that will help.'

'I've changed my mind,' he said. And disappeared.

Lydia put the fire extinguisher down next to the

wheelie bins and considered her options. Then she went back into the kitchen and located a large stainless-steel mixing bowl. If nothing else, this would definitely make Angel pay more attention.

Outside, she closed the door and put the bowl on the floor, away from the plastic bins. She put the envelope in the bowl and doused it with lighter fluid before getting her phone and starting to film. 'Stop sending me stuff,' she said, for the benefit of Paul and then put the phone in her jacket pocket for a moment while she lit a match and dropped it into the bowl. It would have been better with Jason holding the camera, but she managed to get her phone back on target in time to catch the envelope burning merrily. Black smoke whooshed up into the air and the flames reached an impressive height. Lydia mentally congratulated herself for having the foresight to commit arson outside. She filmed a few seconds more and then sent the video to Paul Fox's mobile.

Almost immediately, her phone rang. 'There goes a grand's worth of cocaine.'

'Hilarious,' Lydia said. 'Don't call me again. We're done.' It was the closest to happiness she had been in days. With strange misfirings of her power, throwing up in Alejandro's office, bad dreams, Emma's marital problems, and the knowledge that Yas Bishop had attempted to break into her flat, there was a horrible sensation that felt suspiciously like panic. Except she was Lydia Crow. She didn't do anxiety. 'I just need to sort it,' she said out loud. That made her feel better. She would sort it. She always did.

AFTER CHANGING her outfit for something that didn't smell of smoke, Lydia tried to find Jason. She knocked on his bedroom door a few times and tried to coax him out, but there was no response. She opened the door a crack and looked inside, expecting to find him writing on the wall or lying on his bed, but he wasn't there.

Just in case he was listening, she spoke out loud, detailing where she was going and when she expected to return. She hovered by the door, expecting him to appear and ask questions, maybe tell her she was being foolish. Lydia was faintly disgusted with herself for feeling bereft. She had lived on her own since leaving home aged eighteen and she didn't know why she was suddenly being so pathetic.

DOWNSTAIRS, Lydia was threading her way through the cafe tables, when the light abruptly changed. Visible through the big windows, the sky turned from cornflower blue to gunmetal grey in an instant. The colours of the street were turned up to high definition, as if lit by hidden lights. Outside, there was an electric feeling in the air, as if the weather was about to finally break. Lydia thought about going back up to the flat to find an umbrella before remembering that she wasn't the kind of person who owned such things. It would be handy for stakeouts, though, and something she should probably buy on her way to Bayswater.

She had decided to visit Yas Bishop, her sneaky visitor. Repay the favour, and find out what Yas had been looking for. Plenty of people would be freaked out by a phone call from a private investigator, not many responded by trying a little B&E. Perhaps she would find out why Yas had sent an expensive silver statue to Robert Sharp, too. And if she could glean some details about the mysterious JRB, then so much the better.

By the time she emerged from the Edgware Road station, fat drops of rain were falling. Lydia had picked up the free Metro paper and she held it over her head as she ran down the busy thoroughfare of Edgware Road, dodging pedestrians wielding umbrellas or similarly hurrying to beat the rain, which was coming down heavier and heavier. Skidding past a retro-styled laundrette on the corner of Star Street, Lydia found herself on a suddenly quiet road. Lined with cars, of course, but with the classic yellowish brown London stock bricks. They were handmade bricks, Lydia remembered being told in school, which gave them a distinctive appearance. And in-demand now, for restoration work. They were the same colour and type as the half bricks found stuffed in Robert Sharp's pockets. A detail that would be more useful if there weren't hundreds of similar buildings in the capital.

Yas Bishop's house was halfway down the street, which was a no-through road, the end blocked by bollards. Lydia was glad she had decided not to drive as she would probably have had to drive to Kilburn to find a parking space. Not for the first time, she wished she was a copper and could park wherever the hell she liked. It would almost be worth going through the physical training. On the plus side, Uncle Charlie would probably disown her.

As far as she knew, Yas lived alone. The curtains in the windows facing the street were closed upstairs. The downstairs windows had venetian blinds with slanted slats, half-open. Lydia stepped up to the tastefully-painted sage green door and rang the bell. She could hear it inside but no answering footsteps. After trying it three times, Lydia leaned as far as she could over the black iron railings which edged the space leading to the basement. She tried to peer into the downstairs window which was above this space, but the distance and plain voile curtains scuppered the attempt. She cupped her hands around her eyes, anyway, and looked for movement.

The rain was pouring, now, and there was a rumble of thunder in the distance. Lydia cursed the fact that Yas had bought a mid-terrace. There was no easy way to get round the back of the house, with a locked door at one end of the street which likely led to the back of the terrace. There was a little gate in the railings and steps down to the basement. There were a few plant pots with earth and no visible plants, and a bright green plastic crate with empty bottles and jars, and a plain white door with obscured glass panels. It didn't have a separate doorbell or number. It looked like Yas owned the whole place, which was impressive. Although she could be sub-letting it under the radar. Lydia knocked on the wooden frame and peered through the small window which looked onto the terraced area. It was fitted with white metal security bars and fully obscured with a thick white blind.

After a moment of hesitation, she called Fleet.

Karen had always said that a good investigator used every resource available, was never too proud to ask for help. She hadn't openly advocated lusting after those resources, but then who knew? Perhaps Lydia simply hadn't got to that module in the course before she'd left Aberdeen and started her own firm. 'Can I ask a favour?'

'You can always ask,' Fleet's voice was distracted and there were noises in the background. Beeping, voices, something mechanical which suggested construction work.

'It will stop me from committing a crime.'

A slight pause. 'You are a stressful girlfriend, you know that.'

'I'm not your girlfriend,' Lydia had walked a little way down the street, not wanting a concerned neighbour to call in that she was loitering outside Yas's property. It was London, so pigs would likely fly first, but the intent to commit crime had the side-effect of making a person paranoid.

'And that there is a prime example of what I'm talking about,' Fleet's tone was hard to read. 'Is that official?'

'Yes. Officially, I'm not your girlfriend.'

'And unofficially?'

'I like you.' Saying the words was like pulling teeth, and they made Lydia feel like a stupid school kid.

'I like you, too, Lyds. Which is why I will prevent you from ending up in jail. What's the problem?'

She could hear the smile in his voice and knew she was about to wipe it away. 'You know there was a woman trying to break into my gaff? I've come to visit her but she's not answering the door.'

'And?'

'I need to get in. I have a bad feeling.'

'What sort?'

'The Crow Family sort. The spidey-senses sort.' In for a penny... Uncle Charlie could warn her all he liked, she needed help and Fleet had done nothing but show that he was on her side. Besides, she needed to prove she wasn't Martin Blank. She gave Fleet Yas Bishop's address.

'Bayswater? I'm not far, as it happens. I'll be there in twenty.'

'Thanks,' Lydia walked back along the road and found a cafe. She bought a takeaway cup of coffee and by the time she had walked back to Yas's, Fleet was pulling up in his Honda Civic. She handed him the steaming cup. The rain had passed as quickly as it had come and the smell of wet brick and tarmac competed with the faint odour of drains and the ever-present exhaust fumes. Lydia filtered the lot through a whiff of Fleet's coffee. London's bouquet.

Fleet knocked on the door. He rang the bell several times, then fixed Lydia with a steady look. 'I don't have cause to enter. And this isn't my manor.'

'I know,' Lydia said. 'But what if I was a concerned citizen who had seen someone in distress waving from that window?' She pointed to the upper storey sash.

'Through the curtains?' He raised an eyebrow.

'I have very good eyesight.'

'If I was following a tip from a concerned citizen that

somebody was in immediate danger then, yes, I could, in theory, enter the house without permission.'

'Great, then.'

Fleet sized up the door and took a couple of steps back. Then he put his coffee down next to the step, pulled a set of picks and a bump key from his pocket and proceeded to make short work of the lock. 'No deadbolt,' he muttered. 'Sloppy security.'

'Better than having your nice painted door kicked down, though,' Lydia said. 'This looks expensive. Nice skills, by the way.'

'YouTube,' Fleet said. He had the door open and had announced himself loudly. 'Ms Bishop? Are you home? Ms Bishop, don't be alarmed. Are you all right? I'm with the police, my name is DCI Fleet and I am entering your property on suspicion of...' He hesitated. 'In case you need a hand with anything.'

'Wait here,' Fleet said, turning back to Lydia.

Ignoring this, Lydia followed him inside. Within seconds, she could feel the same creeping nausea as she had felt in Alejandro's office.

'You okay?' Fleet was looking back over his shoulder. 'Go outside, you look peaky.'

Fleet had a hand over his own mouth and he pulled a clean white handkerchief from his jacket pocket and held it over his mouth and nose. Lydia was stunned for a moment, thinking that he could also sense the grey metallic edge in the air. The tang of silver. But then she realised that there was another scent, a far more organic odour. Rot.

The staircase faced the front door and a corridor led

deeper into the house, with doors off. Fleet opened the nearest. He looked back and shook his head 'Looks like a renovation project.'

The front room was empty apart from a lumpy shape covered in a white dust sheet. The floor was stripped oak, original floorboards with dark knots in the wood. The walls were painted white and bare wires hung from the ornate ceiling rose. At the end of the corridor was the kitchen. It was a sixties monstrosity with peeling blue paint on the walls and cabinets and scratched orange lino on the floor. Through the window, Lydia could see an overgrown garden. The smell in the kitchen was clean, though. Bleach overlaying the mustiness of the old cupboards and flooring. 'I'm going upstairs,' Fleet said, he filled the kitchen doorway, hands stuffed in his pockets. 'Wait here. Don't touch anything.'

Lydia nodded so that Fleet would move. Once he did, she waited a beat and then followed him.

The stairs were bare and splattered with paint but, more pressingly, the smell was getting worse. The house had an echoey, empty feel, but Lydia knew that somebody was waiting for them on the second floor. The door to the right on the landing was ajar. The smell was thicker, here, it caught in the back of Lydia's throat. Fleet pushed the door with his elbow and poked his head inside. 'Ms Bishop? It's the police. Can you hear me?' He was speaking loudly and moving quickly, now. Lydia followed him into what was obviously Yas's bedroom. She took in the wide-striped gold and cream wallpaper, the padded velvet headboard and French-style furniture. Her eye refusing to settle on the figure lying on the floor between the bed and the spindly legs of the dressing table. Fleet was by the woman's side, he wasn't speaking to her anymore and was, instead, holding his head just above her face, the expression on his face serious as he concentrated. 'She's long gone,' Lydia said, her gaze skittering over the body. Its unnatural stillness. The waxen look to the skin. The open eyes with one eyelid at half-mast. Frozen.

'I know,' Fleet said. 'Gotta check, though. Procedure.' He straightened up to a crouching position and looked carefully around at the body and the room. Lydia kept quiet. She tried to do the same, to focus her mind on the details of the scene. She had wanted a change from adultery, Lydia reminded herself. This was different. The blood which had soaked into the front of Yas Bishop's silky blouse and turned dark brown was different. The burgundy pool beneath Yas Bishop's turned cheek was different. The way it had a tactile surface, like the skin on a custard. That was different, too. That half-open eye. If she were alive, it would be mid-wink. In death, it was obscene. Yas Bishop didn't look surprised or frightened. Truth was, she didn't look anything human at all. That was the thing with a dead body. They were no longer a person, just a facsimile of one.

Lydia swallowed and took out her notebook. *Details, Lydia. Notice the details.* She jotted down her impressions. Used her phone to take multiple pictures of the scene. She felt like she was playing at being a detective. Enacting the procedure gleaned from a thousand television shows and books, backed up by the dry instructions of her meagre investigative training. The training hadn't covered a crime like this, let alone being on scene. The instructions had stopped abruptly with the advice to touch nothing and to call the professionals.

'Clean cut,' Fleet said, his voice startling her. 'From behind, maybe. Definitely a sharp blade and it looks like one slice. Takes a lot to do that first time. So, maybe not their first rodeo.'

'Not suicide?' Lydia said, her voice feeling as if it was coming from very far away.

Fleet straightened up. 'Doubt it. There are easier ways to go.'

'Unless she was disturbed. In her mind.'

Fleet had his phone out. 'I'm calling it in, so you might want to make yourself scarce.'

Lydia was surprised out of her numbness. 'Don't you need me to be the concerned citizen?'

'Nah,' Fleet said. 'I'll sort something. Say I was passing. Or that I got an anonymous call.'

Lydia opened her mouth to say something smart about him bending the rules and then closed it again. Fleet was doing her a favour, protecting her from getting involved with the law. Her phone was still gripped in one hand and she snapped a final few pictures of the body and the room. Now that she was released, free to leave, she felt rooted there. As if this horror was a web and she was caught.

'Get going,' Fleet said. 'Seriously. This clearly didn't just happen, but you said you called her before? That links you to her. You'll be high on the list of suspects if you're the one to find her.'

'Right,' Lydia forced her feet to move. She moved

away, feeling strangely unwilling to turn her back on the body.

'And don't touch anything on your way out. Leave the front door open.'

Lydia retreated a few steps and then stopped.

'What is it?' Fleet looked genuinely worried. Lydia could see that he was at an active crime scene and his brain was processing that, plus he was about to lie, to put his job on the line to protect her from the possible wrath of her dodgy family, and he still had enough mental capacity left to focus. On her.

'Nothing,' Lydia said. 'I was just thinking, I can stay. I'll explain why I was here. What I do. You can name me as an informant or whatever you need to do to cover yourself.'

'You don't need to do that,' Fleet said. 'Honestly, I'll be fine.'

'I'll tell them I called you because I heard noises and was concerned for her welfare.'

'What about your family? You don't really want to be on our database, do you?'

'I'm a private investigator. That means I will deal with the law. And I'm legit.'

Fleet shook his head.

'I am,' Lydia said. 'I'm not my uncle.'

'I know,' he said softly.

Then it happened. Lydia's concentration had been distracted by talking to Fleet, she had stopped processing the sight of the poor, dead woman, lying on her high-end carpet, and the background thought, the part of her that had been interpreting her sense impressions, was now front and centre. Screaming in her mind. Silver tang. Metal on her tongue. Not sharp like a beak, all hardened keratin and organic warmth, but sharp and clean and cold.

'I said 'all right' then.' Fleet was staring. 'Did you hear me? Lydia?'

'Sorry,' Lydia was turning, now, fleeing. 'I'm sorry. I've got to go.' She stumbled down the stairs, running from the leftover energy which was everywhere, making Lydia's nerves jangle painfully. The unmistakable calling card of a Silver.

CHAPTER FIFTEEN

Lydia walked the streets blindly, processing the scene and trying, unsuccessfully, not to replay the image of Yas Bishop covered in blood. Her memory of the scene was jumbled; the copper stench of the blood was overlaid with the bright tang of Silver. Lydia couldn't shake the sense of horror which came with it. The rain turned heavier and Lydia welcomed the cool water; it felt cleansing. Lydia imagined it rinsing away the metallic sheen she had picked up at Yas's house.

Later, after the rain had done its worst and then cleared up as quickly as it had appeared, Lydia finally felt calm enough to head home. Her feet were aching and the pavements were steaming lightly as Lydia walked from the station towards The Fork. She had cleared away the shock and the tragedy of Yas Bishop's death to reveal the puzzle underneath, and found herself almost disappointed that she hadn't received a phone call from the police, calling her in. She knew it was better to be kept out of it and she was grateful to Fleet for doing so, but she wanted to be in the thick of it. To have as many details as possible.

Now that her brain was firing again, she realised something else; she still had other work to do. Yas Bishop's death or not, Dr Lee was still an active case. And a paying client. Checking her watch for the third time in a row, just to confirm that Fleet would definitely not have finished his working day and that it was too early to have heard anything about Yas, Lydia decided to distract herself with her actual job.

THE BLOCK of flats that Mrs Lee had visited looked more dismal than the last time Lydia had seen it, when it had been bathed in perfect sunshine. The sky was dirty white, now, the sun layered behind cloud and the promise of rain in the air. A classic English summer's day.

Lydia checked her phone as she walked, as if looking at directions. At the main door, she pressed the bell marked 'Nails' and waited. After a few seconds the intercom crackled.

Lydia stepped up and spoke into it. 'I'd like an appointment. I haven't...' She had been going to explain that she hadn't booked, but the intercom went dead and the door buzzed. 'Nails' was the bottom buzzer in a stack of four, so Lydia assumed the flat was on the ground floor. She knocked on the first door and it opened quickly. The tiny woman in front of her was wearing a neat tunic in soft sage green and matching trousers. Her black hair was tied back in a sleek pony tail and she had expertly-applied eyeliner. Lydia hadn't been expecting someone who looked so professional and healthy. She looked like the employee of a high-end salon. Not that Lydia had much experience in that area.

'You want nails?'

'Uh,' Lydia really didn't want nails.

'Acupuncture?'

Well, that was worse. 'Um, I'm not...'

'Must be energy healing, then,' she said brightly, beckoning Lydia inside. 'Come on through. It's twenty-five for the first session, special rate, and then I will advise you on the course needed. Usually a six-week treatment, but it depends on how your chakras respond to the healing. Your first session includes a full health and wellbeing assessment and is non-refundable. Do you have any allergies?'

Lydia had been following the woman and trying to take in her surroundings and she didn't realise, for a moment, that she had been asked a question. 'No. No allergies.'

They had walked down a short hallway and Lydia had glimpsed a kitchen with a small boy standing on a chair to pour milk into a bowl of cereal. A television was playing somewhere in the flat. The flow of words continued as the woman ushered Lydia into a small room which had a massage table set up in the middle and a narrow white desk covered in bottles of jewel-coloured nail polish. The wallpaper was wine and cream and there was a matching wine-coloured blind at the small window. The bed was draped in matching dark red towels, giving it an unfortunate, sacrificial vibe.

'Great,' the woman picked up a clipboard with a piece of paper attached and a pen and handed them to Lydia. 'Fill out this health questionnaire.'

Lydia did as she was told, signing the name Lydia Brown at the bottom. The form had a pleasingly professional look, although the clause which stated, 'the therapist, Kirsty Thomas, bears no responsibility for conditions, symptoms, or effects arising from the treatment received', was a little worrying.

While she did this, Kirsty moved around the room, pulling the blind down and switching on a large salt lamp which gave off a warm pink glow. Gentle, tinkling music began to play and Kirsty squeezed hand sanitiser gel into her hands and began rubbing them together as if preparing to pummel something.

'Take off your shoes and any clothes which will be uncomfortable and lie down.'

Lydia took her time untying her Doctor Martens, trying to engage the woman in general conversation. 'Have you been a therapist for long?'

'It's important to drink plenty of water after the treatment, and not to do anything strenuous. You must rest.'

'Right,' Lydia said. 'I'll cancel my marathon.'

Kirsty stopped moving and eye-balled Lydia. 'Have you had energy treatment before?'

'First time,' Lydia said. 'Can you tell?'

She seemed to relax again. 'And what is your main area of concern? Do you have pain? Discomfort? Feelings of sluggishness or exhaustion? How is your digestion?'

Lydia pushed down the impulse to retort 'mind your own' and said, instead, 'I've just been like, really tired.'

Kirsty nodded. 'I'm going to start with a body scan. Remain still.'

Lydia wondered how she could casually ask about her other clients. Kirsty was moving her hands in flowing movements, inches above Lydia's torso, an expression of intense concentration on her face. It was weird and Lydia wasn't sure she would be able to keep a straight face so she closed her eyes. 'I can really feel that,' Lydia said, making her voice full of wonder.

'The scanning is completely painless,' Kirsty said sharply. 'You will feel a warmth when I begin the chakra work.'

'Right. Yes.' Lydia had an urge to apologise. 'I just meant I was glad I was here. My friend recommended you, she said you've worked miracles.'

'No miracles,' she said, but her voice was more gentle. 'Just energy healing. I can sense there is a lot of tension in your shoulders and neck. And the bones of your skull and your face are mis-aligned. It is just a small fraction, but it causes tension and tiredness. You get headaches.'

'Yes,' Lydia said, playing along. 'Terrible ones.'

'Six weeks. I will cure them. But you must drink eight glasses of water every day.'

'My friend,' Lydia tried again. 'Jane. She talked so much about your treatments, I just had to have one.'

The woman was touching her now, gentle pressure on her ankles and then a light touch smoothing up her leg before a gentle grip of the knee, and on upwards. Lydia tensed every muscle in her body to stop herself from jerking off the table. Or punching something.

'Deep breaths,' Kirsty said, sounding kind of testy. 'In for four and out for four. Count it. You will feel the energy warming you.'

Lydia did a few dutiful breaths, making plenty of noise to show willing. A funny thought crossed her mind; what if the therapist really could sense energy through her hands? What would she make of her Crow power?

'Are you ticklish?' Kirsty's voice was sharp, accusing.

Lydia hastily turned her smile into an expression of deep relaxation. 'Jane's really ticklish,' she began, 'I bet she was a nightmare to treat-'

'You don't need to talk,' Kirsty commanded. 'Just relax. Concentrate on the energy flowing and relax.'

Lydia spent another twenty minutes listening to the New Age music and inhaling the smell of Ylang Ylang and lavender and trying not to flinch or laugh as Kirsty ran light strokes up and down her body, occasionally tapping or gripping. Eventually, Kirsty moved away and there was the sound of chiming. Lydia opened her eyes expecting to see Kirsty wielding a tiny gong and mallet, but it must have been a recording on her phone.

'That was great, thanks,' Lydia said, sitting up and swinging her legs off the side of the table.

'Don't move too quickly,' Kirsty chided. 'You might feel light-headed.'

Lydia was surprised to find that she did, a bit. The power of suggestion?

'You've got a very strong energy field,' Kirsty said. 'You're lucky, it will keep you very healthy.' She flushed. 'Sorry. That was a bit-' For the first time, she looked uncertain. 'How is Jane doing?'

Lydia had been about to automatically reply 'she's fine' but then her brain caught up. 'She's okay. You know, good days, bad days.'

'It's a terrible thing. The body's energy turning against it like that.'

Lydia made a non-committal sound and counted out twenty-five pounds in cash. She didn't want to seem too keen, in case it closed the subject down. Kirsty struck her as a woman who liked to be in control of the conversation.

'I did warn her,' Kirsty said, checking the notes and slipping them into one of the large pockets of her tunic.

'Warn her?'

'About the chemotherapy. It's poison, you know. Literal poison.'

'Jane is very strong-willed,' Lydia said. 'You can't change her mind once she's decided something.'

Kirsty nodded. 'I definitely got that impression. And I could see it in her energy field, of course. Her aura is very dense.'

They were walking back down the hall, now, Kirsty showing Lydia out. 'I'll tell her you were asking after her,' Lydia said. 'And thanks, again, for the treatment.'

'Do you want to book your next appointment now? You need six sessions, thirty each. You can pay in a block booking if you like? You'll save five pounds.'

'That's all right,' Lydia said. 'I'm going on holiday next week, but I'll look at my diary after that.'

'You don't want to leave it too long,' Kirsty said. 'Don't take chances with your health.'

Heading back to The Fork, Lydia's phone buzzed. She checked the message before taking a detour in her route. She pushed open the door to The Hare and inhaled the familiar mix of hops and sweat, old perfume and sawdust, feeling the tension ease from her body as she approached the bar and ordered a drink. When it came to soothing anxiety, Kirsty's energy healing had absolutely nothing on Lydia's favourite boozer.

Within minutes of settling in her favourite corner seat and texting Fleet to let him know she had arrived and would wait, the door opened and admitted a tall, beautiful detective chief inspector. She watched him buy a pint of dark ale, exchange a joke with the guy behind the bar, a regular, and weave his way through the other punters.

Lydia tipped her head back to look up at Fleet and he bent down and kissed her on the mouth. Firmly, and with a casual intention that stopped the breath in Lydia's chest. 'I didn't think you'd get away tonight. Don't you have to work late?'

'Not my case.'

'Even though you found it?'

'Not my manor. And I wasn't on duty. I'm down in report as first on the scene but in unofficial capacity. Not sure how it will play out and neither was the SIO. Wait and see what tomorrow brings. Top brass might have an opinion on the matter.'

Fleet raised his glass to his lips, then lowered it again. 'Did you see the room?'

'No sign of a struggle,' Lydia said. 'And gold jewellery in a dish on the dressing table. Real stuff, too. Not junk.'

'So not a burglary, then.'

Lydia shook her head and took a large swig from her soda water and lime. She was trying to cut down on alcohol in case it was causing her senses to misfire. Plus, keeping a calm head and all of her inhibitions securely in place seemed like a good idea. Even with a crime scene fresh in her mind, Fleet was a distracting presence. Especially after he had come through to help her, again, and without a moment's hesitation. And then lied to his beloved force to keep her safely apart from an official investigation. To distract herself from these dangerously mushy thoughts, Lydia turned her mind to the scene at Yas Bishop's house.

Yas Bishop had been wearing skinny jeans and a silky top in emerald green. Unless JRB ran a very casual office, she hadn't been dressed for work. She hadn't been wearing shoes. Lydia closed her eyes and recalled Yas's bare feet. Her heels and toes rubbed red raw from new shoes, or some seriously uncomfortable heels. One gold and pearl earring visible, the other missing or hidden by the angle of her head. Snap shot images. Details that were easier to look at than the whole.

When she opened her eyes, Fleet was watching her. 'SOCO's report will be out tomorrow. Post mortem, too, with a bit of luck.'

Lydia nodded and sipped some more soda water. She wanted a whisky.

'I'll let you know.'

'Thank you. I appreciate that.'

A flicker around his mouth. 'You are most welcome.'

A pause in which Lydia wondered if a whisky would help or hinder. Maybe it would take her mind off the day. Take her mind off Fleet. 'I'm sorry I left. Are you going to get into trouble?'

'Nah,' Fleet said easily. 'I told you. I'm not worried.'

'I am,' Lydia said. 'I don't want to mess things up for you. For your career.'

'Did you want to come back to mine? It's closer.'

'No,' Lydia said, blinking at the sudden change of subject. 'No, thank you'. Ignoring the heat which was already low in her stomach and fast moving south.

'Early night for you?'

Lydia hoisted her soft drink in answer. 'I'm making smart decisions.'

'I'm not,' Fleet said and leaned over so that his face was barely an inch from hers. Lydia held her breath and didn't move. Most of her wanted to move forward, to close the tiny gap between their mouths.

His eyes were boring into her own, light reflected on

the copper brown of his irises. Despite her best intentions, she was breathing in his scent, the powerful pheromones of DCI Fleet. And that gleam. The mysterious bit of shine that she couldn't identify. She had never had that problem before. The thought hit her like a bucket of cold water; was Ignatius Fleet the reason she was misfiring? Was he her kryptonite?

He moved away, now. His face closed.

Lydia felt disappointment, relief and fear all at once. 'Sorry,' she said. 'I just can't.'

A smile, then. Forced, but friendly enough. 'No worries. Another time, maybe.'

OUTSIDE ON THE STREET, the pavement was filled with people necking drinks after work. Shirts were untucked and ice cubes clinked against glassware. She took a deep breath and then another. Leaving Fleet was a good idea. She didn't know what the gleam meant. He was a cop and she was a Crow. She was trying to build her business and already needed to duplicate herself in order to get everything done. She was misfiring. Maybe she wasn't such a weak link in the Crow bloodline after all. But she didn't know what that meant or how to find out more without alerting the wrong people. She didn't know who were the wrong people. Lydia walked home on autopilot, her thoughts churning. The Fork was closed and, for once, there was no sign of Angel. Lydia was surprised to feel a stab of disappointment. She realised that she had been looking forward to exchanging a couple of words with her. With that realisation came fear. She was getting comfortable, feeling at home.

Lydia went to the kitchen and opened the freezer. She picked up a bag of frozen peas and held it on the back her neck while she delved further with her other hand. There was a catering size tub of vanilla ice cream. Raspberry sorbet. A massive lemon cheesecake. Ready-to-bake croissants and pain au chocolat and then, at the back, a pint of mint choc chip. Bingo.

Peas safely stored and the ice cream tub in one hand, Lydia crossed the dark cafe. The knocking on the door made her jump. The shape in the glass of the door was large enough to give her a moment's hesitation and she put the safety chain on before opening it. It certainly looked like DCI Fleet, but Lydia wasn't taking any chances. Not after seeing a woman lying in a pool of her own blood.

'I forgot to give you this earlier,' Fleet said, ducking his head a little as he spoke. He held out a small bundle.

'Lame excuse,' Lydia said, stepping back anyway to let him inside. 'What is it?'

'Gloves,' Fleet said. 'For the next time you're illegally at a crime scene.'

'You're enabling me,' Lydia said.

Fleet put his hands on either side of Lydia's face and locked eyes. 'I'm trying to keep you safe.' He let her go and turned to shut the door.

'Did you want some ice cream?'

'Are you trying to distract me?'

'From your mission to save me from myself?' Lydia put the tub on the nearest table. 'Maybe.'

'There are better ways.'

Lydia's breath caught in her throat. 'Do you want the ice cream or not?'

'Yes, please,' Fleet smiled, then, and gleam or not, cop or not, Crow or not, Lydia couldn't help but smile back. 'I'll get you a spoon.' Lydia went behind the counter to the canisters of cutlery.

'Are we not going upstairs?'

Lydia shook her head. 'Too dangerous.'

'I see,' Fleet slid into one of the window booths.

'Actually... Sod it.' Lydia picked up the tub and headed for the stairs to the flat. 'Come on if you're coming.'

The curtains were open and the glow of the street lights, combined with the dying light of the summer sun, lit the living room. 'You want to sit outside?' Fleet said, 'it's still really hot.'

The door to the terrace was in her bedroom and, halfway to it, Lydia lost her nerve. Instead, she opened the door to let the evening air cool the room and sat cross-legged on her unmade bed.

'I'm not complaining,' Fleet said, accepting a spoon. 'But why are you avoiding the terrace?'

Lydia ate some minty deliciousness and ignored the question. 'Thank you for your help today.'

Fleet stilled, a spoon of ice cream halfway to his lips. 'You're welcome.'

'I know this isn't what you want,' Lydia gestured around at the room. The unpacked boxes in the corner, the door she was too afraid to step through, the weird-ness that was her life.

'How do you know that?'

'Well...' Lydia stopped. Unsure. 'It stands to reason.'

Fleet ate his ice cream and nodded, swallowing. 'Well, then. That seems conclusive.'

'It is,' Lydia dug in the tub with her spoon, suddenly unable to look at Fleet.

'And you're not at all curious?'

'About what?'

'About what I think,' Fleet said. He held his spoon loosely, and was watching her with an expression which was a mix of exasperation and attraction.

'I know what you're thinking,' Lydia said. 'And it would be fun. It would be amazing. But then we're back to square one, again, and it's awkward and just making things complicated and I need to concentrate on work and my family and I can't give you what you want.'

'Back to that, again,' Fleet said. 'What do I want? And why can't you give it?'

Lydia blew out a long sigh. 'You want a normal life. With a normal person. Or maybe you don't. Maybe you want uncomplicated occasional sex. Or semi-regular sex. With no strings or emotions. And I can't do either. Not with you. I wish I could, but I can't. It's annoying.'

Fleet propped up a couple of pillows against the headboard and sat with his legs stretched out. Lydia did the same and they sat like that side-by-side and passing the ice cream tub back and forth without looking at each other. After a few minutes, Fleet put the tub and his spoon on the bedside table. Lydia could feel him looking at her, but she didn't face him.

'What needs to change?'

'My life. My family. Your job.'

'What if you just trusted me? Wouldn't that work?'

Lydia squeezed the handle of the spoon tightly in her fist. She forced herself to look at him. 'You have never let me down. I believe you have my best interests at heart. I believe you are a good person.'

'But you don't trust me?'

'I don't trust you to still like me.' Lydia looked down at her hands. 'If we got to know each other properly. If you really knew me.'

'Because you're so dark. So terrible.'

Lydia forced a smile. 'Maybe.'

'Bollocks,' Fleet said. 'Don't dress up your fear of intimacy with some superhero shit.'

'You love my superhero shit.'

'I love everything about you.' It wasn't the same as saying 'I love you' but it was a hell of a lot closer than Lydia had ever come to declaring feelings. She felt her yawning sense of inadequacy. He was brave. It made her want to be brave. She bit her lip. 'I love everything about you, too. So far, anyway.'

'Well, then,' Fleet said. 'How about we stop messing about?'

Lydia didn't trust herself to speak, so she leaned over and kissed him instead.

His hands were instantly on her, on her neck, knotting her hair, running over her shoulders and arms. She leaned in and let her hands follow suit. The tightly curled hair at the nap of his neck, the muscles of his chest and arms, the blood under his skin. Singing to her own. The gleam getting warmer and warmer until she felt her own blood thumping in response. Could feel a glow which must be shining out of her own skin.

His mouth on hers felt like the most natural thing in the world. Lydia didn't want to think anymore. She didn't want to feel afraid. She just wanted Fleet. She could be normal for him. Or she could pretend to be.

CHAPTER SIXTEEN

The next day, Fleet got up early and left for work. He kissed Lydia goodbye and she pretended to be sleepier than she was to avoid any 'morning after' awkwardness. Once the door had closed behind Fleet, Lydia got up and showered. Then she made coffee and pondered her options for the day.

Lydia was sipping her coffee next to the open door of the roof terrace. The air flowed over the bare skin of her arms and she wished she could take a chair out there to work. Jason appeared from behind her, making her jump a little, the coffee sloshing over the rim of her mug.

'Sorry,' he said. 'I didn't mean to do that.'

'Do what?' Lydia was aiming for sarcasm as she sucked coffee off her hand.

'It's nice out,' Jason was looking out of door. 'Disappear like that.'

It took Lydia a second. 'It's the sudden appearances

that are tricky. If other people could see you it would be a handy interrogation tactic.'

A brief smile. 'I could shout "boo!", too.'

'Where do you go?'

Jason rubbed at his face with one hand. It was the action of a tired toddler and it made Lydia want to put her arms around him. 'I don't know. Mostly it's like I haven't been anywhere. But I come back and time has passed and I'm in a different part of the building so I know it's happened. Sometimes it's...' He trailed off.

'What?' Lydia prompted.

'It's like a bad dream. It doesn't really make sense and I don't think I can describe it coherently. It's scary, though.'

'I'm sorry.'

Jason's smile was a little stronger this time. He reached out as if he was going to touch Lydia's cheek but then dropped his arm. 'Thanks.'

Lydia's mobile rang. It was Uncle Charlie so she picked up, getting no more than the start of her greeting before Charlie cut across her. 'Come to the house. Now.'

BEING SUMMONED in such a terse way by the head of the Crow Family ought to have put the fear of Feathers into Lydia. Instead, it made her regress to teenage Lydia and she had a full internal battle with the urge to simply not turn up. She wasn't an idiot, though. And Uncle Charlie always brought out her old nature, her primary instinct was to fight, not flight. Fleet would probably smile at the term 'old nature', he would probably say she hadn't grown out of it one little bit. She could feel her whole body relaxing, curving into a smile just at the thought of Fleet. She banished him from her mind as she walked up the path to Charlie's front door. *Not the time, Lydia.*

The door was open and Lydia knew to walk in and close it behind her. She headed straight for the living room, figuring that Charlie would have chosen a formal room to match his mood. He was standing in front of the empty fireplace, hands by his sides and the blankest, coldest expression Lydia had ever seen on his face. She had glimpsed Charlie's shark-side before, but she realised, in this moment, that she had never seen it in full force.

'I can explain,' Lydia said. She hadn't planned to say the words and she snapped her mouth shut as soon as they escaped.

There was a silence in which they regarded one another. The tattoos on Charlie's arms were writhing and Lydia made sure she didn't look directly at them. Her left hand was clenched around her coin, but the fingers of her right hand stretched wide, pointing toward the earth. The taste of feathers was thick in the air and Lydia was having to use all of her concentration not to take a step backward. She knew if she did, she would keep on moving until she was far away from Charlie's stare. She felt a tingling in her fingers which travelled up her wrists and arms to her shoulders. Another urge was creeping in, the desire to stretch her arms wide, like wings. She kept them by her sides with enormous effort. Unbidden, Maddie appeared in her mind, and she heard her voice whispering into her ear. 'You can fly.'

The staring contest was still going on. 'In your own time.' Charlie's voice was low and calm. Lydia saw the slight widening of his eyes and realised that he hadn't intended to speak. The terror ebbed a little. The creature in front of her became, marginally, familiar. Her Uncle Charlie emerging and the capital-letter Head of The Family receding.

'What were you thinking?' He said at last. 'Barging in on Alejandro Silver.'

'I thought we were allies?'

'There's being friendly allies when we're up against the Pearls or the bloody Foxes, and then there's being the kind of pals who can go wandering into their place of business and asking questions about their clients. Hell Hawk, Lydia, I thought you were smarter than that.'

Lydia was still using half of her brain to stop her arms from raising from her sides. She was proud of herself for having a steady voice when she replied. 'I'm an investigator. I was just doing my job.'

'Bollocks you were,' Charlie said. 'You were asking about Robert Sharp and you have no business doing so. He's not your client.'

'No, he's dead,' Lydia retorted.

'Lyds,' Charlie said. He gave a little shake of his head. 'You've got to be sensible. I know you don't like it, but you're a Crow. That means you can't start a pissing match with the Silvers. You just can't.'

'Even if I think they're guilty of something.'

Charlie blew out an exasperated sigh. 'Of course

they're guilty. But this Sharp guy, he's nothing to do with us.'

'He's not one of us, you mean?'

Charlie shrugged. 'I'm just saying we're not going to war over him. I read the papers, they're saying it was a professional hit. That means he was into something which drew attention. You get a visit from a professional, likelihood is you did something to deserve it.'

Lydia felt a spark of anger. 'Now who's talking bollocks? You know that's nowhere near true.'

The tattoos had stopped moving and Lydia was relieved that Charlie seemed to have calmed down. She had no wish to ruin his forgiving mood and she didn't want to reveal any more than was strictly necessary to Charlie, but there was absolutely nobody else she could ask. 'There's something else.'

Charlie stilled.

'You know I went into Alejandro's private office? There was this cup.'

'Cup?'

'Yeah. Silver. Big. Like a football trophy but it looked really old. there were flowers and stuff moulded on it and engraving, too, but I didn't see it up close.'

Charlie moved from the fireplace, crossing the room to stand inches from Lydia. An explosion of movement. His gaze drilled into Lydia's eyes, searching for the truth. 'That's impossible.'

'What is it?'

Charlie's olive skin looked suddenly sallow in the sunlight. 'It doesn't make any sense. It can't-'

Lydia swallowed her impatience and waited.

'It sounds like the Silver Family Cup,' Charlie said, refocusing on Lydia. 'Which it can't be. That ought to be in the British Museum.'

'So, Alejandro took it back? Can he do that?' Lydia knew that part of the truce had involved the Families donating their treasures to the British Museum. It had been a show of unity and of openness. A symbolic gesture to demonstrate that the old ways were now relics and curiosities, academic artefacts and nothing more. The Fox Family hadn't agreed, of course. They had spread their devious paws wide and shrugged, saying that they didn't own anything museum-worthy. The Pearls had donated a pearly King coat, and a heavy gold necklace dripping with creamy yellow pearls, fat as peas.

'That's not it...' Charlie had taken his phone from his pocket, he looked at it with a blank expression and put it on the table. 'Hell Hawk. I can't believe... Maybe it's a replica?'

'Why does it matter?'

'The cup was stolen from the museum forty years ago. Alejandro didn't get it back from the curators. I guess he found who nicked it and got it back from them.'

'Ah.'

'Yeah,' Charlie was still looking into the distance, his brow furrowed. He rubbed a hand across his face.

Lydia wasn't sure how to ask the question without alerting Charlie to the very thing she wanted to keep secret. She felt as if she had a great big flashing letters above her head, spilling her inner thoughts. 'Is the cup just symbolic?'

'How'd you mean?'

'I get that it's important to the Silvers. It's a Family symbol. It's their heritage. I was just wondering whether it was more than that?'

Charlie shrugged. 'You know the stories.'

'Not really,' Lydia said. 'Dad didn't talk about the Silvers much.'

'Well,' Charlie said. 'What did Alejandro say?'

'Nothing. I didn't ask.'

'Smart girl.' Charlie looked around, as if he was checking they were still alone. 'You know the Silvers have a facility with language?'

Lydia nodded.

'And you know that back in the day they were very persuasive.'

'A Silver could make you think that black was white, up was down, left was right.'

'And that if you stepped off the side of a tall building you would float down to earth like a feather, land on your feet with a big smile.'

Lydia shuddered. The idea of having her own will taken like that was terrifying. The thought that a person could make you think things, make you do things because you believed them utterly, shook her at bone deep level.

'Well, there were other rumours, too. That they had an affinity for silver. Could imbue the substance with, I don't know, some sort of ability or effect. Enchant it, I guess is the best way to put it.'

Enchanted silver. Of course. Lydia resisted the urge to roll her eyes. She remembered the waves of sickness which had broken over her again and again. And the silver knight she had been chasing. 'Theoretically speaking, if an object was enchanted like that, could it alter a person's behaviour? Or their personality?'

Charlie shrugged. 'Yeah. Seems like that would be the least of it. Even if an object wasn't enchanted but somebody believed it was, believed it had power, that could be enough to change their behaviour.'

Like the Crows and the other Families. It didn't matter that their power was mostly a memory, people still believed enough to give them respect. Or a wide berth.

'How do Crows feel about silver?'

'The family? Well, we've been allies for a long time. You know that.'

'Not the people. The metal.'

'Did you feel something?'

'No,' Lydia lied. 'Just that I was near a Silver.'

For a moment Lydia thought Charlie could detect her dishonesty, but his frown was for something else.

'Speaking of that,' Charlie said. 'I was going to bring someone round this evening. After the cafe is closed.'

'You want me to identify them?'

'It won't be until late. Eleven-ish.'

Lydia did not want to start a precedent of being at Charlie's beck and call. But he was Charlie Crow. And this favour might be exactly why he had reigned in his anger over her visit to Alejandro.

'I know you might have to rearrange social plans,' Charlie was saying. 'Or are you working? Staking out some cheating husband?'

'Not tonight,' Lydia said.

'It won't take long,' Charlie said.

'Good.'

'Anything else you want to tell me?'

'Like what?' Lydia wasn't falling for that.

Charlie smiled fondly. 'That's the way, Lyds.'

THE AIR HAD COOLED off after the rainstorm and Lydia pulled on running gear. At the park, she did slow laps, while the cases swirled in her mind. Robert Sharp had been given a silver statue by a company called JRB. Yas Bishop, employee of JRB, had handled the statue and had since been killed. Lydia wanted more information on JRB but had hit brick walls. Stopping at a bench to stretch, Lydia realised something; she couldn't do this alone. And to get proper help from Fleet, she was going to have start being honest with him. Before the terror of that realisation could immobilise her vocal chords, she hit the speed dial.

'You know that knight statue?'

'Weird greeting,' Fleet said. 'The antique? You still think it's significant?'

Lydia took a deep breath. 'I swear there is something strange about it. And the place Yas Bishop bought it from has disappeared.'

There was a short pause. Then Fleet said: 'Disappeared?'

'Shut up shop. Like it was never there.'

'It's an empty shop, now, or the actual physical space has vanished?'

'Are you laughing at me?'

'No. I'm trying to get clarity.'

'Clarity on my madness.'

'I did not say that.'

'I want to examine it,' Lydia said. She did not want to say *I want to hold it and see if I can sense something weird in its energy. Like a Silver Family vibe.* 'If nothing else, it's a known link between the two victims.'

'Family might have been allowed in to box up his possessions. Or the cleaning crew. I'll ask Ian.'

He rang off and Lydia resumed stretching. She was just thinking about whether to run a bit more while she waited for Fleet to call back when he did. 'No statue,' Fleet said.

'Weird greeting,' Lydia said.

'Hilarious,' Fleet said, and she could hear the smile in voice. 'Sharp didn't have family in the country who were willing to come and clear out. They paid a company to do it and they took an inventory of his possessions. I'm looking at it now and there's no statue listed.'

'Someone is tidying up,' Lydia said. 'I should have taken it when I had the chance.'

'No,' Fleet said. 'You shouldn't have stolen the valuable item from the murder victim's house. I can't believe I have to say it.'

Lydia had been walking briskly, but she stopped. 'The point is, we don't know where it is, now.' *And I can't test it.*

'What do you think you would discover by examining it? You got a valuation from that shop, already.'

214

Lydia focused on the ground while she hesitated. *Was she really going to say this to Fleet?* 'You know Sharp changed behaviour? Before he was killed?'

'Uh-huh.'

'And Yas was really spooked and anxious when I called her. Then she tried to break into my flat. I know we don't know much about her personality before, but that sounds pretty erratic. What if it was the statue which made them both, I don't know, experience an altered state?'

'So you want to examine the statue for its special crazy-making properties.'

'Exactly. I was going to show Uncle Charlie. See if there was something-'

'But it might have affected you. Or Charlie.'

Lydia shrugged, her eyes on a group of teenagers walking across the park, their hoods up. 'I would have been careful.'

'Well it's a moot point. Thank God.'

'Wait,' Lydia hearing real concern in Fleet's tone. 'You're serious. You would really be worried about a magical statue?' Feathers. She had used the 'magic' word.

'You're worried, I'm worried,' Fleet said. 'And besides, you don't police Camberwell for this long without accepting a few things. And seeing a few things. Things that you can't always explain but you'd damn sure better be careful of.'

'So what do we do, now?'

There was a short silence on the line. 'I need to tell Ian.' Fleet sounded almost apologetic. 'I need to think of a way of doing that that doesn't involve you, but... I will manage it.'

'You should tell him to speak to Alejandro Silver.'

'Because the statue is silver?'

'That. But mainly because their clients, JRB, were looking after Sharp. And Yas Bishop worked for JRB.'

'That's good to know.'

There was another pause. 'But?' Lydia prompted.

'MIT won't be able to question the top man in one of the fiercest law firms in the city without solid evidence. Especially not considering that same man plays golf with the Deputy Commissioner. It's just not going to happen.'

CHARLIE ARRIVED at The Fork at ten forty-five. As promised, he wasn't alone. The woman he was towing had braided hair in an unnatural shade of pale orange and a grey Adidas tracksuit which was either retro cool or just old. She didn't look pleased to be attending the party, and Lydia could see fear behind her careful mask of indifference.

'Meet Candy,' Charlie said. 'Not her real name.'

'Hi, Candy,' Lydia said. 'You want a cup of coffee?'

Candy spat a wad of chewing gum on the floor in response.

Charlie heaved a sigh. 'So?' He said, looking at Lydia.

'I ain't done nothing. This is fuckin' outrageous. You've got no right.' Candy's words were a stream of disjointed sentences, peppered with more swear words than Lydia used in a year. And she was pretty proud of her own ability to curse.

'Now?' Lydia was surprised he was being so open about her ability. She grabbed a paper napkin from a nearby table and used it to scoop up the gum.

'None of us are getting any younger.'

'I need a favour,' Lydia said, raising her voice slightly over Candy's continued tirade. 'In return.'

Charlie was gripping Candy around her bicep. Her arm looked like a stick in his gigantic hand. If he wanted truth from Candy, Lydia had no doubt he had the means to get it. On the other hand, it was perfectly possible that Candy didn't know what she was. She could tell Charlie her truth and still be feeding him a lie. Lydia wrapped the gum carefully, held it out.

Charlie took the small package and tucked it into the nearest pocket of Candy's tracksuit. He barely glanced at her, black eyes on Lydia. 'What favour?'

'A name,' Lydia said. 'And a cordial introduction.'

'Fine,' Charlie said. He was wearing a dark jacket, but Lydia could almost sense the tattoos moving beneath it. Candy seemed to, too, she was shrinking away from him and the tirade had slowed to a trickle and reduced considerably in volume. 'No... Fuckin'... Right.'

Lydia hesitated.

'So?' Charlie said. 'Chop chop. We've got a deal.'

'What's she done?'

Charlie smiled and Lydia felt the skin on the back of her neck go cold. 'You want to get involved?'

'No,' Lydia said. She hesitated for a second more and then said: 'No power. No family connection.'

'Nothing at all?'

'Nothing.'

'I'm a Pearlie,' Candy said, panic clear in her voice. 'She's a fucking liar. I'm a Pearlie. My mother was a Pearl. I'm one. I swear to god.'

'Pearls swear to the sea,' Charlie said, 'everyone knows that.'

He dragged Candy to the door, ready to leave. Out of The Fork and away from Lydia. No longer her problem. Just the way she wanted.

Hell Hawk.

'Wait,' Lydia took a couple of steps, put a hand on Charlie's other arm.

The look he gave her was a challenge. And it was excitement, too. And greed.

'Don't hurt her.' Lydia knew she was playing into his hand in some unknown way, but she also didn't know how to avoid it. This was the problem with her family. The only way to be sure you were out was to be out completely. Aberdeen, or preferably the moon. Anything less and they just pulled you in.

'What do you care?' Charlie said. 'You're out. Henry fixed that.'

'Well, you've made me part of this,' Lydia gestured to Candy. 'And I'm running a legit business, here. Above board. I can't be involved in criminal activity.'

'I'm offended at the suggestion,' Charlie said. 'But, fine. You have my word. Candy here, will be delivered safely to her own front door. To live her life however she chooses.'

218

Candy had gone silent. She turned wide, frightened eyes from Lydia to Charlie and back again.

'Well, I say front door,' Charlie said, turning a large and dangerous smile onto Candy. 'I mean the pavement I picked you up from.'

'She's homeless?' Lydia felt sick.

'Nah, it's her place of business.' Charlie said. 'But not anymore, isn't that right, Candy darling? No more sweeties for the kiddies.'

Candy's mouth was half-open but instead of swearing, she nodded.

'Good girl,' Charlie said. 'And you,' he said to Lydia. 'I'll be in touch.'

'I'll call you tomorrow for that favour,' Lydia said.

Charlie made a little mock bow. 'Your wish is my command.'

Lydia locked the door behind Charlie and climbed the stairs to her flat. She didn't knock on Jason's door or wash her face, just fell face-first into bed and was asleep in seconds.

LYDIA WAS on the roof terrace. Not again, she thought. Not tonight. She walked to the edge of the terrace, ignoring the fear. *Let's get this over with. Get back to dreaming about skateboarding kittens or getting stuck in quicksand.*

'Everyone thinks I'm the bad guy,' Maddie's voice was so clear that Lydia turned around. Even though she was never there to see. Just a voice in her ear before she felt the shove, or during the following, sickening fall.

Maddie was next to her on the terrace. She looked the same as she had the last time Lydia had seen her in real life. When Maddie had tried to kill her. She was wearing the same clothes and her hair was falling across her face at exactly the same angle. She still had enviable eyebrows and the most-perfect flick of eyeliner Lydia had ever seen. She raised her hands and smiled. 'Surprise!'

'What do you want?'

'Oh, don't be like that,' Maddie said, her mouth a twist of disappointment.

If Lydia hadn't known she was a stone-cold psychopath, she might have felt bad.

'Isn't it obvious?'

Lydia turned away, sick of playing games. Dream or not. She gripped the railing and leaned over. The pavement looked closer than it did in reality. Or her dream eyesight was strangely acute. She could see every detail of the concrete slabs. The marks and divots, the patch of liquid that was probably urine.

'Are you going to jump?' Maddie sounded genuinely curious.

'Why not?' Lydia kept her eyes on the pavement. 'This is a dream. I can't die. And I want to wake up.'

'Suit yourself,' Maddie said. 'But don't come crying to me. Don't say I didn't warn you.'

CHAPTER SEVENTEEN

The next day Lydia updated Jason over her morning coffee before phoning Charlie. 'I don't like it,' Jason said. 'I thought you weren't one of those Crows. I thought we were staying independent.'

'We are,' Lydia said. 'But Charlie has his uses. And it's not like I know anybody else with contacts in organised crime. I can't just start asking randoms whether they happen to know anybody who could organise a professional hit. I'm pretty sure that would be a bad idea.'

'I know. You're right. It just... It feels like a bad idea.'

'Aren't you the same man who was telling me I needed help, that I couldn't do everything on my own?'

'I didn't mean him,' Jason said. He went back to his room. 'And I need more pens.'

'Right,' Lydia said to the empty air. The sun was up and shining through the blinds. She stabbed the call button on her mobile, and felt her shoulders tense up at the sound of her uncle's voice.

She walked through the flat as she spoke, needing the movement to release the pent-up energy that was suddenly fizzing through her body. Too much caffeine. A thought which floated through her mind approximately three hundred times every single day.

'Always good to hear from you,' Charlie was saying.

Lydia cut across the niceties. 'I need that name.'

'Who do you need?'

Lydia told him, while being careful not to spell it out in incriminating language. It was a phone call, after all, and she knew at least that much. She was in her bedroom now, and she crossed to the external door, pulled aside the thin curtain and looked out on the terrace, drenched in the early morning sunshine.

'Any point in me asking why? Or warning you not to tangle with them?'

'None at all,' Lydia said, A fat London pigeon landed on the terrace and began its distinctive bobbing walk.

'At the risk of stating the obvious, these are not people to mess about with.'

Lydia stayed quiet. That pigeon wasn't going to last long. Lydia might have been a weak link in the Crow Family line, but she was still a Crow. And this whole building belonged to the family. Sure enough, a raven swooped down and landed a foot away from the chubby grey bird.

'Fine,' Charlie said. 'But tread carefully.'

'Can you arrange for me to have a friendly conversation? Is that possible?' As Lydia expected, phrasing the request in such a manner spiked Charlie's pride.

'Of course,' Charlie said.

The raven took a step toward the pigeon and it flew up in a panicked flutter, leaving a couple of dusty down feathers in its place. 'Today would be perfect.'

'I bet,' Charlie said, his voice dry as kindling. 'I'll see what I can do.'

Ready to finish the call, Lydia hesitated. 'About last night-'

'Our mutual friend is perfectly healthy.'

'Right. I know,' Lydia said, as if the idea that Charlie might have chucked Candy in the Thames had never crossed her mind. 'What was that about, though?'

'She was selling without a permit,' Charlie said. 'Running a whole crew doing the same.'

Lydia tried to match the vision of Candy with her idea of a drug lord. 'And she told you she was Pearl?'

'Which would have caused complications, yes.'

'Gotcha.'

'Be careful today,' Charlie said. 'These are not our people.'

It wasn't until late afternoon that the text from Charlie came through. A time and a location. Lydia looked it up on StreetView and found herself gazing upon the perfect murder spot. A warehouse district in north London, just off the Seven Sisters Road. Jason also had reservations. 'I wish I could go with you,' he said, adding quickly. 'I'm not trying to start an argument.'

'I do, too,' Lydia said and she meant it. Adultery cases seemed suddenly alluring. But she was damned if she was going to flinch. She was a Crow. And what had happened to Robert Sharp and Yas Bishop wasn't right. It was that simple.

She allowed plenty of time to get across the city in the Volvo. It didn't feel like quite the right make of car for the job, but her finances were going to have to improve a great deal before she could change up her motor. Pulling up on the designated location, Lydia distracted herself by trying to work out what would be the ideal car for a private investigator. Something roomy and comfortable but not too ostentatious. Not memorable.

The meeting place was on a quiet back road running behind three large, low warehouse buildings. The first building had a fleet of vans parked behind it, but the other two had the sad air of desertion. Empty car parks, a few broken windows. Sparse security. Lydia looked around for cameras, but she knew they would be disabled by the crew she was meeting if they had anything planned. They weren't amateurs.

Idling the engine and trying not to freak out, Lydia heard the car coming before it turned onto the road. A black SUV, sunlight bouncing off its highly polished panels and the windscreen, making it difficult to see inside at a distance. The car had turned onto the road at a crawl and continued at the same pace, exhaust roaring as it came. It was either an intimidation tactic or they were checking the vicinity. Eventually, the car slid alongside and Lydia found herself locking eyes with the driver, a young man with a shaved head and a neck tattoo. She wound down her window. His was already open.

'Dhruv?'

He smiled showing very white, even teeth. Like a movie star. 'Ms Crow.'

There were two white men in the backseat of the car. They were huge and wearing bulky jackets, despite the warm weather. They looked wedged in and they were staring straight ahead, like they were in power-down mode. Lydia didn't really want to see them animated.

'Beautiful day,' Dhruv said. He had a surprisingly soft and pleasant voice.

Lydia produced her gold coin in one closed hand, gripping it so hard the edges were digging into her palm. 'I want to ask you about Robert Sharp.'

'What about him?'

'I think it was a professional job and I'm wondering if you know the crew responsible?'

Dhruv tilted his head. 'And why would I tell you? If I did know anything, that is.'

He pronounced 'anything' with a thick Laahndahn accent. 'Anyfink'.

'I'm not after the crew,' Lydia was trying to keep her voice matter-of-fact. Reassuring and professional. She had no idea if it was the correct tactic or not. 'I know it was just a job.'

'Oh, you know that, do you?' The beginnings of a smile played on Dhruv's face.

'But I want the person responsible. The one who made it happen, ordered it. I'm hoping you might have heard something.' Lydia didn't know if she was insulting or complimenting Dhruv with this suggestion. She hoped, fervently, that it was the latter.

'I don't have much to do with Camberwell, but I know your uncle. Owe him a favour so I'm here to answer one question. You're not recording this meeting and anything I say will not come back on me or my people.'

'Understood,' Lydia said.

'And you're sure that's your one question? Nothing else is coming to mind?'

Lydia opened her mouth to say 'yes', then paused, searching for the trick. Had she phrased it correctly? Was Dhruv going to get away with giving her no information while simultaneously satisfying his 'one question answered' favour? He was staring at her, a challenge in his face. The two men in the back were still looking blankly ahead, as if they were running cartoons in their minds for entertainment or were heavily sedated. Lydia wasn't fooled. Then it occurred to her, why was he giving her this chance? He could have answered her first question and been done. She re-ran the brief conversation, gripping her coin to keep herself from spinning away with the fear of the situation. If this went badly, the three men could kill her easily. They would all be armed and the thought of meeting another loaded gun turned every part of Lydia to liquid. She had asked if Dhruv knew the crew responsible. He could say 'yes' or 'no' and be done. He clearly didn't want to take advantage of that loophole. Which meant he wasn't worried about incriminating himself or his crew. And that he didn't care much about protecting the person Lydia was searching for.

'In your own time,' Dhruv said. 'I've got places to be.'

'Who tried to engage your services with regard to Robert Sharp?'

Dhruv smiled as if she had passed a test.

LYDIA KNEW SHE WAS DREAMING. She was almost sure she was dreaming.

She was on the roof terrace and there was cool air on her skin. She could sense the man behind her. He wasn't pressing anything into her back, but she knew he had a gun and that it was pointed at the base of her spine, and her fear was thick like feathers stuffed into her mouth. The sky was black as a wing, but then it split with crackling lightning which lit up the terrace in stark white light. This isn't how it happened, she thought. *I'm definitely dreaming.*

'Go on,' the man spoke although Lydia didn't hear his words. Just felt them. Next thing she was at the edge, the railing pressing into her stomach and the grey concrete far below. Maddie was next to her and she knew that this was when she would be tipped over. Sent screaming through the air and she willed herself to wake up early. She would wake before she hit the ground, so why not avoid those horrible few seconds of terror. Wake up, now. She tried to say the words, but nothing came out.

Maddie had a hand on her shoulder and another

around her waist. She was hauling Lydia up and over the railing with impossible strength.

'No,' Lydia said. 'Please. Don't-'

'Fly!' Maddie screamed in her ear.

And she woke up.

Clammy with sweat and shaking with adrenaline, Lydia stared into the darkness of her bedroom. Orange light from the street lights spilled through her curtains and the noise of the city slowly covered the hammering of her heart, the clamour of fear and the sound of Maddie's harsh voice in her head. She had left her window open, trading quiet for air flow, and the sounds of a fox or rat scrabbling through rubbish floated in. An unearthly female screech, not unlike dream-Maddie, solved the puzzle. Definitely a fox.

Enough. Lydia rose from the bed and pulled on cotton pyjama bottoms and a shirt. She would exorcise this nonsense once and for all. She stepped into her unlaced Doctor Marten's and unlocked the door to the terrace. Not letting herself hesitate, she walked through the doorway and into the night air. Her hand slid automatically into her pocket and found the coin she knew would be waiting there, and she gripped it for strength.

There was a full moon riding low in the sky, wisps of cloud flowing across it. The roofscape was just as she remembered, and so were the unloved-looking terracotta pots along the side of the building. Minus one, of course, which had been used by Jason to protect Lydia from the hit man. Despite being the middle of the night, it was still mild. The heatwave refusing to release the city from its grip, even in the darkness. Nevertheless, Lydia's skin was goosepimpled and she had to clench her jaw to stop her teeth from chattering. That was fear, not cold, and Lydia had had enough. She was a Crow and Crows did not jump at shadows. Henry Crow's daughter would not remain hostage to a memory, however bad.

She walked deliberately to the edge of the terrace. Gripping the railing, she leaned over it and yelled 'piss off' as loudly as she could.

Lydia straightened up, feeling faintly foolish, but no longer frightened. It was just a place. There was nothing here to be afraid of. A beat of wings and Lydia looked up in time to see a raven swooping low over the roof. It landed a foot away and fixed her with a beady stare. Lydia felt a shudder rip through her body. It was a raven. Just a normal bird. The night raven had no eyes, just black holes where they ought to be. This wasn't Madeleine Crow. This wasn't a mythic horror. This was just a raven. A beautiful sleek majestic raven. 'Greetings,' Lydia said, bowing her head in respect. 'I hope you are having a good night. ' As soon as the words were out of her mouth she felt ridiculous.

The raven cocked its head, as if listening. Then took what looked like a deliberate hopping step closer to her. The feeling of foolishness fled in the face of the bird. It was looking at her intently and Lydia was overcome with the sense that it was waiting for her to speak. She cleared her throat. 'Did Uncle Charlie send you?'

The bird stayed motionless.

After another moment, Lydia said: 'Maddie?'

The raven shifted, its black feathers ruffling.

'What do you want?' Lydia tried. She was frustrated

at her own inability to communicate. The air was thrumming and every nerve ending felt alive. This was important, she knew that much. Three crows, cut-out black shapes against the ink-blue of the night sky, circled the terrace, cawing.

The raven let out a screech and then took off into the air.

'Come back!' Lydia felt a sudden desperation. And the dreadful notion that she had just missed something vital. She waited for a while, her arms wrapped around her body against the sudden cold, hoping the raven would return. The three crows wheeled in the sky, like a patrol, but there was no sign of the raven.

KNOWING something was no good without being able to prove it. Not what Charlie would say, of course. He had a thousand ways of extracting justice and not a single one of them involved anything resembling due process, but Lydia was not her uncle. She didn't know if it was the desire to prove this or just her innate pig-headedness, but she was determined to do this according to the official laws. The ones her new boyfriend believed in and had dedicated his life to upholding.

The SOCO report and post mortem had both come in. Fleet wasn't supposed to be sharing the details with Lydia. He wasn't even supposed to know them, but his friend Ian seemed keen for his opinion on the case.

'Knife was recovered from the scene. It's confirmed as the murder weapon.'

'Definitely ruled out suicide, then?'

Fleet nodded. 'It looks like she was taken by surprise. No defensive wounds on arms or hands.'

'That's some surprise. The killer must have been very quick.'

'And the move must have been very unexpected. It wasn't even from behind. Forensics show an arcing movement, taken from somebody who was probably taller than Ms Bishop. Now, she's not short for a woman, so someone taller is likely to be a man. Plus, you know, violent crime statistics skew for that probability.'

'Or a woman in high heels,' Lydia said. 'Yas didn't have shoes on and presumably the killer did.'

'True,' Fleet said. He chewed for a moment, staring into space.

'House wasn't broken into, right?' Lydia said to Fleet, putting thoughts of sorting this out via a handy backchannel like Dhruv's gang firmly out of her mind.

'Right,' he dug around in the takeaway carton of Kung Pao chicken with a pair of chopsticks and Lydia tried not to get distracted by his manual dexterity. It took effort.

'So, Ms Bishop either knew her attacker or was presented with a good enough reason to trust them and open the door. Depends on her level of security consciousness, but that could include someone posing as a gas or broadband engineer.'

Lydia speared a wonton. 'Not a woman living on her own. Not likely.'

'Fair enough,' Fleet said. 'Whoever it was, they got her upstairs with minimal fuss. No signs of a struggle, so either they were large enough to overpower Yas immediately and leave no evidence, or they were invited to her bedroom.'

'Or they showed her the knife and the threat was enough to make her comply,' Lydia said, thinking about her brush with the gun-toting hitman. She took a slug of cola to wash down the wonton. 'But you think it was a love interest?'

Fleet shrugged. 'Worth considering. No relationships have emerged as yet, she seems to have been married to her work, but you never know. Could be something new, or a bit of wish fulfilment.'

'Wish fulfilment?'

'Professional services,' Fleet said. 'Or a casual pick-up online.'

'Doesn't feel right, does it? What line is Ian taking on it?'

Fleet shrugged. 'Could be a breakdown of some kind. Irrational behaviour. Her family haven't seen her for weeks. They're in Norfolk, so it's not particularly unusual, but her sister did say that she hadn't been Face-Timing on Sundays, the way they usually did.'

'So I was right about another change of personality? Altered behaviour pattern, just like Robert Sharp?'

'Seems that way,' Fleet said, nodding. 'Which reminds me, I spoke to Ian about your mysterious statue.'

'Not my statue,' Lydia said.

'Yas Bishop had several pictures of the statue on her mobile phone. Not just plain shots, like you might take to show the object to someone else, but these weird tableau and selfies. In one of them, she was naked and cuddling it.'

232

'That sounds like altered behaviour. Unless she had a fetish about statuary before this whole thing began.'

'You don't want to know where its sword was pointing,' Fleet said.

'Any news on her job?' Lydia asked. 'Did the police have any more luck with the elusive JRB?'

Fleet pulled a face. 'Not a lot. Company directors claim no knowledge, say that it's HR's job, middle management don't actually manage stuff, just client accounts.'

'They're saying they don't know her at all? When they employ her? What about Human Resources? Records? They have to know.'

'The number given for HR is just an answer machine.'

'Well that's dodgy.'

'As fuck,' Fleet agreed. 'But it's also an effective stonewall. If we don't have enough details or a name, we can't get a warrant. And without a warrant we can't get more details. And you know we can't go to the Silvers. Top brass wouldn't be too pleased. Not without a hell of a lot more due cause.'

'You know who else Yas would trust?' Lydia had been waiting, hoping the Murder Investigation Team had more to go on, that she wouldn't have to reveal what she knew in order to push them in the right direction, but there was nothing for it.

'Who?'

'Her lawyer.'

CHAPTER EIGHTEEN

Lydia decided to pay a housecall to her client. It didn't feel like the kind of conversation she ought to have on the phone and she really couldn't put it off any longer. She rang first, to check it was a good time. 'Not really,' Dr Lee had said, but Lydia told him it was important.

Dr and Mrs Lee's garden flat in Denmark Hill was tastefully decorated and had an enormous modern extension at the back with a bright open-plan kitchen and dining room. Following the current trend, the rear wall was all glass, giving a view of the neat garden with a covered seating area at the bottom. The sun was belting through the vast expanse and had made the kitchen uncomfortably warm. Lydia wondered if, in ten years' time, the monied middle-classes would be busy bricking-in glass walls all over the city when the fashion changed. Dr Lee offered tea and Lydia accepted to give her a moment to look around the kitchen while he made it.

There was a landline on a console table in the dining room part, and above it a small pinboard with takeaway menus, business cards, and an emergency contact list. Lydia could hear the kettle boiling at the other end of the massive space, and she searched methodically through the layers of pinned papers, not really sure what she expected to find. Until she found it.

'Milk? Sugar?' Dr Lee said when Lydia joined him in the light-filled kitchen.

'Why didn't you tell me your wife wasn't well?' She held up the hospital appointment slip, which had been half-buried on the board. The clinic was in the oncology department, the date next month. Terrible though it was to admit, she was filled with relief that she wouldn't actually be breaking the news of his wife's illness. 'This process works a lot better if I have all the available information.'

'She is well,' Dr Lee said, frowning at the paper. 'I mean, she wasn't well. Breast cancer. But they caught it early and it was successfully treated. She has to have a regular check-up, that's what you've got there, but it's only once a year, now. She's been completely clear for six years.'

'Well, that's good news.' Lydia kept her tone neutral, hiding her confusion.

'Why did you think she was ill? Have you seen her go to the hospital?' Fear was gouged into the lines on Dr Lee's face.

'No, nothing like that,' Lydia waved the paper. 'I just saw this. That's all.'

Dr Lee sagged against the counter. 'Oh, thank God.'

Lydia wasn't sure what to do or where to look but Dr Lee was already straightening his spine. He occupied himself with the business of the kettle and the mugs. Lydia didn't bother to say that she wasn't going to stay for tea, now, she knew it was more important that Dr Lee had something on which to focus. 'I'm sorry,' she said. 'I didn't mean to upset you.'

'That's quite all right,' Dr Lee said, putting a used teabag into the compost bin. 'What was it you wanted to discuss. What have you found?'

And there it was. Lydia has a responsibility to her client, the broken-looking man who was wiping a pool of tea from the counter, but there was no reason to make things worse within a marriage than they had to be. Do no harm didn't just apply to doctors. Lydia's old boss, Karen, had often said that being an investigator was like being a therapist half the time. Lydia wasn't a fan of that half, but looking at Dr Lee she knew she couldn't let that make her thoughtless or cavalier. She had chosen a job which inserted her into people's lives, into their most intimate relationships. Lydia had to work out a way of doing that that would still allow her to sleep at night. 'I haven't found anything to suggest that your wife is having a romantic or sexual affair.'

Dr Lee smiled hesitantly. 'Is there a 'but' at the end of that sentence?'

'Nope,' Lydia said. 'I can send you a full report of my surveillance, but it might be better if you take the details on trust.'

'What do you mean?'

'When your wife asks you if you trust her, you can look her in the eye and say 'yes'.'

Dr Lee still looked confused and Lydia wondered if he thought she was trying to wriggle out of writing a detailed report, or whether he was starting to wonder if she had, in fact, done the work she was going to bill him for. She tried again. 'Right now, you have a choice. You've already breached your wife's trust by hiring me. But I'm the one who has invaded her privacy, I'm the one who has followed her and observed her without her knowledge. That's my job. As her husband, though, you can choose not to invade her privacy in that way. I'm not married and I've never had a long-term relationship, but I've seen a fair few in my professional capacity and I know this; there is a line in every marriage that, once crossed, breaks it. You might have already done so, but if there's a chance you haven't, don't you want the chance to avoid it?'

Dr Lee looked stricken and Lydia honestly wasn't sure if he was about to shout at her for lecturing him or start sobbing. Finally, he nodded. 'How much do I owe you?'

'I'll send over my invoice in the next couple of days,' Lydia said, already heading for the door.

LYDIA HAD FOUND a parking space for her tank-like old Volvo and had no wish to lose it unless absolutely necessary. Instead, she walked back to Church Street and waited in a cafe until Mrs Lee finished work. Bang on time, she emerged from the office and headed to her car.

Lydia was ready, though, and intercepted Mrs Lee with one hand on the driver's door.

'Can I have a quick chat?' Lydia said. 'I'm an investigator.' She handed Mrs Lee her card.

'What is this about?'

'Can I buy you a cup of tea?' Lydia indicated the cafe she had just left. 'Or a coffee? This won't take long but I'd rather not stand in the street.'

Mrs Lee shook her head and opened the car door. She got in quickly and Lydia stepped back, expecting her to drive away. Instead, she stared out of the windscreen, motionless, for a minute and then wound down her window. 'Get in.'

Lydia walked around to the passenger side and obeyed the command.

'Five minutes,' Mrs Lee said. And, then. 'I know why you're here.'

Lydia tilted her head. 'And why's that?'

'I assume it's about Gerald.'

'Gerald?'

'Gerald Horner. My boss.' When Lydia still looked blank, Mrs Lee added. 'I work at Horner Insurance. You're not here about Gerald?'

Lydia shook her head. 'Why would you think that?'

'No reason,' Mrs Lee said quickly. 'I just assumed he was dodgy. He comes across that way. You know the type. And he's been having meetings with some very rough-looking people recently. I thought he must have got into trouble. He visits casinos, that sort of thing.' Mrs Lee's lip was curled in distaste.

'Right. Well, no. It's not about Gerald. I shouldn't be

here, really. I'm looking into alternative therapists and I believe you have been visiting Kirsty Thomas. On Tindal Street.'

Mrs Lee's eyes widened in shock. 'How on earth do you know that?'

'Trade secret,' Lydia said. 'It's nothing to worry about and I'm not looking into Kirsty specifically, it's a wide-ranging case and she has come up as a peripheral. I'm working for a journalist who is working up a big piece on alternative health care, stuff like acupuncture, aromatherapy, energy healing.' Lydia was making up this nonsense on the fly but Mrs Lee seemed happy enough to take her word for it. 'It would just be really helpful to get a patron's view and my job is to rustle up a few leads, members of the public who would be happy to chat to the journalist about their experience. Whether it's helped you, how you feel about the process, whether you would be interested in seeing regulation across the industry, that kind of thing.'

'Would my name appear in the article?'

'Not unless you wanted,' Lydia said. 'And you'd be paid for your time, of course.'

'I don't want to get anybody into trouble,' Mrs Lee said. 'Kirsty has been brilliant.'

'May I ask why you've been seeing her? I'm trying to source a range of interviewees.' Lydia flipped open her notebook. 'Don't worry if it's too personal. Or too painful. If you'd rather not say-'

'I was ill a few years ago,' Mrs Lee said. 'Breast cancer.'

'I'm sorry.'

'Six years clear,' she said. 'I still feel frightened, though. It changes you. And not the way they show on the TV. It's not always bucket lists and seizing the day. Sometimes it's just fear. I get a sore back and I think it's a spinal tumour.'

Lydia nodded sympathetically. 'Is that what you see Kirsty for? The anxiety?'

'Sort of,' Mrs Lee looked away, embarrassed.

'It's completely understandable. After what you've been through.'

Mrs Lee took an audible breath in and then let it out slowly. 'I go for help with the cancer.'

Lydia made a squiggle on the pad, not making eye contact in the hope that Mrs Lee would continue to open up.

'When I was really sick, my husband was amazing. Everyone was. And now I'm not... I sort of miss it. I know that sounds awful. I mean, I'm not ill and I should be grateful, but I'm supposed to just get on. Like it never happened.'

'Have you talked to your husband about how you feel?'

Mrs Lee was staring out of the windscreen. She shook her head slowly. 'I can't have my name in this piece. He doesn't know I go to Kirsty. He wouldn't understand. And I am grateful. I really am. I know I'm lucky to be here.'

'Maybe he would,' Lydia began. 'Maybe-'

'No. He's a doctor. He hates alternative medicine. Says they're all charlatans and crooks. Besides, it would look like I was dismissing his career choice, his life. He'd say I was being ungrateful to the real medics who saved my life. And he wouldn't understand why I'm pretending to still be ill for an hour a week... I mean, who would understand that? It's completely mad.'

'It's giving you something you need,' Lydia said briskly. 'It's none of my business, but I think you should tell him.'

Mrs Lee snapped back to the conversation. Her shoulders straightened. 'When will I hear from the journalist? What's their name?'

'If you're chosen as an interviewee, it will be tomorrow.'

'And they won't use my name?'

'Definitely not,' Lydia said.

Mrs Lee was chewing her bottom lip. Lydia could see her brain catching up with the situation, now that the surprise was wearing off, her self-preservation was kicking in. Lydia tried to calm her down. 'If this is going to stress you out, I don't have to pass on your name. You don't have to take part, either. It's completely up to you.'

'Maybe not, actually,' Mrs Lee said. 'Is that okay? I'm not sure I want-'

'That's fine,' Lydia said quickly. 'Thank you for your time.' She made to get out of the car, pausing halfway out of the door. 'Sorry. Can I just give you some advice?'

Mrs Lee had already turned on the engine and flicked the indicators.

'Don't invite strangers to get into your car with you. That's a really bad idea, safety-wise.' She smiled to soften the words, but Mrs Lee just gave her a blank look, like she wasn't really listening. 'And talk to your husband. Trust me, it's better coming from you.'

'Wait, what do you mean?' Mrs Lee stopped mid-manoeuvre and focused on Lydia, but she was already walking away.

CHAPTER NINETEEN

Lydia was dreaming. The sun was shining onto the roof terrace and the sky above was the perfect blue of childhood memory. There was a pressure at the base of her spine but instead of a gun pressing into her back, she knew it was just her Dad's hand, steering her over to a cluster of white plastic garden chairs with some familiar figures.

Maddie was sitting next to Jason. She was smoking a cigarette and holding one elbow like a fifties starlet. Jason looked entirely solid and alive. He was smoking, too, and clouds began billowing across the terrace. He smiled and stood up when he saw Lydia, wreathed in grey blue smoke. 'Have you met everyone, yet?'

'What?' Lydia felt relaxed.

'Everything is going to be different, now,' Jason was saying, as part of Lydia's brain recognised that the dream had changed. Nobody was throwing her off her terrace, which was a great improvement. Maddie was calm, although she was looking studiously away from Lydia. Jason was here and chatting happily.

Lydia wanted to turn her head to look at her Dad, see the man she instinctively knew would be young and whole. The father of her memories. She wanted to talk to him, but her attention was caught by a third seated figure.

The man from her circuits class. The one who had brought with him a burst of unidentifiable power. Maddie was blowing extravagant smoke rings, obstructing her view so she couldn't get a good look at him. Then she exhaled a stream of smoke which formed into the unmistakable shape of a raven in flight. It was larger and more detailed than was possible from a cigarette, and it floated through one of the dissipating smoke rings. Lydia's eyes were stinging badly, now. They began streaming, so she blinked to clear them. And woke up.

THE NEXT DAY, Lydia prepared the invoice for Dr Lee and emailed it over. She was relieved the job was complete, but felt an overwhelming sadness which took her by surprise. Mrs Lee was cheating on her husband in one sense; she was lying to him about where she was going after work and all to cover up the fact that he wasn't giving her something she needed. Why couldn't people just talk to each other? It would be so much cheaper and easier than hiring Lydia. Of course, then she would be out of job, so there was that.

LYDIA MET Fleet in The Hare. He was just off work, but had taken off his suit jacket and his tie was loose. He had a pint of something dark and stood up when she arrived. Lydia waved away his offer of a drink. 'I can't stay.'

Fleet sat down. 'You wanted to talk, though?'

Lydia took a deep breath. 'I think the Silver Family paid a professional crew to carry out the hit on Robert Sharp.'

Fleet had been lifting his pint to his lips but he put it back down onto the table untouched. 'Why do you think that?'

Lydia shook her head automatically and then stopped. She had to trust him sometime. She had to trust somebody. So she told him about her meeting with Dhruv.

'And he told you that Maria Silver tried to engage his services to kill Robert Sharp?' Fleet took a sip of beer. 'You know that's not the most reliable testimony I've ever heard?'

'Yes, but he didn't take the job. He doesn't know who did, but he could hazard a guess.'

'What a surprise. Rival gang, by any chance?'

'No,' Lydia said. 'He said it was a professional set-up. Nothing personal. I didn't ask him for the name, though.'

'Why not?'

'I'd already used my one question.'

Fleet nodded, thinking. 'It's your word. That's all we've got. I'm assuming your contact will deny all knowledge if we haul him in?'

'You haven't got my word, either,' Lydia said. 'I can't

be involved. Not officially. If I'm seen attacking Maria Silver it could break the truce between the Families. That can't happen.'

Fleet nodded to show his understanding. 'You won't get credit, either, though. I thought you wanted to work this case so that you could raise your profile, get criminal case work rather than domestic stuff?'

Lydia shrugged. 'Can't be helped. You can pass stuff to Ian, but MIT can't know it came from you. We're connected, now, and people might think I'm involved in the case.'

'We're connected?' Fleet's mouth twitched at the corners.

'Don't get excited.'

Fleet went to take another sip but Lydia got there first, stealing a couple of mouthfuls of foamy beer before giving him back the glass.

'So, let me get this right,' he said. 'You think that Maria killed Yas Bishop. That she gained entry to the house easily because Yas knew her as JRB's lawyer? And you are basing this on... What, exactly?'

Lydia closed her eyes. 'I could sense the Silver Family at her house.' She opened them, ready to see disbelief, maybe fear, in Fleet's eyes. Instead he just nodded.

'But why would Maria Silver want Robert Sharp dead? And in such a public way? Who was that message intended for?'

'I don't know,' Lydia said. 'The mysterious JRB, again? They're clients of the Silvers. If Sharp was ripping them off in some way, perhaps JRB expected their hotshot lawyers to step in and make an example of him.'

'It doesn't seem like the obvious place to go.'

'If the Silver Family are anything like the Crows, then JRB wouldn't have to ask them to take action like this.'

'What do you mean?'

'Let's say Sharp was screwing their client. That reflects badly on their power, their influence. Alejandro Silver wouldn't hesitate to make an example of him. It's a matter of pride.'

Fleet tilted his head. 'I can see that. But if Maria ordered the hit on Sharp, what makes you think she would get her hands dirty with Yas Bishop? It's a big step from ordering a hit to carrying one out.'

'I've been thinking about that,' Lydia replied. 'What if Maria didn't want her dad to find out about Yas? Maybe the statue was a mistake on Maria's side and she was covering her own tracks.'

'So, JRB were looking after Sharp. Then he messed up somehow and they wanted him out of the picture. The Silvers sort that out, but it transpires that the reason he went off the rails was because he had a crazy-making enchanted statue that shouldn't have been on the open market at all. How does that link to Maria?'

Lydia slumped. 'I don't know. And I can't ask Guillaume Chartes, the silver shop guy who sold the statue, because the place has disappeared.'

'You said that,' Fleet said. 'Have you been back since?'

'It was like it was never there. The shop next door

had never heard of Guillaume and said the place had been empty for months.'

'It's possible she was lying. Messing with you.'

'True,' Lydia said. She felt like an idiot. Of course the woman had been lying. Lydia had been so thrown, she hadn't questioned it. She wasn't sure what it said about her psyche that she had been happy to accept a shop had vanished into thin air, disappeared from history. It was a hazard of growing up a Crow, she supposed. She was used to accepting the fantastical. But still, she was going to have to watch that tendency if she wanted to make progress as an investigator.

Fleet had his notebook open and was scribbling things down. 'The statue went to Sharp via Yas Bishop. And we think it altered her behaviour, in the short time she had it. And then it had a bigger effect on Sharp, because he had it much longer.'

'You're really running with that theory, aren't you?' Lydia still couldn't believe it. The relief of his acceptance and belief was overwhelming.

'You're not crazy,' Fleet said, not looking up from his notebook. 'Do you mind if I come with you to re-cover some ground, though? A second conversation in the vaults. And maybe a trip to JRB? An in-person visit will be harder to dodge.'

'Won't you get into trouble for that?'

'Won't you?'

'Oh, yes,' Lydia said. 'Most definitely.' Then, because Fleet wasn't rearing away from her as if she were deranged, she leant across the table and kissed him.

THE OLD BAILEY was built on the site of the infamous Newgate Prison and some of the bricks from the medieval prison had been used in the current building. Waste not, want not, even in the finest architecture of the city. Its grand facade, faced with Portland stone and topped with a grand dome echoing the one on St Paul's cathedral nearby, was designed to inspire reverence. And obedience. A shaft of sunlight caught the gold statue of Lady Justice which presided over the court, scales of justice in one hand and the sword of retribution held aloft in the other, pointing toward heaven. Unlike most representations of justice, the figure watching over the Old Bailey didn't wear a blindfold. Lydia had always supposed it was because no self-respecting Londoner would wander about with their eyes closed.

Maria was hurrying out of the old court, still in her horse hair wig and black gown. Instead of scales and a sword, she was carrying files and a takeaway coffee. Lydia stepped in front of the barrister as she turned onto the pavement. 'Quick word?'

Maria didn't break stride, her heels striking the pavement with a sharp click-clack. She spared a single glance in Lydia's direction. 'Aren't you supposed to be on a tight leash?'

Lydia fell into step alongside. 'Not really my style. Besides, I need to talk to you about Yas Bishop.'

'Look at you,' Maria said, her lips thin. 'Running around the city, playing detective. It would be quite sweet, really. In a ten year old. A Harriet the Spy kind of deal. In someone approaching thirty it's just embarrassing. Poor old Charlie,' Maria shook her head. 'You must be such a disappointment. I know he had high hopes...' Maria broke off to look both ways before crossing a road, a taxi swooped past and she picked up speed again. Lydia couldn't help but be impressed at her speed in four-inch stilettos. Her calf muscles must be like rocks.

'You would know all about disappointing your family,' Lydia said. 'I don't suppose Alejandro is very forgiving of failure. Your lot are all about high achievements, aren't you? Straight As at school, first-place trophies, all of that rubbish.'

'Spoken like a true C-grade student,' Maria said.

'Fun as this is,' Lydia said. 'I was more interested in what you were doing on the third of this month? I know what you lawyers are like, you'll have it down in a schedule somewhere. You have to know so that you can bill by the hour.'

'By the minute, darling,' Maria said. 'I know what you're asking and why. That's the date Ms Yas Bishop was found dead at her home. Suspected foul play, I believe.'

'And yet you don't seem concerned. Despite the fact that Yas Bishop was an employee of one of your most important clients. There is a link between the two of you and Yas let her killer into her house, suggesting a personal relationship. You should be concerned, or interested at least. Or is the inbreeding finally catching up on your family? It's tragic when mental capacity just degrades like that.'

Lydia's superior tone was doing its work and there was the smallest crack in Maria's breezy demeanour. She slowed her pace and said: 'I'm not concerned because I had a hospital appointment on the morning of the third. And I believe it is the morning which is of interest to the police.'

'How exactly would you know that?'

'Word gets around. It's all a matter of who you know and what favours they owe. Plus,' Maria shot Lydia a smug smile, 'everyone wants me as a friend. Everyone with any sense, that is.'

'You are useful, I'll give you that,' Lydia said. 'Speedy, too. Is there some kind of emergency? Are you training for the Olympics?'

Maria stopped and faced Lydia. 'What do you want? One word to my father and all hell will break loose. A Crow harassing a Silver? It's not smart. And you know it.'

A man in gown and black suit, files under one arm, swore as he had to abruptly swerve past them on the pavement. There was a steady stream of legal types in this area, rushing to and from the Old Bailey, the Royal Courts of Justice, and the Chambers housed behind high walls, where cases were given. Those with the knowledge and background, the legal language and training, the special costumes and the academic papers, they all belonged here. Barristers and solicitors and legal flunkeys flowed through the veins and arteries of the London legal system, just as they had for hundreds of years. They were in Maria's world and she was wearing her suit of armour. And she knew it.

What Maria didn't realise was that she was surrounded by a silvered aura, and that it was perfectly visible to Lydia. Looking past the gown and the white bands and the wig, Lydia concentrated on the power behind the clothes, trying not to alert Maria to her scrutiny. Maria's energy was nothing like as strong as that she had felt in Alejandro's presence. Lydia wondered how aware Maria was of her father's power, whether she knew anything about the Silver Family cup. She licked her lips. 'Are you after another trophy? I know how much you like a shiny bauble. Do you often shop down in the vaults?'

Maria's face stayed fixed, the smug smile didn't slip, but Lydia felt a tremor in the Silver energy. A tiny ripple of discontent. She pressed on. 'Was it hard to kill Yas? Reading about murder has got to be different to carrying it out. Was there more blood than you expected?'

Maria's smile was back to full wattage. She turned and began walking toward the entrance to one of the Inns of Court. Lydia knew she didn't have long left. Once they reached it, Maria could slip through the archway and lose Lydia in the warren beyond. 'Why did JRB want Robert Sharp dead? I know you ordered the hit on him, but not why. What had he done to piss off your clients so badly? And is that a service you often provide for your top clients?'

'What wild accusations you are making,' Maria said. Her voice was steady and she looked utterly calm and confident again. It made Lydia want to scream. She knew that this woman had ordered a man's death, on the orders of somebody else, but still. And then she had casually cut the throat of a woman who had done nothing except have the bad luck to handle a magical object that should never have been in public circulation.

As far as Lydia knew, Maria hadn't even attempted to sort out the mess in any other way. Which suggested Maria felt beyond the law, beyond the usual morals of mere mortals. 'You've been doing this job for too long,' Lydia said. 'You think you're invincible.'

'I'm untouchable,' Maria said. 'Which is much the same thing. I'm too valuable and I'm too good at my job. Nobody wants to see me on the other side of the law because I'm too useful right where I am.'

'You're right,' Lydia said, abruptly changing tack. 'I'm not going to risk you running to Alejandro and I'm not about to piss off Uncle Charlie. I'm on my last warning with him, as it is. And I don't want trouble between the Silvers and the Crows.'

They were almost at the archway and Lydia made herself sound as frustrated as possible. It wasn't difficult. 'I just want to know, for my own satisfaction, that I was on the right lines. I can't work out why you would want her dead. I mean, Yas was a nobody, as far as I can tell.'

'Nobodies can still talk,' Maria said. 'And when they start behaving erratically, they quickly become liabilities. You have to be able to predict behaviour, that's what makes the difference between most people and those who are truly successful. If you know how people are going to react, what they're going to do, you can manoeuvre yourself accordingly.'

'And you knew Yas was a big enough threat to your reputation to warrant a death sentence?'

'I said no such thing,' Maria said. She stopped walking and leaned in close, giving Lydia a blast of her perfume. It smelled heavy and expensive, with citrus, cedar and cloves, but was no match for the sharp Silver that was hitting the back of Lydia's throat, filling her senses with a cool metallic sensation. Maria's eyes lit up and Lydia wondered if it was in response to her feeling of natural superiority or whether she was, somehow, aware of the effect she was having on Lydia. 'But if I did, if I acknowledged that I played a part in Ms Bishop's demise, there would be absolutely nothing you could do about it.' Maria straightened. 'Take this as a valuable lesson in learning your limits.'

CHAPTER TWENTY

As the first on scene, even in his off-duty capacity, Fleet was able to get decent access to the Yas Bishop murder enquiry. As he said, there were plenty of rules about the flow and containment of information, but cops were still cops. They talked to each other.

'No CCTV, unfortunately,' he reported back to Lydia. 'No suspects. No prints from the scene.'

'What about Maria Silver?'

Fleet pulled a face. 'An anonymous tip with no supporting information or evidence gets filed under 'unlikely'. They'll get to it, but given her legal skills and well-connected family, her name is going straight to the bottom of the action list. Top brass will want a solid reason to drag her in. You're sure it was her?'

'Ninety-nine per cent. I told you, I could sense Silver at Yas's house.'

'Could it have been another Silver? Isn't it more

likely that someone like Maria would enlist someone else to do her dirty work?'

'When I confronted her she practically admitted it.'

Fleet went still. 'You confronted a woman you suspect of murder? On your own?'

'It was the middle of the day in a public place. I'm not a complete idiot.'

Lydia could see Fleet's mind working. 'On the bright side, you might have spooked her. Make her do something daft. If she did the actual killing herself. Which I still find hard to imagine...'

'She would take care of it herself,' Lydia insisted. 'She couldn't ask someone else in the Family, or one of their professional contacts. She wouldn't want to risk it getting back to her father. Trust me, that fear is a powerful motivator. Maria would think that doing it alone would be safest. No collaboration means nobody to rat on you, nobody to let you down.'

Fleet's mouth twitched. 'I think you might be speaking from the heart, there.'

'There will be evidence,' Lydia ploughed on, ignoring Fleet's snark. 'She must have got blood on her clothes. No way to avoid it.'

'Maybe she'll panic, now that she knows you suspect. If she's hidden her bloody clothes somewhere, maybe she'll try to get rid of them now.'

'I love that you think that, but there is no way Maria Silver is concerned about what I know or suspect. You should have seen her.' Lydia felt the sick rage rise up again. 'She thinks she's untouchable.'

'And she's been trying criminal cases her whole

adult life, she must know a hundred ways to get away with murder.' Fleet tapped his lip. 'Mind you, theory is one thing. The physical reality quite another.'

Lydia nodded absently. There was something tugging at the edge of her thoughts. She pulled her computer onto her lap and opened the research tabs she had bookmarked when looking into Maria Silver's career history.

Fleet looked over her shoulder. 'I'll make some coffee.'

LYDIA SPENT the next hour reading through every case she could find, following links to news stories and follow-up pieces. Lots of Maria's cases involved corporate law and were so dense that Lydia felt her mind actively rebelling against the sentences. 'This makes no sense,' she said, at one point.

Fleet had joined her in research-mode and he rubbed a hand over his face. 'This is why they make the big bucks. It's a boredom tariff. Any joy?'

'She doesn't really represent murderers. At least, not openly. Her clients are dodgy in other ways. Take this one.' Lydia angled the screen to show Fleet. Aden Naser had been up on cartel charges and Maria had, miraculously, got him eighty hours of community service. Fleet sat forward, energised. 'That's exactly the kind of thing.'

'How do you mean?'

'There has to be more to it than just Maria's keen legal skills. He must have made a deal. Unless the evidence collapsed at trial. That happens. But if it was a deal, he must have been giving up something worse. Give me a minute.'

Fleet stood up and paced while he made a call. Lydia heard him asking for a file, laughing with whoever was on the other end. 'Yeah, mate. I know. Consider the slate cleared.'

'You pulled in a favour?' Lydia said.

'Got to. Can't just go poking around in files these days without a good reason. Everything is logged. It's a right pain in the arse.'

'Was it a valuable favour?'

'Helped him move into his flat.'

Lydia looked at him for a moment. 'You're joking.'

'Course.'

'And you're not going to tell me what the real favour was?'

'I don't want to tarnish your view of me as squeaky-clean upstanding member of the modern policing community.'

'Right,' Lydia said, ready to continue, but Fleet's phone beeped.

He tapped for a moment and then came to sit next to Lydia, showing her the open file. 'Naser made a deal with the CPS. He gave evidence in another trial. A murder case. Hang on... John Owen. Hit man for over thirty years, got life last year after a trial for killing a gang boss in Liverpool. Currently serving in Belmarsh.'

'Naser gave evidence?'

'Yeah, most likely he'd been a client at some point or knew him in a professional capacity, but needs must... CPS obviously thought the trade was worth it. You'd be surprised at how often cases don't even come to trial if they're not deemed strong enough.'

Lydia was already Googling John Owen. She skimmed the press reports, feeling very happy that John Owen was safely behind bars. Dodgy deal or not, a truly nasty character was off the streets and serving time for his heinous crimes. A sentence snagged Lydia's brain and she went back up a paragraph to find it. After reading it and digging a little deeper, she posed a question to Fleet. 'You know how John Owen evaded prosecution for so many years?'

Fleet didn't raise his gaze from his phone screen where he was still reading the file. 'Fear, professionalism, and a dose of being a lucky bastard.'

'All that. Plus, he destroyed incriminating evidence, including a few body parts, by slipping them into medical waste at Liverpool General.'

Fleet looked up, then. 'And it ended up in the incinerator?'

'Yep, back when hospitals dealt with their own mess. Nowadays it's done by waste management companies under contract, apparently.' Lydia held his gaze. 'Maria's alibi was a hospital appointment that morning. What if she lied about the time by an hour or so?'

'I don't get you...' Fleet began.

'What if she took a leaf out of his book?'

THE NEXT AFTERNOON, Lydia was massaging her temples, trying to get rid of a headache. She couldn't blame the weather anymore, and she didn't have any pressing cases. Much as she wanted to storm into Maria Silver's office and accuse her face-to-face, she knew it wouldn't help. And Fleet had taken her hunch to MIT. He promised her they would take it seriously. That he would make them take it seriously.

April Westcott had replied to Lydia's emailed report with a couple of terse sentences. Lydia didn't blame her and didn't take it personally. That was the nature of being the bearer of bad news. It sucked. Lydia logged into her business account and saw a transfer from April for the final invoice amount. A case closed. Another payment gained from the slurry of messed-up human relationships. Lydia stared into space for a moment, trying to work out if she truly felt bad about the Westcott case or whether it was something else bringing her down. It was something else. Emma.

IT WAS strange to see Tom. Lydia couldn't remember the last time they had spoken, and it was stranger still to see him without Emma. 'Thanks for meeting me,' Lydia said, as Tom slid into the seat opposite Lydia. It was a little Italian place just around the corner from Tom's office, halfway to the tube station he would use to get home to suburbia, and his wife and children.

At some point during the debacle of the Lee case, Lydia had realised that she had a third option with Emma's request. Refuse to investigate Tom and just talk to him as a friend. It gave her a tilting, terrified sensation in her stomach, but she knew it was the right thing to do. At least, she hoped it was the right thing to do. She didn't want to make things worse, or betray Emma's confidence, but at least if she messed up it would be because she was muddling through as a friend, not treating their lives as a case to be solved.

The smiley Hungarian who had brought Lydia an intense cup of coffee appeared to take Tom's order. He asked for hot water with a slice of lemon and Lydia raised an eyebrow.

'Cutting down on caffeine.' Tom put his work bag on the empty chair next to him and folded his hands on the table. 'I know what this is about.'

'You do?'

'Emma said you were worried that I didn't like you.'

Well that was blunt. 'Oh. Right.'

'I won't lie,' Tom said. 'I was concerned about her getting involved with your life. Your work. It sounds a bit, I don't know, like it might be risky. But I know you wouldn't put her in any bad situations and I'm not saying-'

'That's not why I'm here,' Lydia interrupted him.

Tom's hot water arrived in a slim glass mug on a saucer and Lydia waited until they were alone before continuing. 'This is difficult. I never get involved like this, unless it's in a professional capacity, and I don't want to stick my nose in, but you and Emma are my friends and I want to help. Emma's worried about you and her mind is going through all kinds of wild possibilities. I've told her that she's got nothing to worry about but I wanted to let you know, so that you can reassure her.' Every part of Lydia was hoping that Tom was going to say 'oh, yeah, I've been a bit stressed at work' or 'I don't know what you're talking about, everything's fine.' Something simple. Not serious. Something, if Lydia was being honest, to let her off the hook cleanly and quickly. Instead, Tom crumpled in front of her.

'Oh, God.' He bent low over his drink, the steam from the water fogging up his glasses, and then took them off to polish them.

Lydia waited. When he spoke next, his voice was thick and he had to clear his throat and start again. 'I thought I was hiding it. I thought she hadn't noticed. I mean, we're pretty busy. It's not like we get much time together.'

'It's Emma,' Lydia said, as gently as she could. 'Of course she knows something is wrong.'

'I didn't want her to worry. She's got enough with the kids and everything. It's not fair on her.'

'I've been away a long time, and I know I'm the last person who should be advising on relationships, but you two have always been a team. That means you can lean on each other. What can be so bad that you can't tell her?'

'I've been having tests,' Tom said quietly. 'They thought it might be colon cancer.'

Lydia sat back. 'Hell Hawk. That's stressful.'

He nodded. 'It's okay. It's not. Cancer, I mean. They think ulcerative colitis but I'm seeing the consultant next week to confirm. I was going to tell Ems, I was just waiting for the diagnosis, getting through the tests and stuff, first. I didn't want to freak her out when it might be nothing. And I didn't want to talk about it.'

'Telling Emma would have made it real,' Lydia said.

Tom looked at her then. He wasn't crying but his eyes were damp. The expression on his face was pure naked relief, though. 'Exactly.'

'But why not tell her now? I mean, I don't know much about colitis...'

'It's a chronic condition. Lifetime of medication, but the symptoms shouldn't be as unpleasant when they get it under control. If it gets bad or the medications don't work, there's surgery to remove part of the colon and there's a slightly increased risk of bowel cancer. I could end up with a stoma bag.' He pulled a face. 'Sexy.'

'You shouldn't be dealing with this on your own. What were you thinking?'

'I'm lucky,' Tom said, quickly. It had the ring of words which had been rehearsed, repeated. A mantra to help Tom through a life-altering diagnosis. 'I mean, it's not a lottery ticket, but it could be much worse.'

'It's shit, Tom,' Lydia said. 'I'm really sorry.'

He managed a weak smile. 'You have no idea how apt a statement you just made.'

'See? You've been depriving Emma of all your toilet-based gallows humour. She'll be furious.'

'You think?' He was suddenly serious.

'No, you idiot. She will be relieved you're talking to her. Have you told your work?'

He nodded. 'I've needed time for appointments and stuff. And I needed to explain my longer-than-usual toilet breaks. Didn't want to get the sack for slacking.'

'I'm sorry,' Lydia said, wincing. 'I'm really sorry you are going through this. Is there anything I can do?'

He shook his head. 'I'll talk to Emma tonight. What must she be thinking?'

Lydia decided not to mention infidelity or talk of strip clubs. 'She's just worried about you and she knows you're hiding something which worries her more. She's been imagining the worst.'

'It's not fair on her,' Tom said. 'She's got so much on her plate already, looking after two kids, working, everything. She doesn't need this.'

'Still. You've got to tell her. She's your wife, she deserves to know what's going on. And she will feel better knowing. And you'll feel better, too. This is something you two need to face together. That's the deal with marriage, right?'

On her way home, Fleet texted to say he was going to finish late, but that he wanted to see her. Lydia ducked out of the stream of people on the street and texted back. 'Come to mine whenever you're done'.

Seconds later, he replied. 'You still haven't seen my place. I have a coffee table.'

Smiling, Lydia texted back. 'Boasty McBoasterson.' Then she called into the Tesco Metro at the end of her street and bought some good bread and cheese and a bottle of red wine. She would show Fleet that she wasn't a complete animal.

The Fork was closed for the day and she unlocked the door to get inside. The hairs stood up on the back of her neck as she did so, the unmistakable sensation of being watched. She looked around, but the street was deserted.

Not long after, Fleet arrived with a six-pack of beer and a takeaway pizza. 'I assumed you wouldn't have any food in.'

Lydia considered taking offence but she didn't want to jeopardise future pizza offerings. After they had eaten, chatting about their days in a way which felt entirely natural, Lydia chucked the box into the recycling tub and washed her hands in the kitchen. She hadn't told Fleet about the business with Emma and Tom, it was private, but she had alluded to finishing up a client case and told him how relieved she was to have found a resolution which hadn't made her want to scrub herself in bleach. 'I had started to think I wasn't cut out for this job, so it's good to work out my own way of doing it. I can have my own code and, if I stick to that, I will be able to run my business and sleep at night.'

'You're providing a service for people,' Fleet had said. 'If you didn't do it, somebody else would. Better they come to you for help than someone with fewer scruples.'

After drying her hands with a tea towel, Lydia walked back into the living room. The subject they had both been avoiding over dinner was front and centre in her mind.

As was so often the way, Fleet's opening words let her know he was on the same page.

'Are you sure you want your name kept out of the Yas Bishop report? It doesn't feel right that you won't get any credit.'

'It's fine,' Lydia said. 'You know and that's enough.'

He raised an eyebrow. 'You're gutted really, aren't you?'

'Little bit,' Lydia said. 'I would love to look Maria Silver in the eye and let her know that I sussed her.'

Fleet was stretched out on Lydia's sofa, cradling a bottle of beer to his chest. It had been an exceedingly long day, even by his standards, and there were dark shadows under his eyes. For her part, Lydia felt keyed-up. Fleet had explained that MIT had taken the information seriously enough to get the details of Maria Silver's hospital appointment and were in the process of reviewing CCTV from the area. Lydia had been so worried that they still wouldn't have agreed to go after somebody as powerful and respected as Maria Silver, but the relief was tinged with a sense of anti-climax. 'Tell me again,' she said, twisting the top off a cold bottle of lager. 'Tell me how you convinced Ian.'

'You're insatiable,' Fleet said. He smiled fondly but then dug in his pocket for his phone, which was vibrating. He stood up from the sofa and paced the room as he spoke. Lydia didn't even pretend not to be listening. Fleet's responses were short, though, giving nothing away. 'Thanks, mate,' he said, finishing the call, and turning to Lydia with the second-biggest smile she had ever seen on his face. 'Bloody got her!'

'Tell me.' Lydia was pacing, too. Unable to stay still, energy fizzing.

'Right. So. The waste management company for the Bayswater district is First Hygiene. They visited this afternoon and located a bag filled with a heavily bloodstained blouse and skirt. They've just rushed the lab work and it's Yas Bishop's blood. No doubt.'

Lydia felt a rush of adrenaline and relief. She wanted to shout, to punch the air, to hug Fleet.

He was still talking, clearly as keyed up as she was. 'Maria must have taken a change of clothes to the scene and changed before leaving Yas's house. The bloody clothes were contained in a plastic bag from a boutique. Then the CCTV shows her attending a women's health check-up appointment at her private hospital, cool-as-you-like. She's captured going in with several shopping bags, presumably to hide the fact that one of them contains gore.'

'While in the facility, she found a medical waste bin and added the clothes she had been wearing earlier. Probably during her appointment with her doctor, as the bins are only in treatment rooms or wards.'

'CCTV,' Lydia said, 'so the police would have found her eventually.'

'They wouldn't have been looking at her for a long time, possibly never. And by then, the clothes would have been long-since incinerated. Don't explain away your achievement.'

Lydia could feel her wide smile. 'Okay,' she said.

It was a nice moment. Something like pride was flooding her body and, for the first time in months, she felt like she was taking a full and satisfying breath. There was a cold beer in her hand and a ridiculously hot man lying on her sofa... A hot man who was suddenly looking very tense. He slowly put his beer down and swung his legs around until he was sitting up right. The whole time, his gaze was fixed just to the left of Lydia. 'What?'

Fleet didn't stop staring and Lydia twisted around to follow his gaze, into the corner of the room. Jason was there, in his pale grey eighties-tastic suit, looking like an extra from a Wham video. He was standing stock still, a look of sheer panic on his face.

'Um,' Lydia said hoping that something helpful would follow. It didn't.

'Sorry,' Fleet said, dragging his gaze back to Lydia's face. 'I'm sorry. I thought I saw something for a moment.' He shook his head, then frowned. 'Light playing tricks or something.'

CHAPTER TWENTY-ONE

'Y ou're exhausted.' Lydia ushered Fleet out of the flat. 'You should head home and get some sleep.'

Fleet attempted a half-hearted leer. 'I'd rather stay here and *not* get some sleep,' but he ruined it by yawning at the end.

'See? Go sleep. I'll see you tomorrow.'

After the door closed behind Fleet, Jason stepped out from his room where he had been waiting. 'What. Was. That?'

'I have no idea,' Lydia said. 'Did you do something different?'

'Like what? Sparkle? Shout? Smile?'

'I don't know,' Lydia snapped. She was shaken and trying not to show it. It made her cranky.

She followed Jason back into his bedroom. 'Okay,' Jason picked up a blue Sharpie from his bedside table and began writing on the wall, his movements fast and jerky. Jason's writing had become smaller as his fine motor control improved, but number, letters and symbols covered almost every inch. Lydia knew she would have to start painting over some of his older work to give him more space. Or convince him to start using paper. He turned back and Lydia realised he had been writing a small list of possibilities. 'Either I've got stronger and more visible. More widely visible to the general population, I mean. Or there's something weird about your man Fleet.'

'He's not my man,' Lydia said automatically.

'This is not about your strange relationship,' Jason said severely. 'This is about whether DCI Fleet can see ghosts. You need to focus.'

'I know,' Lydia said. 'He couldn't before. So something has definitely changed.'

Jason tapped his lip with the end of the pen. 'You know, this makes perfect sense. If our original theory is correct and you are like a battery, powering up latent ability. Like the way your dad is worse around you and the way that I'm stronger. If Fleet has some small ability or potential, then the more time he spends with you, the stronger it gets.'

'That's a big 'if'. It's not like magical potential is common, that's why the Families are so crazy about it. And Fleet isn't Pearl, Silver, Crow or Fox. I would know. And what do you mean strange relationship?'

'There was high emotion,' Jason said, his voice thoughtful. 'You had a breakthrough with the Maria case, right?'

Lydia nodded, the tiny flame of pride growing a little brighter.

'Will they be able to get her for Robert Sharp, too?'

The flame extinguished. 'I doubt it. Nobody is going to talk on the record, which means there's no evidence of her ordering the hit. Professional jobs rarely get successfully prosecuted.'

'And why did JRB have him killed, again? Wasn't he working for them?'

Lydia shrugged, hating the incompleteness of it. The gaps in her knowledge itched like half-healed wounds. 'He was a valuable asset for JRB until he wasn't. Either he made a mistake or he tried blackmailing them or he tried to get out of the business. Could be anything, really. Anything which pissed them off.'

'It seems a bit extreme. Especially if he just made a mistake.'

'JRB wanted to send a nice public message. Make an example of him for all the other people they have in their pockets. It's a power thing.'

Jason was quiet for a moment, thinking. 'Maria ordered the hit on behalf of JRB because Silver and Silver represent them?'

'Bingo.'

Another silence.

'What is it?'

'I don't want you to investigate me,' Jason said.

'Okay,' Lydia agreed, wondering at the change of topic and the look of guilty panic which was plastered across Jason's pale face.

'You know my wife?'

Jason had died on his wedding day. All Lydia knew was that it had happened at the wedding breakfast which had been held at The Fork which was, presumably, why he was tied to the building. 'Sure. Amy.' Lydia said, keeping her voice respectfully soft.

'Yeah. Amy.' Jason wasn't looking at Lydia directly. 'Her maiden name was Amy Silver.'

Lydia sat in the ground-floor bar in the neighbouring office block and waited for Milo Easen to leave Silver and Silver after a long day fielding phone calls. She sipped at her soda and lime and thanked Feathers for the trend in massive plate glass windows. Through the lightly smoked glass of the bar, she could see across the narrow street and into the reception area of Silver and Silver. Of course, there was every chance that Milo would take a different exit out of the building and Lydia would miss him, have to try again the next day, but that was half of her job. Waiting and watching and hoping. You didn't have to be particularly skilled to be an investigator. Just really patient.

Half an hour later, when Lydia was chasing the last of her drink around the ice cubes with her straw, Milo pushed out of the front entrance. He had a canvas rucksack slung over one shoulder and was carrying his suit jacket.

Lydia followed him along Fetter Lane toward Fleet Street, waiting until the junction before walking smartly up behind him and tapping him on the shoulder. 'Quick word, Milo?'

'Jesus!' Milo went whiter than he already was and then red. 'I can't talk to you.'

'Course you can,' Lydia said. She spread her arms. 'It's a beautiful day for a stroll.'

Milo was looking over Lydia's shoulder, panic in his eyes. Lydia knew he would be scouting the street for other Silver employees. She had expected him to be concerned, but it was interesting that it was terror she was sensing instead.

'The Hare in Camberwell. See you there in an hour.'

'Why would I-' Milo began and Lydia cut across him, taking a tiny step closer. 'If I don't see you there, I'll have to come back here tomorrow. And the day after and the day after that. I'll wait in reception next time.'

LYDIA WAS happy to be on home ground. She sipped an orange juice and settled back to scroll through her phone while she waited. The bar was busy and filling fast, but Lydia had snagged her favourite seat in the corner. When Milo walked in, shoulders hunched, Lydia had the perfect view. He wore a hunted expression as he looked around the pub. Lydia raised a hand and he crossed the room.

'Would you like a drink?'

'I don't want to be here.'

'Fair enough,' Lydia said. 'Let's get it over with then. I want to know about Maria Silver's relationship with Yas Bishop.'

'What do you mean?'

'You don't deny that they knew each other, then?'

'That's...' Milo looked flummoxed. 'JRB are our clients.'

'Right. Did Yas come by for meetings? How much contact did they have?'

Milo frowned 'None, really. JRB never came into the office.'

'You keep referring to the corporate entity. I would like some names.'

'I don't have any,' Milo said. He saw her expression. 'I swear. I don't have any. Ms Bishop was the only listed contact. And I don't recall any meetings with Maria. If I showed you her diary, you would see. Nothing was ever booked in.'

'We both know that doesn't mean it didn't happen.'

'You don't know Ms Silver's schedule. If it's not in the diary, it doesn't happen.'

Lydia caught a glimpse of the steel that had to be necessary to work as Maria's assistant and smiled. 'Have the police spoken to you?'

Milo shifted in his seat. 'Yes. Will there be more?'

'Probably,' Lydia said. 'And I know you won't talk. You can't and I understand that. The Silvers run a tight ship.'

'So what is this, then?' Milo gestured between them. 'Why are you harassing me?'

'For my own satisfaction,' Lydia said. 'I'm not interested in making trouble for you and the police don't need any further tips, they have a solid enough case with Maria's bloody clothes. But I know I don't have all the details. I don't understand where Yas fits in and I need to know.'

'Why?'

'It will annoy me. Nag at me.'

'Not my problem.'

Milo started to get up and Lydia plucked her coin out of the air, flipping it and slamming it down onto the back of her left hand. 'Heads or tails?'

Milo had frozen. He didn't take his eyes from the coin and lowered himself back onto the chair.

'I have a theory,' Lydia said, keeping her hand over the coin. 'Stop me if I get anything wrong. I think Yas Bishop was told to look after Robert Sharp by JRB. Whether it was because he was helping them or blackmailing them, I don't know. I don't really care, either. So, JRB wanted Sharp recompensed. The company didn't use bank transfers to pay him, though, at least none that the police have found in Robert Sharp's records. My guess is that they used gifts, instead. Gifts and favours. Maybe Yas helped him find the flat in Canary Wharf, helped him choose the godawful décor, she seemed to have a thing for interiors. But I think she had to find high-value gifts to pass along, too.'

Milo nodded very slightly.

'And the reason none of this is news to you is because your boss, Maria Silver, had a bright idea. She recommended a place where Yas Bishop could purchase items for JRB and give them to Robert. I don't know if that was Yas's sole job, her entire purpose on the pay roll of the mysterious JRB, but she accepted the suggestion readily enough and trotted off to the Silver Vaults. How am I doing?'

Milo kept his eyes on Lydia's hands. 'Ms Silver asked me to call Ms Bishop with the address of the vaults and a shop name. She said it was for a christening present.'

'Maria must have thought it was a neat solution. An easy way to scratch a back, gather a favour which might be handy later.'

'Nothing wrong with recommending a shop to someone,' Milo said. 'It's not a crime. It's not anything.'

'Absolutely,' Lydia agreed. 'I just wanted to know I was right. I told you, I'm just scratching an itch. Can I ask one more thing? Did Maria specifically tell Ms Bishop to purchase a silver knight statue?'

Milo frowned. 'Not to my knowledge. But I didn't hear them talking about it directly. Which is it?'

'Sorry?'

Milo nodded at Lydia's hands. 'Heads or tails?'

'Neither.' Lydia revealed the gold coin, wondering what the image would be. Her coin often showed the profile of a resting crow, but sometimes it was smooth and blank and sometimes it just had the silhouette of an empty tree branch. They both looked. The coin was engraved with the image of a crow in flight, its wings spread wide.

CHAPTER TWENTY-TWO

Walking back to The Fork, Lydia wondered when Maria had realised her mistake. From the outside, it didn't seem as if she could have known that Guillaume Chartes would sell Yas a statue with supernatural powers. It was interesting that Maria had tried to clear up the mess without drawing on the powerful influence of Alejandro, though. Either Maria feared his anger, or she had been hoping to keep knowledge of the existence of the statue's power to herself.

Something was very clear, though; the more Lydia uncovered, the more she wanted to keep digging. The restless feeling in her guts was reassuring. The endless parade of adultery cases and her accompanying fatigue had made her worry, just a little, that she hadn't found her true calling after all. Now, however, she knew that she was driven by the desire to unravel knots, to see the whole truth behind the obfuscation, to know, if not understand, as many details as possible. And she felt the satisfaction which came from knowledge.

In her flat, she washed out her Sherlock Holmes mug and flipped the switch on the kettle. While she waited for the water to boil, she summoned her coin. It was still showing the same image. The crow in flight. Putting it on the worktop, Lydia attempted, for the first time in her life, to scoop another coin out of the air. Nothing happened. She tried again, concentrating on the feeling in her fingers and trying to remember how it felt when it worked. She felt faintly ridiculous. She hadn't been lying when she had explained it to Jason. She didn't summon the coin or create it, it was always there. Part of her.

'What are you doing?' Jason had appeared in the doorway of the kitchen.

'Nothing,' Lydia said, picking up her coin from the counter. 'Just trying something.'

Jason's smile was infectious. 'With your powers?'

'Such as they are,' Lydia said, pulling a wry smile. 'I'll try talking to my dad. See if I can get some background information.'

Jason closed the gap between them with a couple of steps and wrapped his arms around her. Lydia returned the hug, feeling the strange cool energy of Jason's form. As she held him, she could feel his body becoming firmer under her palms. She flexed her fingers and felt the material of his suit jacket. He pulled back slightly, not letting go, and they looked into each other's eyes for a moment. Jason looked more alive that she had ever seen him. His cheeks were pink and there was a spark in his eyes. Lydia could see every detail of his face, with no shimmering or blurring; each eyelash glistening with moisture, the individual pores of his skin. They broke apart and Jason scrubbed at his face with his hands.

'You okay?' Lydia asked, thinking the ghost was crying. 'Have I upset you?'

'No,' Jason said from behind his fingers. 'I just feel... Feelings. It's like I've been drugged, tranquilised, and you just woke me up.'

'Just now?'

'Well, it's been building, I think. But, yeah. I felt something. Didn't you?'

Lydia bit back her immediate urge to make a joke, to make light of it. Instead she looked Jason straight in the eyes and nodded. 'Yes.'

SINCE THE RAIN STORMS, the temperature in the city had returned to the classic summer in London; mild, damp, and smelling of drains. Lydia stood out on her roof terrace, her hands resting lightly on the railing. She was wide awake and she wasn't afraid. Turning around to survey the space, she found herself thinking about getting some outdoor furniture. Maybe rigging up a light or two.

DCI Fleet was coming round after work that night and Jason was occupied in his bedroom with a new packet of Sharpies. For now, Lydia was alone and free. She went and fetched a beer before sitting at her desk. She could do a bit of paperwork or she could read a book or watch some television. There was nothing pressing to do, no overdue bills, and Uncle Charlie had taken a welcome step back.

He was still suspicious, of course. He wasn't stupid and suspected that Lydia had played a role in the arrest of Maria Silver. As long as it wasn't proven or whispered by anybody else, though, he seemed willing to let it go. There was a new look in his eye when he spoke to her. A mix of wariness and respect that Lydia hadn't seen before. She had to admit that she liked it.

Feeling mellow, Lydia treated herself to a look at the news stories about Maria Silver's arrest. Somebody must have tipped the press as there was a photograph of her being taken from Silver and Silver LLP's offices and into custody. Below it was the glossy headshot used on the company's website and another one of her in some tropical paradise in happier times. Maria had been formally charged with murder and was on remand while awaiting trial. Despite her good standing and lack of prior convictions, bail had been denied due to the serious nature of the charges and because she was considered a flight risk. Her father had already appealed this ruling, and had launched a number of other counter appeals and a civil case against the Met for harassment. It was far from over, but it gladdened Lydia's heart to see the Crown Prosecution Service working even when the accused was a monied, privileged insider like Maria Silver. Maria had been right, England really did have a decent legal system.

Lydia was still smiling to herself when there was a knock on her door. Her proximity alarm hadn't sounded, which meant Lydia was on high alert as she walked up her short hallway. She kept to the side of the passage, had her illegal can of Mace ready in one hand, and put the security chain on before opening the door. Lydia felt the power before she could see through the gap in the door, it felt like a physical blow and she staggered, half-falling against the wall.

Standing in her hallway was the man-boy who had been staring at her in her circuits class. The class when she had felt a burst of power that had been like nothing else she had encountered. The one which had made her worry that her own ability was misfiring. So much had happened since, that she had almost forgotten about it and now here he was. Short, young, and twice as wide as she remembered. And outside her home. 'You,' she managed.

He smiled as if pleased she recognised him and passed a brown padded enveloped through the gap in the door.

'You're a courier?'

He shrugged. 'I am today.' His voice was unbelievably deep and Lydia felt it reverberating through her bones. Which was impossible.

He was already moving away and Lydia found herself gasping for breath and trying to right herself from a sudden wave of dizziness. By the time she had recovered he had disappeared back down the stairs. Lydia forced her legs into action and followed, but by the time she made it to The Fork and then out onto the street, there was no sign of the stranger.

Back upstairs, her landline was ringing. The problem with the retro-style phone was that it didn't have a caller id display. Still, the envelope was familiar and Lydia fancied she could sense the tang of Fox even before she snatched up the receiver and heard Paul. 'Don't burn this one, Little Bird.'

'I think I'll just shred it,' Lydia said. 'Who was the courier you booked?'

'No shredding. No burning. No ignoring me. That's all done with.'

'Is that so?' Lydia said. 'What on earth makes you think I'll change my–'

'Maria Silver.'

'What about her?'

'I know it was you.'

'You know what was me?' Lydia was aiming for confused innocence.

Paul laughed and it raised the hair on Lydia's arms. 'The things I could tell dear old Uncle Charlie. Not to mention Alejandro. How do you think that would play out? How many of your friends and family would die before that score was settled? And that's if it doesn't provoke outright war.'

'You don't want that any more than I do,' Lydia said.

'Oh, I don't know. Bit of a rumble. Might be fun. And you know us Foxes... We always stay safe in our dens. It's the knights who fall on the battlefield. And the birds who get shot out of the sky.'

'Let's say I believe you, which I don't. What do you want?'

'One little job. That's all.'

'I definitely don't believe that.'

Paul laughed again. 'Maybe a little more friendliness

thrown in. The Crows could do with a new ally, don't you think?'

Lydia paused. 'What's the job?'

'Read all about it,' Paul said. 'Then give me a call.'

The line went dead and Lydia replaced the receiver. She picked up the envelope and weighed it in her hands, before dropping it back onto the surface of the desk and giving it a hard stare. After a moment she got up and walked to Jason's room. She didn't want to be alone to open the envelope and, thankfully, she didn't have to be. 'Jason?'

The ghost was motionless in front of the far wall of his bedroom. 'Can you come through for a minute?'

He started as if shaken from a deep reverie.

'Sorry,' Lydia said. 'Did I startle you?'

'You're all right,' Jason said, turning round. His easy smile disappeared. 'What's wrong?'

'Nothing, it's fine. Just come see.'

'What is it?' Jason followed Lydia back to the main room. Lydia pointed to the envelope. 'We've got a new job.'

THE END

ACKNOWLEDGMENTS

This time last year, my beloved mum died. The past twelve months have been extremely tough, and I am so grateful for my wonderful family and friends for helping me through it.

I also feel incredibly lucky to have work which I care about deeply; writing fiction has been a welcome escape and comfort. Heartfelt thanks to you, dear reader. Without you, I wouldn't get to do this as my profession and I am grateful every single day.

Thank you to Catherine Shellard, Keris Stainton, Clodagh Murphy, and Sally Calder for wine, writerly chats, research trips to London, and plentiful hugs. And for providing love and cheer whenever required.

Much love to Lucy Golden-Taylor, Nadine Kirtzinger, Rachel Moorhouse, Katie Bass, and Emma Ward for their kindness and friendship.

A book is always a collaboration and you would not be reading this book without the vital work of my editor, cover designer, early readers and wonderful ARC team. In particular: Ann Martin, David Wood, Beth Farrar, Karen Heenan, Melanie Leavey, Paula Searle, Judy Grivas, Jenni Gudgeon, Kerry Barrett, and Stuart Bache. Thank you, all.

Love and gratitude to Holly and James. You are always happy to talk through plot points and to offer encouragement, and you put up with 'deadline Mum' with grace and understanding.

As always, this book would not exist without the steadfast support, wise counsel, and infinite love of my Dave. Thank you, darling.

ABOUT THE AUTHOR

Before writing books, Sarah Painter worked as a free-lance magazine journalist, blogger and editor, combining this 'career' with amateur child-wrangling (AKA motherhood).

Sarah lives in rural Scotland with her children and husband. She drinks too much tea, loves the work of Joss Whedon, and is the proud owner of a writing shed.

Visit the web address below to sign-up to the Sarah Painter readers' club. It's quick and easy to join, and you'll get book release news, giveaways and exclusive FREE stuff!

geni.us/ReadersClub

47374759R00177

Made in the USA
Middletown, DE
06 June 2019